A Quiet Rebellion: Posterity

M. H. Thaung

Cover image by **Creative Covers**

ISBN-13: 978-1-912819-12-6 (ebook)
ISBN-13: 978-1-912819-10-2 (print)

mhthaung.com

A backwards glance

After the debacle with Silvers, it would have been almost impossible for the Council's secret use of those with psychic powers (deplorably labelled as "cursed") to remain unchallenged. Knowledge would begin to spread about the agent transmitted by some "beasts" (carnivores, although all mammals were feared). All this would have happened even without Queen Eleanor's fledgling plans to reintegrate the cursed back into society.
At last they realised that pain wasn't essential to trigger powers. They became far more sensible about the whole matter: indeed, quite innovative within their limitations...

From Queen Eleanor: The Early Years *by D. Brigham*

Isabel's letter to Eleanor

My dear Eleanor,

If you're reading this, it means I messed up somewhere and won't be coming back. I don't want to leave you wondering, so this is, I guess, a confession.

You see, I killed your father. Not on a whim, but because, in my judgement as a human being, he was a danger. As king, he was in a position to do a lot of damage.

You'll see from the notes I've hidden with this letter that he believed we will be invaded, sometime over the next several years. I can't speak to the truth of that. His proposed solution was to manufacture more afflicted, more people like me. I could just about understand that idea though it sticks in my craw. What I couldn't countenance was his plan that curse victims be forced to undergo training, using blackmail and threats to their families, and that the current training based around pain should continue as it's supposedly proven to be effective. I could be charitable and suggest your father's beliefs may have been born of desperation. But he would have transformed society, and not for the better.

Susanna tells me she has ideas for training powers that don't involve pain. I wish her luck with those. As to your father's claims, you can consult these notes and make your own decisions.

Rest assured, even if I am alive, I won't come after you if you conclude that the realm needs more people with

powers. However, if you follow your father into cruelty, I shall not rest until you follow him into death.
Your affectionate cousin,
Isabel xx

Chapter 1

*So what? We know pain's a reliable trigger. They'll be
given no choice but to cope with it...
To have any chance of repelling... how best to rapidly
increase numbers of cursed?
multiple bites? captive beasts??
What will future historians say if I'm the king who loses
his realm? This is not the time to pander to squeamishness.*

From the private notes of King Frederick of Numoeath

Curled up in a chair in her private sitting room, Eleanor
rubbed bleary eyes. She'd stayed up all night to read her
father's notes, but despite their disturbing contents she had
dozed off. Shivering, she tugged the quilted silk blanket
over her shoulders and burrowed deeper into the faded velvet cushions. All she'd confirmed was his strong belief in an
imminent threat to the realm. His fragmented scribbles
held no further clues or evidence.

Isabel might know more, but her disappearance was yet
another problem. Cousin Isabel, pyrokinetic and murderer.
And a regicide, at that. Her confession note had expressed
no regrets about her betrayals. It even included a warning:

*If you follow your father into cruelty, I shall not rest until
you follow him into death.*

"You should know me better than that," muttered

Eleanor. "Fool that I was, I looked up to you. Even confided in you. I am not my father."

For decades, those researching the curse had insisted that the only reliable method for controlling curse-bestowed powers involved pain. Recent events had disproved the need for pain, but she suspected her father wouldn't have cared.

He'd even recruited one scientist in a secret, desperate ploy to generate more curse victims. How *could* he? Rather than hatching such a chicken-brained plan, why hadn't he instead encouraged research into alternative methods for training the current afflicted? Settlers' teeth, he could have *ordered* the scientists to change the training system, using his King's Discretion. Wouldn't that have been a better use of his absolute power than scheming to inflict more cruelties on his subjects?

Well, not quite absolute power. The Queen's Discretion Eleanor wielded couldn't override one specific law. Regicide carried an automatic death penalty. She drew a shaky breath. Despite Isabel's treachery, Eleanor couldn't face the idea of her execution, especially after learning of her father's intentions. Only a few people knew of that confession note, and they were all sworn to secrecy. Isabel's absence was a relief; her arrest would sorely test Eleanor's obligation to uphold that law.

Picking up her mug, she sipped her stone-cold tea, its chill seeping into her chest. There was also the rest of the realm to consider. Although she'd been on the throne for a whole year, she'd foolishly left the Council to govern undirected. Her only personal achievements were blimp surveys of dubious value. Even with Isabel's assistance, her last one had been a disaster.

But no point wallowing in self-reproach. From now on she would actively reign. Time to use her wits and judgement, starting with judgement of the fallen king. She stalked over to the wall where his portrait hung. Her arms trembled as she lifted it down, letting it clunk on the threadbare carpet.

"I'm disappointed in you, Father." No, not just disappointed. That was too small a word for her crashing sense of disillusionment. Like a stone dropped from a blimp, she'd plummeted from complete trust in his judgement to suspecting all his actions. "Maybe you were losing your mind, becoming paranoid in your middle years, obsessed with the idea of external danger. Blaming someone else for your own faults. We have enough problems without panicking over something imaginary." What had happened to his lauded perceptiveness, that he had reacted with so little to go on?

Still... She cocked her head to one side. Could she use the pretext of an external threat to further her long-term plans? The events of the last few days—a murder trial, implication of a previously reputable scientist and his death, plus what she'd learned about her father's plans—had been symptoms of the problems she wished to correct. Once she made knowledge of cursed powers public—carefully, of course—cursed practitioners would no longer need to ply their powers in secrecy. They need not fear exposure: or having to kill to prevent that exposure. Maybe Isabel wouldn't have been driven to desperate measures. And there would be less danger for people like Artur, the blimp engineer who'd been cursed indirectly through Eleanor's actions.

She tossed the blanket on to the chair then gathered the

papers scattered on the floor, stacking them in some semblance of order. The problem would be getting Council support. Although they would have to obey her directives, they'd place innumerable obstacles in her way because they held her in low esteem. She frowned at her father's portrait. However, they'd offered *him* respect. If she told them of King Frederick's private notes referring to danger, they'd not question it. She could even build upon his vague allusions and say he predicted an attack in the near future. *That* would shake them out of their stagnant complacency. Their condescending, heavy-lidded expressions would change, and their eyes would bulge... A smile curved her lips. And then Eleanor could use the supposed emergency situation to push for her own agenda, killing two birds with one flechette, so to say.

Sneaky, but justifiable. Nobody knew what lay outside their borders. In theory, external hostile forces could exist, so she wasn't really lying to the Council. Just taking an oblique approach. Far better that than an unplanned exposure and public panic about how cursed powers were used. And if Eleanor's misdirection were later revealed, the benefits of her actions would already be apparent.

With a grimace, she picked up the portrait and wrestled it back into place. She couldn't afford gossip about its removal. Time to prepare for the Council meeting. Heading towards her bathing room, she pulled a sober blue jacket and dress from her wardrobe. She paused to glance back at the portrait. Maybe her father had also not believed in an attack, merely using it as a pretext for his own plans. She'd better take care: those plans had led to his untimely death.

"I'm sorry?" Stifling a yawn, Eleanor shifted uncomfortably

in the central seat at the Council room's U-shaped table. Unlike the lived-in upholstered furniture in her suite, this hard oaken chair wasn't conducive to sleep. Probably a good thing. Why had she called this meeting in such a rush instead of scheduling it to allow herself some rest? She had only herself to blame.

Seated beside her, Chief Councillor Hastings gave her an avuncular smile. His well-groomed appearance suggested that *he* hadn't worked into the small hours of the morning. "As I was saying, Your Majesty, your calling an emergency session is quite without precedent. That is, your father never saw fit to do such a thing, and he expressed no concerns about how the Council handled matters he delegated. Particularly if there are trying times ahead, it will no doubt be necessary to reassure the populace that they are still being governed by a steady and experienced hand."

Like yours, you mean. At least he didn't go as far as patting her arm, as he once did when she visited here as a child. Then, she might have giggled, but today she'd have been tempted to hit him. "I totally agree, Chief Councillor. My father often praised your competence. Your oversight of Council meetings while I dealt with other matters has been invaluable."

He adjusted his spotted silk cravat. "So you'd agree—"

"It's truly admirable how you have yielded the chair so graciously, now that I have time to attend." Time to push a little. "A lesser man might have resigned from his position in disappointment. I'm delighted to have your continued loyalty and support."

Hastings' jowls wobbled as he closed his mouth. Had he truly been a boxing champion in his youth? His three long-standing Council colleagues—representing history, logistics and security—watched Eleanor with polite neutrality, as if waiting to side with the winner. How tempting to replace the lot of them. No, that wasn't fair: they'd simply maintained the status quo. It was *her* role to lead progress. She'd better make up for lost time.

Or maybe they were watching the new Council member beside her: Susanna Longleaf, a former captain of the guard. Eleanor had appointed her just a couple of days ago. If the other councillors had concerns about *why* a mind reader was now the Chief Scientist, that was their problem. It shouldn't be necessary to call upon her powers during these meetings, but that might explain why the men clustered on one side of the table, with Susanna sitting opposite in lonely splendour. While the men and Eleanor wore sober suits, Susanna's borrowed nectarine wrap dress added a splash of elegance to the room. Would Eleanor cut such a figure when she reached middle age?

Historian Gauntlett cleared his throat. One of Hastings' contemporaries, his soft, vague expression was compounded by thick glasses. "What is the problem, Your Majesty?"

Concentrate! This ought to be a pivotal moment and the start of major reforms. Wishing she weren't quite so petite, Eleanor pressed damp palms to the table and leaned forwards. "Several things. Logistician Randall, you weren't at Captain Jonathan Shelley's murder trial earlier this week, so I'll briefly update you. He has been exonerated of all charges. He was framed by former Scientist Silvers, who was scheming to curse people deliberately." At Randall's puzzled look, she added, "I'm just setting some context. You needn't do anything."

"Presumably Silvers has been fully interrogated about

this." Security Councillor Martek scowled at his bandaged wrist. The lanky old man had suffered a minor sprain when Silvers attempted to escape from the courtroom.

"Partly," said Eleanor. "He provided information about his motives and methods at an initial questioning." Silvers had been open enough about that, though he had no awareness of being manipulated himself.

Pushing those ugly glasses up his nose, Gauntlett wrinkled his lips in disapproval. "Might I be able to speak with him? Unpleasant chap, and shocking behaviour, but if his ideas tally with some clues in our archives, the afflicted might have alternative training methods open to them. In fact, I remember Captain Shelley approaching me with a similar hope. Independently of Silvers, of course."

Poor Jonathan's good intentions had contributed to the mess. Out of a sense of responsibility, he'd tried to help the teenager Tabitha with her training, much as it—literally—pained them both. Silvers had then kidnapped the girl in order to blackmail him.

"What's the problem with the current methods?" asked Hastings. "Most captains and other people with powers perform their tasks with reasonable efficiency. Captain Shelley's unconventional ideas are not the norm."

Susanna inhaled sharply.

No wonder, given her closeness to Jonathan. Eleanor nodded at her. "Chief Scientist Longleaf, would you care to answer?"

"Pain, Councillor Hastings." Susanna pursed her lips. "You don't appreciate the pain the afflicted have to put themselves through in order to learn control of, and subsequently trigger, their powers. Powers they then use in support of the Council's aims. I plan to change that by implementing a new, non-traumatic training system. I'm pulling all the mind readers from their other duties to help. I would welcome Historian Gauntlett's input as well."

Eleanor hid a smirk. Susanna's précis of the issue would lead the discussion exactly where she wanted, and without excessive queenly input. It would have been nice to confide in the woman—to a limited extent—but she'd have enough on her plate with the recency of her appointment.

Hastings still wore a frown. "I suppose it might encourage more Keep residents to cooperate. But is it prudent to deprive other departments of the mind readers' services? On another point, Captain Longleaf... I beg your pardon, Chief Scientist Longleaf. No offence, but I don't fully understand the decision to appoint you as a scientist, never mind as the most senior one, given your lack of experience. Maybe I'm slow on the uptake, but I would have imagined Kenneth Staunton to be a better candidate. Particularly if Her Majesty is seeing fit to call this emergency meeting. There must be matters of great import."

Would the man not stop bellyaching? He was worse than a scratched phonograph. Still, it was a useful reminder that Staunton was one of his cronies. Eleanor rapped the table. "Need I remind you that Staunton has only recently been reinstated as a scientist following his retirement last year? His approach to research is now outdated." To be fair, Hastings had no idea Staunton had been manipulating Silvers, never mind that it had been at her father's insistence. Still, she shouldn't make things awkward for Staunton, given that he'd been carrying out a royal request. "The training method Chief Scientist Longleaf has pioneered is the greatest scientific advance in recent years. I fully support her decision to reassign all mind readers to training.

Historian Gauntlett, going back to your original request to speak with Silvers, I'm afraid you can't. He's dead."

Hastings stiffened.

"What?" Gauntlett removed his glasses and polished them on his tie, as if that would help him assess her words better.

"Indeed." Eleanor raised her voice. "He was being held in the Council detention cells. Charges including murder, kidnapping, unlawful imprisonment, theft... He was found devoid of life shortly afterwards." She waved a hand at Hastings. *I shouldn't enjoy this, but I will.* "I'm sure that Councillor Hastings intended to address the matter later in the agenda. And that he will be able to explain how it happened, since his area of responsibility covers the Council building and the security and welfare of those within. Especially prisoners, even those facing execution." The obvious culprit would be Isabel, assuming she was still alive. Her note had suggested she would target people who exploited the curse, uncaring of the suffering they caused. But Eleanor couldn't stomach exposing her, so she'd leave Hastings to a fruitless investigation instead.

"It could have been natural causes?" At the other councillors' doubtful looks, Hastings swallowed. "Well, I have little to report right now, but obviously I will assess the evidence more closely after this meeting. The number of people familiar with our procedures is quite limited, and it should be straightforward enough to eliminate those who are blameless. In addition to the guards on rota, we could look at others with access to the Royal Compound. Captains in particular—"

"Thank you." Eleanor's pulse raced. Her poke at Hastings had steered him in a dangerous direction. "I'm sure you will deal with matters capably. Now we should move on."

Hastings closed his mouth.

Time to see if her idea would work. "All of us feel my father's loss keenly." After the murmurs of agreement died down, she continued. "He had the best interests of Numoeath at heart, and we flourished under his leadership. I valued his opinion in all things." *Well, I used to.* "I have just come into possession of some notes he wrote, dated from just before he passed on. They caused me considerable disquiet."

Martek clutched his fountain pen. "A threat to our safety?"

"I fear so." Her stomach fluttered. "According to his notes, our realm faces an external threat. He believed this would manifest within the next few years. An attack of some kind." Might as well be bold with her claims.

"An attack from where? The south?" Shrugging his bony shoulders, Martek looked confused rather than worried. "Nobody's approached us in the centuries since our ancestors arrived. I'd have guessed that those who didn't make the Great Journey all died. But even if they survived, why would they be hostile?"

"I don't know. I suspect he didn't have time to look into matters further before he went to Settlers' Rest."

"Hmm," said Hastings. "The timing is suspicious. Might he..." He glanced at Eleanor. "Could his passing and his intentions have been related?"

Eleanor licked her lips. It would take an idiot not to make the connection, but for once she didn't want them thinking about murder. "As you know, a full investigation was made. There was no evidence his death was unnatural.

I concede it is a possibility"—she strove to keep her voice unconcerned—"but an unlikely one."

Hastings raised a silent eyebrow.

Her gaze swept the table. "Gentlemen, and Chief Scientist Longleaf, this matter concerns us all. We must make the most of the resources at hand, which surely include the abilities of the afflicted. If it comes to the worst and diplomacy fails, we may end up in combat, those with cursed powers fighting alongside the unafflicted. We *cannot* afford hesitation or panic among those on our side, and we cannot expect our citizens to continue in ignorance. Therefore, we must pre-emptively obtain public acceptance of cursed powers. We must integrate the afflicted—and their powers—back into society, where they can work openly. Where they can work for the benefit of everybody."

Susanna's lips parted, then her eyes crinkled. A dimple appeared on her cheek.

The other councillors murmured and regarded Eleanor speculatively. At least they weren't recoiling in horror. But why would they? They already deployed captains with powers to detect potential troublemakers. Rarely, the Council demanded more permanent solutions—*neutralisations*, such a sanitised word—but that was almost always to ensure that powers remained secret. She clenched her fists under the table. Such killings wouldn't be needed if her plans worked.

"But they would still be answerable to the Council?" asked Hastings.

How typical of the man. "They would be under the supervision of the scientists, as is currently the case. With Chief Scientist Longleaf's new initiative, I'm confident that more afflicted can be released from the Keep. I'm sure we could provide incentives—*attractive* ones—for them to work for the Crown." And they shouldn't be slaves.

Eleanor nodded at Logistician Randall. "Additionally, the isolation of our outlying settlements is of concern. Imagine if one were overrun by invaders, and we had no way of knowing?"

Randall raised a finger, his cuff slipping back to expose a hairy forearm. "Just to remind my fellow councillors, twenty thousand people—nearly half the population of Numoeath—live in rural settlements."

"Exactly," said Eleanor. "We must not ignore the welfare of the ruralites, merely because *techne* and learning are concentrated in the capital."

"It would seem only fair," said Gauntlett, "to allow villagers to benefit from new developments."

Martek frowned. "Certainly, should some peripheral population come under attack, they need to be able to defend themselves as well as warning the rest of us."

A tightness in Eleanor's neck eased. They weren't as stuck in their ways as she'd feared. She'd just had to present her reforms in a way that didn't threaten their positions. Emphasising an attack might have been unnecessary, but she couldn't backtrack now. "I completely agree, and we need to improve communications. That means better messaging systems as well as roads so everyone can travel more easily. I can understand a past mismatch of *techne* level between settlements and the capital because of transport issues. The settlements are hardly poverty-stricken or suffering from lack of resources, but there's no good reason to leave them disadvantaged when it comes to knowledge."

"But what about the week's quarantine?" asked Martek. Of course he'd be concerned about security.

"True, this might increase the risk of beast attacks and

exposure to the curse, if people are tempted to travel more frequently and independently of the convoy." She wouldn't mention the idea of deliberate cursing, nor the recent discovery that beasts weren't always involved. "But it will be possible to plan routes that avoid cursed mounds. We have evidence that beasts tend to live near cursed mounds. Attacks in other areas are unfortunate but unlikely."

Martek leaned forwards. "Pardon me, Your Majesty, but the scientists hadn't yet passed me that information."

Damn. Although Susanna knew of Eleanor's blimp trips through helping Artur after he was cursed at a mound, there was no official report. Eleanor hadn't dared submit her data following the trip in case it threw suspicion on Artur. Instead, she'd *sidestepped* the official protocol and arranged for Susanna to train him in the palace, rather than having him detained in the Keep. Fortunately, now that his power seemed quiescent, he was no longer in danger of being incarcerated.

Susanna clasped her hands, her knuckles white. "You'll have to forgive me, Councillor Martek, but I've not yet had time to go through the papers awaiting review."

"Staunton would have known already," muttered Hastings.

"I'm sure he wouldn't." Eleanor's voice was sharper than she had intended, and she threw Susanna an apologetic glance. "Even if Staunton hadn't been away for a year, I haven't yet completed *my* written report on the survey I performed personally by blimp. Susann—Chief Scientist Longleaf, I'm sorry it's taken so long. I will send someone over with the papers later today. Let's move on."

The meeting continued. Faced with an external threat, no matter how vaguely defined, even Hastings conceded her plans were reasonable, as long as someone else was involved in the actual work. Eleanor nearly grinned. She already had an engineer lined up to develop roads and communication systems, and the public acceptance was something she ought to handle herself.

Hastings lightly thumped his fist on the table. "And how should we prepare militarily? I'd hate to think of a hostile force trampling over us unhindered. We must fight for what's ours and give invaders cause to regret their actions."

She squelched the impulse to tug her braid. Raising an army to support her pretence hadn't crossed her mind when she had her bright idea. "Historian Gauntlett, can you check your archives for previous invasions or wars?"

Gauntlett nodded. "The pre-Journey archives include references to conflicts. I'd not paid them that much attention. They didn't seem relevant to today. But now I'll assign someone to the task. I wonder if the royal library archives might also have records?"

His suggestion made sense, even if the whole investigation was a farce. Still, it would be good to get some help in her library. Those two rooms of dust-covered old books and journals reproached her every time she entered. Who knew what useful knowledge might be hiding there, just waiting to be discovered? "Do you have someone you could send over?"

"Yes. He's a convoy guard with an interest in history, so he has practical experience of travel."

Hastings drummed his fingers on the table. "Funny, in my boxing days I consulted those old books with an eye to military theory. Thought it might be useful in the ring. Enjoyed many an afternoon in the library. Gauntlett and I were a lot younger then." He raised an eyebrow at

Gauntlett. "With fewer grey hairs. Anyway, the sooner we recruit defence forces, the sooner we can start training them."

"Er, quite right. Just what I was about to say." At least she could give him a sop to his dignity. It certainly wasn't a task she wanted to waste time on herself. "I am creating a new position to lead the army. Chief Councillor Hastings, I think you would make an admirable commander-in-chief."

"Your Majesty! This is a great honour indeed." Red-faced but smiling, Hastings stood and bowed while the other councillors applauded.

It was all Eleanor could do not to roll her eyes. Let him play at being a soldier, and it would keep him out of the way of the real work.

She drew the meeting to a close after telling Susanna to continue with her training work and directing Martek to keep an eye on their southern border. There, Numoeath's fertile land petered out and gave way to barren wastelands. In other directions, the realm was bounded by sea and rocky coastlines which made a natural barrier.

The other councillors departed while Eleanor remained to write her meeting notes. Things had gone more smoothly than she'd expected, considering how hastily she'd thrown together her ideas. Next time she'd suggest expanding the Council. The captains should be represented, as should the engineers. She already had a list of candidates.

Murmuring from the guards—a mix of her own and the Council's—came from the hallway outside.

A bulky figure filled the doorway, his red uniform matched by his eyepatch. "Your Majesty?"

She smiled. Someone she could trust. "Paton, I'm nearly finished. I have a small job for you."

Chapter 2

After leaving the Council hall, Susanna strolled along the paved pathway towards the Keep, avoiding spray from the decorative fountains to either side. She pretended not to notice the brown-clad guards' glances and whispers. *Breathe in...* They'd be wondering why a city captain had been placed in charge of the Keep. *Breathe out...* That was a question she'd asked herself repeatedly since her appointment two days ago. It didn't help that Hastings seemed to regard her as an interloper. On the bright side, sweaty palms weren't visible. *Back straight, eyes ahead.*

Her impending meeting with the other two scientists had promised to be a trial by fire. And that was even before learning of this threat from outside their borders. Being appointed Chief Scientist had been a considerable honour—and an unprecedented one—but the post would be no sinecure. Staunton had played a deep and risky game, advancing the late king's schemes, and he wouldn't be happy to be deprived of his reward.

Unfortunately, she'd never mind-read Staunton as he'd been in retirement during her time working in Ascar. Eleanor's mind readers had confirmed his worthy motivations and support of the Crown, but that didn't mean he was well-intended towards Susanna personally. Now she was Chief Scientist, she shouldn't mind-read him herself, especially for what would be regarded as a petty reason. How could she have anticipated his reinstatement? Nobody could have predicted both the loss of Silvers and the death of Lady Nelson, the previous Chief Scientist.

She raised her chin and regarded her destination.

Nearly everyone dreaded the square intimidating tower she approached: a combination of prison and research facility. It was fifteen years since she'd been detained inside. Despite reporting here as a captain many times, passing inside its grey stone walls still made her breath catch. Today would be her first in this new role, and already she felt the increased pressure. *Breathe in...* Her gaze tracked up to the barred windows of the third floor. If she could help free those inside and alleviate the fear that society had of them, it would mean others didn't have to suffer. Susanna clenched her jaw. She *had* to live up to Eleanor's expectations.

The brown-uniformed boy at the Keep's reception desk stood and thumped a fist to his chest. Her fingers curled automatically, but she nodded instead of returning the salute. The sooner she shucked off her guard habits, the better. No point in confusing people.

After ascending the stairs to the first floor, she took a deep breath, squelched her nerves and donned her captain's mask of composure. First impressions would count for a lot. Ambling along the maze of corridors, she exchanged pleasantries with her new support staff, trying to memorise their names and wondering if she'd be forced to ask for directions. Eventually she stumbled on the office she'd been offered the previous day.

Previously Lady Nelson's lair, the papers inside had remained untouched since the old woman's death. Until some space could be carved out of the tottering piles, Susanna had commandeered the storeroom next door to work in. Silvers' old office had reverted to Staunton, but she wouldn't put it past the man to dump Silvers' notes in her new room. That said, better she be the one to deal with those, given how Staunton had influenced Silvers.

Inside Susanna's cramped temporary office, Jonathan was perched on the edge of her desk. A smile touched her lips, and her breathing eased. Her long-time colleague, friend and *finally* lover wore a borrowed royal indigo robe, his injured arm in a sling. Because Jonathan still had no belongings after Silvers had confiscated—*stolen*—all his assets, he depended on goodwill to keep him clothed. Eleanor's housekeeper certainly had a sense of style. Once Susanna had time, she'd supplement Martha's efforts and treat him to smarter garb than he usually chose.

As she nudged the door shut with her foot, he slid off the desk and took her hand. His pale blue eyes regarded her with concern. "How did it go?"

"Where to start?" She squeezed his hand. "Eleanor kicked off with a declaration of your innocence, so that's a weight off our minds. Gratifying though it is, I was surprised she said that first, since there are more serious matters. She's convinced King Frederick was right, and it's likely someone will try to attack us. In a few years, she estimates."

Jonathan frowned. "But from where? In all my years on convoy, I've never seen signs of—"

"I know. It can't have been information gathered by Isabel, not after that letter she left. But whatever the king's sources, the evidence he set down in his notes was strong enough that Eleanor's decided to act. And it must have been compelling, given her disenchantment with his methods." She grimaced. "I don't blame her. Still, she's a clever girl. Already she's thinking ahead and prioritising infrastructure. That'll benefit everyone, whatever the threat is. Oh, and there's a silver lining."

"I should hope so," he grumbled. "This isn't sounding at all good."

"The good thing is, she's going to dispense with the secrecy about curses. Life will be so much easier for us. She's persuaded the Council to support this. Somehow, she even got Hastings to agree—you know how conservative he is—and that was *before* putting him in charge of the army. Turns out he and Gauntlett once made a study of military matters, so he's a better choice than most. I have high hopes for her as queen, now she's more actively involved in government."

He didn't look as pleased as she'd hoped, but optimism wasn't in his nature. "I guess. Nothing like the thought of war to unite people."

"I know it's a concern, but it's not imminent." She picked up her papers. "Anyway, we need to do our bit, starting now. Let's head for the meeting room."

With the same painted off-white walls as the rest of the Keep and its unadorned cheap furniture, the scientists' meeting room had always struck Susanna as an oddly insipid place, considering what went on there. Curse victims relived their experiences in detail, so the scientists could tease out information about powers. After over a decade as a captain, standing at attention to report, this would be her first time seated behind the table. From now on, she'd allow interviewees to sit as well. When she took the middle chair, Jonathan pulled out a chair at one end. *Breathe in...* Although he was officially only here to talk about painlessly triggering powers, she was glad of his presence.

As Jonathan was settling himself at the table, Staunton

arrived. His tailored charcoal suit—*he* wasn't wearing borrowed clothing—and trimmed grey beard signalled his readiness to return to work. He and Jonathan scowled at each other.

Stomach roiling, Susanna cleared her throat.

"Good morning, Susanna." Staunton gave her a barely polite nod before sitting beside her but away from Jonathan.

Hasty footsteps in the corridor preceded Fellows' arrival. "Susanna, I hope I'm not late, and to your first meeting, too." He eased his plump backside into the seat between Jonathan and Susanna and brushed a few crumbs off his tie. "Oh, hello, Captain Shelley. Good to see you back. I'd heard some rumours, but I guess they weren't true?"

Surely Karsten Fellows wasn't always this socially unaware? Susanna had previously mind-read him during his monthly monitoring. Such monitoring could only detect surface thoughts and deliberate lying, but she'd sensed a focus on his work rather than personal ambition. Properly directed, he should be an asset.

"I've been exonerated." Jonathan glared at Staunton. "No thanks to your colleague here."

Dammit, he wasn't helping. Susanna drew a quick breath. "Let's begin. At the Council meeting I've just come from—"

"Rub it in, why don't you?" muttered Staunton.

Boys! Time for words with impact. "Queen Eleanor has directed us to prepare for an invasion."

Fellows' face went pinker than usual, and his jaw dropped. "But how..."

"Just yesterday, she came into possession of some notes written by her father. I don't know their contents, but she's convinced. Powers will be essential to support the war effort. Because of this, the queen intends to inform the public about the value of powers and obviate the need for secrecy. It's excellent news that we can work openly, but it also means we can't afford any accidents. The last thing we want is a backlash against acknowledged cursed because someone was hurt or worse."

Staunton stopped glaring at Jonathan and tugged his greying beard. "Will she make public the full history of how powers have been used?"

At last the man was paying attention to business. She tipped a hand from side to side. "Presumably she'll need to gloss over things somewhat. Kenneth, you know some of the background already, since you were there when we found the papers in... Isabel's house. Although it's not our business, strictly speaking, I'm sure she'd appreciate any suggestion on how to approach the matter."

"Certainly," said Staunton. "I've offered to read those notes of King Frederick's. I could maybe put together his words with what I remember of our conversations. That might help Queen Eleanor with her strategic decisions. I wish he'd shared his thoughts more fully with me, but at the time, well, who would have believed that he'd be–"

Susanna coughed. Fellows didn't know that Isabel had confessed to killing King Frederick, and Eleanor had made it clear she didn't want the information disseminated.

After a moment, Staunton continued. "That is, nobody could have expected King Frederick to die. And we still don't truly know his intentions."

"Whatever they were, it's up to the queen now." She regarded her papers. "Our job is to continue training the afflicted, easing them into power using the mind-reading feedback system I developed. I can't train everyone myself, so I'm going to reassign all the other mind readers to help. Jonathan will also contribute. Monitoring sessions will be discontinued, as will the use of mind readers in interview rooms." From personal experience, monitoring was a waste of mind reading effort. They rarely caught anyone lying.

"No monitoring sessions at all?" Staunton raised an eyebrow.

"Not as routine. In exceptional circumstances we could—Oh. *That's* why you retired." Routine monitoring was restricted to those in active service. Staunton's retirement would have left him free from the procedure while he secretly worked towards King Frederick's objectives.

"One reason. I can't say I was proud of it."

Fellows' brow furrowed. "Proud of what?"

"Sorry," said Susanna. "Kenneth, would you mind bringing Karsten up to date?"

She sat back while Staunton summarised recent events. King Frederick's request to generate more cursed would have provoked public outcry if revealed. So, Staunton had set Silvers up. He'd allowed Silvers to blackmail him into retirement so that Silvers would do the dirty work. Silvers had found out—using Jonathan's flesh—that whatever caused the curse could be transmitted by extract from a sufferer.

When Staunton finished, Fellows gaped. "I had no idea! I mean, Jed Silvers was a little odd, and I wasn't entirely surprised by his arrest. But I'd assumed it wasn't for anything too serious, although I did wonder when they found him dead in his cell. To think..."

Jonathan leaned forwards. "All true, and I have the scars to prove it. He even implanted a tracking device in my leg. I suppose that was another 'suggestion' from you, Staunton?"

Staunton held up his hands. "I'm responsible for many things, but not that one."

Jonathan's eyes narrowed. "Only because you didn't think of it."

Susanna's temples throbbed. She should have foreseen he would clash with Staunton. Raising her voice, she said, "As a related issue, we have further evidence that the curse might have other modes of transmission..."

She told Fellows about Artur, who definitely hadn't been attacked by a beast or any other animal. He had, however, been hit with a fragment from a cursed mound. The working hypothesis was that the mounds contained some agent that caused the curse. Beasts became cursed from living there, or maybe eating the agent, and then transmitted the agent to other beasts or people they attacked. Eleanor would provide notes and photographs from her blimp trip with Artur, the trip when Isabel had disappeared.

"So *that's* why she wanted my maps." Fellows beamed. "I'm pleased they proved useful, although it's a shame about the blimp engineer. Is he the one you trained?"

"He's one of them." Even if that had been in secret. "There was also Tabitha."

"The young girl? The one who can move things around? Captain Shelley, I remember you had an interest in her. Glad to see it paid off. So, can she use her power at will?"

"Not quite," said Susanna. "My training—supplemented with Captain Lester Black's mind-control ability—helped Tabitha direct her power. But for activation we'd still been using the calibrated stimulus generators. She calls them 'pain boxes'. The sooner we're rid of those, the better."

"And that's where I can help." Jonathan pushed up his sleeves, creasing the velvet fabric, and propped his elbows on the table. "While I was on the run, I learned how to activate my power without pain. Of course, I was already experienced in controlling it."

Staunton frowned at him. "I'm all for non-traumatic methods, but I'm not convinced your method would be safe. We incarcerate the new ones because any stimulus—even something trivial—can set their powers off—"

"But mine's under conscious control. Just don't need pain." A muscle in his cheek twitched.

Staunton's frown deepened. "I read your reports. You nearly caused a blimp crash. And some rural herbal infusion set off your power in front of witnesses. That would suggest your control was precarious to start with. Not a good example for new practitioners."

Jonathan reddened but remained silent.

Blast. This meeting was difficult enough without all the bickering. Susanna tapped the table with her pen. "Our *current* and *immediate* problems are dealing with the newly cursed that Silvers created. There are two new residents upstairs in the infirmary. One's nearly ready to discharge to the residential floor. I'll speak to them both and offer training in how to control their powers, with Jonathan's help. If all goes according to plan, we'll be able to discharge them quickly. And after that, I'll look into the longer-term residents. I'm concerned that some have been in the Keep for so long, they might not cope with returning to regular society."

"What about Silvers' death?" Fellows mopped his brow. "If someone's going after scientists, that's worrying."

Susanna pursed her lips. They'd have to keep him in the

dark that they suspected Isabel, since that would open up a can of worms about King Frederick's death. Fellows had never been involved in Silvers' schemes, so he wasn't at risk. Susanna had to take it on trust that neither she nor Staunton were in danger either. "The death's being investigated by Hastings's people." *Isabel, you've gone far further than I could have imagined.*

Staunton stroked his beard and regarded Susanna. "It seems like there are diverse new matters to deal with, and at a time of instability and external threat, with considerable urgency. I'd be happy to take on some of the work, given your relative newness in a leadership position."

An experienced co-worker would certainly be helpful, but Eleanor didn't trust him enough after all he'd done, even if his motivations had been good. Best to take his words at face value. "Thank you for the offer, Kenneth. I might come back to you about that at some later date."

Jonathan pointed at Staunton. "You're mistaken, Staunton. Captains' duties require a considerable range of skills including leadership and planning. And captains have to think on their feet, under time pressure, and often in full view of the public. None of this hiding in cosy offices, isolated from the world."

"Jonathan," murmured Susanna. After bringing him to this meeting, she couldn't order him around. That would mar his credibility, not to mention her own.

"Though I'll give you this, Staunton." He jabbed a finger towards the scientist again. "Captains do secret dirty work, just like you. Difference is, we accept personal responsibility for it."

Poor Jonathan. He would never overcome his regret at having to murder a man to protect the Council's secrets.

Reaching over, she touched the back of his hand, which lay clenched into a fist on the table. "We're working to move beyond that." Nobody could bring the dead back to life, but with Eleanor's new plans, such measures should no longer be necessary.

Staunton raised a cynical eyebrow. "But she's been in Ascar for the last year, not touring the settlements. And all she's done is mind reading to order."

"Whose fault is that?" asked Jonathan. "She didn't ask to be redeployed. And she's still been working, while you've been sitting at home, scheming. Don't think that'll save you from—"

"Gentlemen," said Susanna. "Can we stick to relevant topics, please?"

"I'm trying to," snapped Staunton. "It would be easier if you could keep your lover under control."

She stiffened. Escalating personal insults—

Jonathan growled. "It wasn't me who let that piece of shit run rampant, who manipulated him. And he didn't just harm me. He fooled those poor Maldonites, and who knows what his intentions were for Annetta and the boy Samuel after dragging them here? I don't like you, Staunton."

"Yes, you've made that abundantly clear." Staunton rose. "Chief Scientist Longleaf, I don't think there is anything for me to contribute if you can't keep even a small meeting running to order. If anybody needs me, I shall be at home. Good day."

He bowed to Susanna, nodded at Fellows and left.

The nerve of the man! Jonathan glared at Staunton's retreating back. How dare he try to undermine Susanna after scheming the way he had with Silvers? That had landed

Jonathan as a fugitive with a price on his head, exposed him to who-knew-what drugs and nearly got him executed as a murderer.

The adjacent chair creaked, and Fellows turned to address Susanna. "Er, I'm not sure I could be of help with a new training system. I've overseen testing and so on, but..."

Jonathan's fists balled. Fellows wasn't nearly so bad, but none of the scientists had questioned how the newly cursed went through their so-called training. Not one of them had wondered why there was such a low rate of uptake, why the afflicted chose to spend their lives in—admittedly comfortable—captivity rather than undergoing training.

Well, it would be different with Susanna in charge. As he peered past Fellows' rotund profile, his gaze softened. That orange dress enhanced her trim figure even better than the ones she usually wore. How lucky he was. Such poise, and she still chose *him.*

Susanna glanced at him, and her lips twitched before she spoke to Fellows. "Not to worry. You can still speak with all the Keep and infirmary residents who have powers. Tell them there's a new training system that they might prefer. The mind readers will help them as a matter of priority."

"I can manage that." Fellows ducked his head.

"You don't need to speak to the residents in Rooms Two, Three and Four. I'll visit them myself. Can you also show Jonathan your maps? He may be able to indicate routes used by beasts."

Fellows' eyes crinkled above his round cheeks. "That would be grand. Captain Shelley, where would you like me to send them?"

"The barracks—" Jonathan closed his mouth. If Silvers had stolen *all* his belongings, there was no point in returning to an empty suite, even assuming it was still his. "Actually, could you leave them at reception downstairs? I'll pick them up."

"I'll go and find them right away." He grabbed his documents and left.

Susanna kept her gaze on the papers she was stacking, her movements slow and deliberate. "Jonathan, these meetings would run more smoothly if you could refrain from sniping at Staunton."

"He started it!" Jonathan's uninjured shoulder slumped. She deserved better support than that. "Sorry, that sounded infantile. But he's so... I don't trust him."

"I know, but we can't always select who we work with, and being at odds with yet another scientist won't help anyone in the long run." She chewed her lip. "I know you've been through a lot recently, and your injuries are nowhere near healed. And I shouldn't have dragged you here, not with Staunton. I'm sorry. But this is a difficult time, and I can't afford to let Eleanor down."

Reaching across awkwardly so as not to jostle his shoulder, he took her hand. A scant month ago, he wouldn't have dared: both because he was unsure of his reception, and because she might be able to pick up his thoughts. This new relationship between them was unfamiliar territory, hinting that they might grow old together. He wouldn't jeopardise it by keeping secrets. Not from Susanna. "It's not your fault. I'm proud she appointed you. I had just hoped we might manage to have some peace. But that's never going to happen, is it? What can I do?"

She squeezed his fingers gently. "As you told Staunton, you can help with training. You can annotate Fellows' maps and report on your observations of beast behaviour. That will help Eleanor's road plans hugely. There's plenty for you to do. But first, you need to take time to recover."

"Whatever you say, ma'am." He kissed the back of her hand.

Her cheek dimpled. "I must say, your robe is very fetching. People will wonder where I found you."

He glanced down and snorted. Fine clothing made him feel like a fraud. "Not quite what I would have chosen myself. But I suppose I should let you get on with the rest of your day. I'll pop up and visit Tabitha then grab Fellows' maps and see what I can do with them. The infirmier wants to see me too."

"Ah…" She sighed. "Would you mind very much not visiting Tabitha *too* often? It's just that, well, she seems more attached to you than is good for her. She's got the others for company. I think it would be healthy for her to form other friendships. And I'll see her myself today."

Jonathan stiffened, then he winced at the memory of his behaviour in the meeting. Not a good example for an impressionable girl. Staunton might be a bastard, but Jonathan was reaping rewards for allowing the man to provoke him. "And I suppose what you're not saying is that you don't want my bad temper to rub off on her."

"Sorry." Pink touched Susanna's face.

He resisted the temptation to run a finger along her cheekbone. "You're right. I guess I brought that on myself. I'm sure the others will keep an eye on her." Tabitha's neighbours on the residential floor were Franka, Annetta and Samuel. Annetta's actions had landed Jonathan in danger, but she'd then recruited the other two to rescue him and Tabitha from Silvers.

Susanna gave him a wavery smile. "Unfortunately, I do

have other things to deal with. Once you've sorted yourself out, perhaps you could return to our suite for a rest? We can't stay in the palace permanently, but it'll take a few days to find other accommodation."

We? His heart thrilled, but he sobered as he regarded the crow's feet around her rich brown eyes. Were they deeper than they had been yesterday? "Of course. I don't want to be a burden on you."

"You're not a burden. You keep life interesting."

He stood and kissed her forehead. Her affectionate glance as he left was ample reward. Time for him to do something for her, to help her do her job. She trusted him, and she hadn't belaboured her concerns about Tabitha. He should show himself deserving of that trust and not visit the child. Instead, he would pay Staunton a visit and have a little chat, man to man.

Susanna returned to her temporary office and dropped off her paperwork, indulging in the privacy to gather her thoughts. She closed her eyes and massaged her temples. Her guilty relief at Jonathan's departure—he wasn't *trying* to make her life difficult—was tempered by regret that she'd deprived him of the opportunity to visit Tabitha. Well, she couldn't blame him for his volatile attitude towards Staunton. And he'd held her hand. Nobody willingly initiated physical contact with a mind reader: not when secret thoughts might be exposed. Her heart lifted. Jonathan truly trusted her.

With a knock on the door, a messenger boy handed her a news sheet. Hastings had somehow got a rush print job done and distributed already. Nobody could criticise him for lack of efficiency.

Calling all patriots: the realm needs YOU!

Susanna sighed. What was she doing, daydreaming about Jonathan when there were serious matters afoot?

On the stairs up to the residential floor, she moved aside when Paton approached. He'd rescued her during her clumsy investigation of Silvers' neighbourhood, and then a few days later he'd arrested her. That had been a stroke of luck because Eleanor had become involved, leading indirectly to Susanna's promotion.

Meeting his one-eyed glower, she tried not to blush. *Breathe out...* Paton might be the Royal Chief Guard, but embarrassment or no, the Keep was *her* domain. She squared her shoulders. "Can I help you?"

He waved a hand in negation. "Her Majesty requested I ask Tabitha if she wanted anything."

That girl had everyone seeing to her comfort. "And did she?" Surely not expensive toys and trinkets, given her rural origins.

"Bird seed. She's feeling cooped up here."

Cooped up? After asking for bird seed? Was that a joke? Susanna opened her mouth, then thought better of replying. At least someone else was looking out for Tabitha. And just as well. She was fifteen, but often acted like a younger child. That was partly because of her confinement, and maybe also due to her—fortunately brief—kidnapping by Silvers. "I'm glad you're taking an interest in her."

"Gotta watch out for potential troublemakers." He continued down the stairs before she could form a snappy retort.

When Susanna arrived on the residential floor, the on-duty guard saluted her. "Good morning, Chief Scientist Longleaf."

"Good morning, Jeremy."

The lanky guard ducked his head. "Beg your pardon, ma'am, but it's Joshua."

Her face warmed. *Damn.* "Sorry. Joshua. I'll remember next time. Any problems?"

"No, everything's fine. Scientist Fellows dropped by briefly, said he'd be speaking with the residents over the next few days." Joshua rubbed the back of his neck. "Ma'am, if all the residents are getting keys to their suites, will the corridor still need guards? It's just that I've kinda got used to working here..."

"I don't think everyone will receive a key. And even if they do, it would be prudent to have someone keeping an eye on things. Your job is secure." That was the best she could offer him, given the possibility of war. "I don't need keys for the people I'm visiting today."

"Ah." His expression brightened. "If you need anything else, just let me know." He saluted, and she walked off down the corridor.

The doors to Franka's and Tabitha's suites were ajar. Hearing laughter from Tabitha's room, Susanna knocked on the frame and slipped inside.

The two-seater couch and adjacent footstool were occupied by Franka, a sturdy woman in her forties. Her broad face wore an expression of good humour, and she chuckled. "He looked at me with horror and said, 'You mean it's going to fall off?' Since he was acting like—" She heaved herself forwards and waved at Susanna. "Well, if it isn't Chief Scientist Longleaf. Good to see you, ma'am. Nice to see you've dressed up so fine just to visit *us*."

Susanna smiled. Franka's years of convoy service would make her a good captain, but she'd never lose that irreverent streak. "It was the least I could do after the queen's housekeeper dragged me to a storeroom and told me to help myself."

Tabitha nodded from her habitual place by the window where she stood feeding the birds with breadcrumbs. Samuel perched on a nearby stool, pencil in hand, sketch-pad on his lap. Both children—and Franka—still wore the white overalls provided to detainees, but maybe Franka could take them shopping soon.

Hmm. Susanna glanced around the room again. "No Annetta?"

"She's down in the laboratory." Franka massaged her leg, which had been injured in a beast attack several weeks ago. "That's why I'm keeping these two entertained. She feels bad about all that stuff that happened, so she's working extra hard. I did say it wasn't her fault that Silvers misled her, but she still feels responsible. And I gather that's not the first time she's got one up on"—she glanced at Tabitha—"Jonathan."

True enough. It was an accident with the Annetta's herbs that had led to Jonathan's first imprisonment by Silvers. The diffident herbalist was someone to keep an eye on, no matter how good her intentions.

"Why's Paton so grumpy?" asked Tabitha. "I only asked him what his first name was."

Franka laughed. "I don't think *anyone* knows that, not even him."

Susanna could well believe that. "You should be glad he's fetching the bird seed you wanted."

"I guess. Even the birds are getting bored here." Tabitha stuck out her lower lip. "Isn't Jonathan visiting today?"

"Er, I don't think so." *Breathe in...* She suppressed the

memory of his disappointed expression. "I asked him to sort some things. I'm sure he'll be over when he can."

Tabitha's face scrunched, then she brightened. "And how about Lester? He's really..." She blushed.

"I'm afraid not." Not if the man could help it. "Remember, he's a captain too, and he has other duties." Just as well Susanna had suggested Eleanor send him out of the city for a bit. Then Tabitha needn't feel offended at his absence.

Seemingly oblivious to the conversation, Samuel slid off his stool and held up his sketch for Susanna to inspect. Thankfully, it was a depiction of Tabitha rather than anything unusual. Samuel's power of "distance-viewing" was unpredictable and disquieting, although he didn't seem disturbed by the drawings he produced. Even allowing for the fact he was only ten years old, such indifference was odd. Had he been not quite right, even before he was cursed? Perhaps Annetta would have more information about his background.

Susanna raised an eyebrow at Tabitha. "What do you think?"

Tabitha squinted. "My hair isn't *that* messy, is it?"

"Well, maybe sometimes, if I'm honest." Despite all the ribbons Susanna had provided, that mass of curly black hair remained out of control. "It does look like you." She addressed Samuel. "Well done."

He beamed, then his eyes turned to the dining table that held the remnants of a cake. "I'm hungry."

Franka shook her head. "You're always hungry, kiddo. Go ahead and finish it off."

A wooden box on the table caught Susanna's eye. A calibrated stimulus generator. *Pain box.* Her breath caught, and she resisted the urge to touch her earlobe where the clip would attach when in use. "Tabitha, have you been practising your power?"

"A little. You did *tell* me to."

"True, but I hoped you wouldn't need to use the pain box." Wasn't this why Susanna was working here, so the boxes need no longer be used?

"Oh, *that*." Tabitha wrinkled her nose. "I didn't need it. Was just showing it to Samuel. He'd never seen one before."

"I should think not!" A hasty glance confirmed the boy to be focussed on the cake. "He's too young for such things. So if you didn't use it..."

"Here, look." Tabitha picked some breadcrumbs from a bowl and scattered them on her palm.

With a grin, Franka swung herself to her feet and approached. "This is fun to watch."

Not daring to blink, Susanna studied the unmoving breadcrumbs. Tabitha closed an eye and squinted in concentration. After a few seconds, the breadcrumbs started to jiggle, individual ones jumping into the air.

Impressive. But... "You're not *blowing* on them, are you?"

"No!" She turned her head away, and the breadcrumbs continued moving. "I'm sort of shaking them, but without moving my hand. But I can do other things as well."

"Such as?"

"Keep watching..."

As Susanna peered closer, a puff of air blew some breadcrumbs into her face.

"Hey!" She rubbed her watering eyes while Franka laughed.

Tabitha smirked. "You did ask about blowing."

"I suppose I did." Outwitted by a teenager. What next? "And you've demonstrated that the principle works. Activation and control. Excellent. And how about you, Franka?"

"Nah, I'm still where I was before. Need the pain box. But really, I can't see my power being much use anyway, so it prolly doesn't matter too much."

"I hope you don't need it, but did you see the *Informer* earlier? The extra edition?"

"Yeah." Franka's face grew serious. "If we do end up going to war, I guess frightening off enemies would be useful. Who'd have thought it?"

Susanna frowned in Tabitha's direction. Her power—the same as Jonathan's—could also be useful in combat. But it wouldn't be right to put a child on the front line. Still, could she maybe help in the medical corps or at least train in the infirmary? After all, Jonathan had saved Franka's life with his power, despite his lack of medical experience. Talking of which... "I'm glad you three are coping, but I can't stay any longer. I should go and speak to Annetta."

"Now you're a bigwig, everyone'll want a bit of your time." Franka waggled her eyebrows. "Jonathan will just have to share."

Susanna opened her mouth then paused. Franka might offer a sympathetic ear about Jonathan's—admittedly understandable—moodiness, but Susanna could hardly offload her frustrations with the two children there. "I'm sure he'll manage to keep himself out of mischief." *I hope.*

Chapter 3

Captain Lester Black of the city guard ran a shaky hand through his hair, inspecting himself for the hundredth time in the gilt-framed mirror. How stupid, he'd used too much pomade: an amateur's mistake. He wiped a greasy hand on his trouser leg while the red-clad guard manning the waiting area smirked. The man had been a visitor at Lester's previous place of employment, though thankfully not one of Lester's customers.

Like it or not, with the captain's uniform came responsibilities. Lester now reported directly to the Council, and citizens gave him cautious respect. He should feign a captain's dignity and carry himself with a composure like Susanna's. Standing in for the mother he couldn't remember, she'd given him a stability he hadn't previously known. At first, he'd been wary of her interest in him, but anyone with eyes could see her attachment to Jonathan. Once he'd reassured himself about that, Lester could relax in her presence. Relaxing in *Jonathan's* presence was another matter, but that was hardly unusual: men never seemed to treat him with friendliness.

He peered in the mirror again. This morning's shaving nick wasn't too conspicuous. Dark hair was all very well, but twice-daily shaving was inconvenient. Maybe he could grow a beard? Nah. Face fuzz would distract people from his green eyes. Not that he was out to seduce any—

"Captain Black?" came a woman's voice.

He jumped and blinked at an elderly woman in a pink pinafore. "Uh, yes?"

"The queen's working in her study." She nodded at the laden tray she held. "I'm taking her some refreshments, so you might as well follow me."

"Of course." *Old lady. Try boyish charm.* He summoned a smile. "Might I carry your tray, ma'am?"

"Ooh, not just handsome, but polite!" Beaming, she handed him her tray then patted his cheek.

The royal guard's snigger was cut short by the housekeeper's glare. "A problem, young man?"

The guard snapped to attention, eyes straight ahead. "No, Martha. Just something in my throat."

Lester followed Martha's well-padded backside up the grand wooden staircase. The palace wasn't completely unfamiliar territory. He'd been to the royal library just two days ago when Queen Eleanor held a meeting about Silvers' crimes and Jonathan's innocence. Lester's presence had been peripheral then, so why was she requesting another visit now? And by himself, seemingly?

At the top of the second flight, Martha halted and wagged a finger at him. "Ah! I knew I'd seen you somewhere before. I'd recognise that cheeky smile anywhere."

"Sure, I visited just a couple of days—"

"No, it was several years ago." She tapped her chin. "Weren't you working in... The King's Pleasure?"

"What?" The crockery on the tray rattled. "What if I was? And what were *you* doing there?"

She sniffed. "Arranging a home visit, of course. As head housekeeper, I'm responsible for the comfort of my employer. And, well, after the former queen passed on... How do you think the establishment got its name?"

Lester gaped. Was she having him on? Surely not.

Martha winked. "But we won't mention that to Eleanor. She's such an innocent."

"Uh, right." He tried to straighten his expression as the housekeeper walked onwards.

She knocked at a door and swung it open. "There you are." Before he could say anything, she was gone.

With a white-knuckled grip on the tea tray, Lester slunk into the room. Its wood-panelled walls were a far cry from the stifling velvet hangings that would have dressed a brothel's interior. No gold-painted chandeliers in this room, and only portraits of various royalty served as decoration. He tore his gaze away from King Frederick's leer and studied the room's occupant.

Queen Eleanor sat behind a well-worn desk, her head bowed over some papers. Maps, by the look of them. She muttered to herself then twirled the end of her loose dark braid around a finger.

No point loitering. Lester's polished shoes clicked across the wooden floor. Damn, he should salute or bow or something. How could he do that with his hands full? "Your Majesty?"

"Oh!" The queen's head jerked up, and she hastily flipped her braid back over her shoulder. "I thought you were Martha. Put the tea tray over there, please." She waved at a low table, and he set the tray down. Frowning, she reached towards the bell pull. "Would you like a cup too?"

Lester gulped. "No, thank you. Your Majesty. Shall I pour?"

"Please. I'll be with you in a minute, just want to get this down while I remember." She scribbled a few notes.

Hand wobbling only slightly, Lester poured tarry tea

into the gold-rimmed cup. He carried the cup and saucer over—*don't drop them!*—and laid them on the desk with a flourish. The queen's eyebrows rose. *Damn!* Old habits reappeared at the worst of times.

She waved him to an adjacent chair and took a sip. Her eyes closed briefly as she swallowed. "Ah, that's better. I expect you're wondering why I've summoned you here."

"Am I? I mean, yes." *Calm down.* She couldn't have heard of his previous occupation. Oh, but Silvers had told everyone at the trial. Barracks gossip had spread about the bastard's death, but that had come much too late for Lester. He couldn't escape from his sordid past. Anyway, surely *the queen* wouldn't need to—

"You tried to help Captain Shelley at his trial, and you witnessed some of the aftermath. I was speaking with Susanna earlier, and she mentioned your power. How you can use suggestion to influence people's behaviour."

Lester flinched. "I wasn't trying it on you, honest!" Why did people assume the worst?

She stared. "I wasn't suggesting that."

"Oh." What an idiot he was. When would he learn to think before opening his mouth?

"But I think you may be the right person for a job I have in mind."

Really? It wasn't often that someone trusted him. He inclined his head. "Happy to help, Your Majesty."

"Please call me Eleanor. Though not in public. I think that might give a wrong impression."

"Absolutely! That wouldn't be good at all, Your—uh, Eleanor."

A giggle escaped her before she coughed into her hand. "Sorry. I'm tired of stuffy formal titles, but that's a trivial issue. I'm wasting your time with my rambling."

Great, now the queen was laughing at him. "In that case, if you don't mind my asking, what *is* the issue?"

She gazed at her father's portrait, and her face grew serious. "My plans depend on public acceptance that cursed powers can be useful, and getting rid of the secrecy that's grown up around them."

He nodded. It had been a strain to keep his power concealed. But if he was openly known to have mind control, that mightn't be good for him either. The last thing he wanted was to get beaten up yet again because someone thought he was manipulating them, whatever the method.

"I'm directing you to visit each of the settlements. Ostensibly, you'll be informing them of future investments in infrastructure. Sound out what they all need. However, while you're there, you are to bring up the idea that curses and powers might be... less of a danger than people believe. Diplomatically, of course. You'll need to judge whether the time is right before you say anything."

"Tell them about *powers*?" He imagined hordes of outraged villagers advancing on him with scythes, and his hands shook. *Keep it together, man!* Of course someone needed to start the ball rolling, and she could hardly tour the settlements to tell them herself. Everyone knew about curses already. This would be a tentative step further. "Anything for the war effort, Your Majesty."

Her forehead wrinkled. "War?"

"Isn't that the reason? I read about it in the *Informer*, special mid-morning issue. Chief Councillor Hastings was calling for volunteers."

"Oh yes, of course." A flush spread across her cheeks. "Sorry, too many things on my mind. Please bear in mind that your own role is at least as important as Hastings'."

"But why me? Why not a convoy captain they already know?"

"Because of your power. Some people might be disquieted to learn of our work to return the cursed to society. I'm sure in the long term they'll appreciate the benefits—especially once I tell them of helpful powers—but there might be an initial risk of causing panic. I'd rather you didn't use your power to manipulate people, but maybe a nudge? If it looks like they might react badly?" She frowned at her papers. "Whether or not you use it, I'll bear the responsibility. You're acting on my orders."

"I really don't know how things with the settlements work at the moment." His shoulders tensed. "In fact, I've only been out of the city once, and that's when I got bitten." From whore to city guard had seemed a great career move, and then he'd chased a murderer into a group of beasts. Lester's wounds healed without even scarring; the murderer hadn't survived the beasts' attack.

Her glance was tinged with sympathy. "I'm sorry about your injury. In an ideal world the curse wouldn't exist. But the fact remains that you have a power that is useful in this situation. Thank you for deciding to train it rather than opting to remain in the Keep."

"It wasn't so bad, really. And Isa—Captain Hanlon really helped me settle in as a captain..."

Eleanor's face froze, and she stared at the desk, reaching up to grasp her braid.

Lester tried not to fidget. The length of Isabel's absence had been quite out of character, and now he was wondering if the cousins had argued. Should he offer some gentle words, or wait until Eleanor spoke first? He'd never explored how to deal with royalty. *The King's Pleasure.* They certainly hadn't mentioned anything to *him* when he worked there.

"We have a hub and spoke arrangement with Ascar at the centre of the outlying settlements." Eleanor's voice firmed as she spoke, and she lifted her head. "Transport is slow and uncertain, and people only get the opportunity to travel to the next settlement every few months when the convoy passes through. Information takes time to disseminate, even with messenger birds. Resources can't be shifted quickly. I want to change all that."

"But I've never been out of Ascar. Are you sure someone else wouldn't be better?" With the couple of dozen captains so thinly spread, he'd expected a rural assignment eventually. But couldn't his first task have been simpler?

"You're the only one with your ability." She regarded him. "Susanna told me about your background. It was her suggestion that this assignment would be good experience for you, expanding your responsibilities. She has confidence in you. And so do I."

He wasn't sure whether to be gratified or terrified. "Sounds like it'll take a long time if I need to travel with the convoy."

"I suggest you commandeer a blimp if you don't mind travelling by air. I have a friend—one of the engineers will be able to help."

"Wow." He brightened. That might be an experience. Not to mention a quick getaway if he messed things up. "Though, uh, the ruries might not be impressed with me. I've no idea about their customs." And he'd end up a laughingstock again.

"Good point. I should assign you a travel partner who

can answer questions you might feel awkward asking the locals." She glanced out of the window towards the Keep. "Ah, I know just the person. Someone who was born in the country, knows rural ways and would appreciate a break from the city."

"Sounds great. Who will that be?" It would be a relief not to take on *too* much responsibility. He could fake it with the best of them, but having someone along who was really in charge, with him as a captain—as a front—that would be much better.

Eleanor met his gaze and smiled. "Someone you've helped already. I'm sure she'll be keen to return the favour. Tabitha."

Shit.

After her visit to the residential floor, Susanna popped down to the laboratories in search of Annetta. She found the herbalist sitting in a preparation room, scribbling in a notebook, surrounded by haze from gas burners and bubbling flasks.

Susanna tried not to cough at the melange of acrid odours. "How is your work going?"

Annetta jumped, her pen leaving a streak on the page. "Oh! Sorry, Chief Scientist Longleaf. If I'd known you were visiting, I'd have tidied up." She wiped bony, ink-stained fingers on her beige infirmier's overalls.

"No need for that—it should be me apologising for interrupting your work. Call me Susanna, please. What's in the flasks?"

Paper rustled. "Let's see... the one labelled '3W-1s' is a combination of thornbush—*waxy* thornbrush—and heart sage, in a three to one proportion. I hope it'll have a quicker effect on infectious diarrhoea, which can really be quite in-capacitating. Not just symptomatic relief, but preventing spread. We certainly don't want transmission. I imagine in a military situation with tents and things, people might not pay so much attention to..."

While Annetta rambled on, Susanna's gaze passed over further flasks with informative labels such as "1W-2s" and "4L-3p". She pointed to a flask at the end of the row. "And what's this one? It's not labelled."

"That's because it's not experimental. It's my knockout powder." Annetta's brow wrinkled. "I used some on the cor-ridor guards when we, um, rescued Captain Shelley. But when I checked my stock earlier, there was less than I re-membered. Don't want to be caught short in an emer-gency."

How could this unprepossessing young woman talk about overcoming trained Keep guards in such a matter-of-fact way? Still, her skills would be useful against anyone with ill intent. "Anything I can do to help?"

"Now I've settled in, I wouldn't mind a couple of assis-tants. Extra hands are always useful, and I can start train-ing them up. I also need volunteers. Cursed ones, I mean, so I can assess my special recipes. Terry's offered already. The equipment here is great, especially the gas burners—so much better than heating bowls over a candle or stove. But I'm running short of some general herbs. And I'm com-pletely out of the ones for neutralising powers." She blushed. "I used my last batch on Captain Shelley."

"I'm grateful you did." At Annetta's surprised glance, Susanna added, "You stopped him from committing mur-der. No matter how evil Silvers was, even though I believe he deserved to die, I don't think Jonathan would have recovered from killing him. He's already suffering a huge amount of guilt from—"

"Old Gerald didn't deserve to die either!" Annetta glared, then she slumped. "He was just in the wrong place at the wrong time."

"I'm sorry. But Jonathan didn't have any choice." He still viewed himself as a murderer, although the Council had retrospectively agreed the old man's death was necessary. "Gerald's power could have put the whole convoy at risk, yourself and Samuel included. It was the lesser evil."

"There's always a choice," mumbled Annetta. "I know the protocols for dealing with the cursed say neutralisations might be needed. We all know that. Just that I thought everything would be more open and official. But... yeah. Captain Shelley would have died in order to save Tabitha, wouldn't he?"

"Yes. He was lucky Samuel's drawing alerted you something was wrong." Susanna shivered. *Breathe in...* Jonathan had been moments away from execution when Annetta interrupted his trial.

"Silvers told me so many lies about him." Annetta's cheeks went pink. "I should remind myself of the good he did. You obviously know him a lot better than I do."

"I've known Jonathan a long time. Since before he became a captain. Even if he hadn't been cursed—that's how most of us end up as captains—he'd likely have been promoted. He takes his responsibilities very seriously." Too seriously for his own good, in fact. Hopefully, at his age—only a couple of years younger than Susanna—he'd be deemed too old for front-line combat. Let him not need to kill again. Eyes smarting, she waved some smoke away from her face.

Using tongs, Annetta repositioned a flask. "Isn't it difficult for the two of you? With one of you being away so much of the time? I left Maldon less than a fortnight ago, and already I miss—" She cleared her throat. "Even though the suites are comfortable, it's not the same living here."

Susanna had to laugh. "I don't know, to be honest. It was only since the Silvers business that we, ah, got together."

"That recently?" Annetta lowered her voice. "It's none of my business, but I can make fertility planning—"

"It's fine. I'm well past that age now. Though sometimes I regret the time we could have had in years gone by." She sighed. Tempting though it was to confide in the herbalist—who surely respected confidentiality—she hadn't come here to talk about Jonathan. "You said you were running short of herbs? Is that something we can find locally?"

"I have a list..."

After some discussion, Susanna agreed to assign Annetta two assistants once she'd gone over the list of Keep staff. She'd also send people out to harvest the more common herbs.

At the mention of a trip back to Maldon, Annetta brightened. "Oh, I know exactly where there's a nice patch of dareth leaf. And there was a clump of bitter pinkweed I was watching last month. Maybe it'll be ready to harvest now. And even if not, I'd love to catch up with Adrian—I mean, with everyone there."

Susanna tried to keep a serious expression. "Take your opportunities while you can. I'm sure we could arrange something."

Chapter 4

Alone again in her study, Eleanor finalised her report about the cursed mound she'd visited. After dispatching it to Susanna, she slouched back in her chair and finished the tea Lester had delivered. When she replaced the cup on the saucer, it rattled. That captain's jitteriness must be catching: he'd seemed so pale when she gave him his final instructions.

Her braid had come loose, and she redid it with clumsy fingers. Or maybe her imminent lunch with Artur was making her anxious. That would make more sense, with her guilty conscience over all his troubles. She'd dragged him on a blimp trip to help with her beast research, and Isabel had blown up the mound. Following the explosion, Artur had been cursed with the ability to sense people's last moments. He'd used it to solve the mystery of her father's murder. Isabel's written confession had confirmed his findings. If they'd found that confession note earlier, Artur needn't have overtaxed himself with his power.

As if that weren't enough, Eleanor had used the poor man as a front for her clandestine explorations. She'd created the impression that they were lovers on a romantic blimp tour of the countryside. After she confessed her ruse to him, his clear disappointment had increased her guilt. Perhaps, if he hadn't been cursed—but no, she didn't dare see him as anything closer than a friend. Not if the curse could be passed between people without a beast vector.

Thoughts of more would only lead to frustration for them both.

She massaged a tightness at the back of her neck. Now she'd set her plans in motion, Artur needn't spend his entire life fearful that others would discover he was cursed. The right thing to do would be to set him up with a funded blimp project and leave him alone. But technical discussions with him were too tempting: a rare chance for intelligent conversation. Was she selfish?

Meeting him in this study felt too formal, and her private sitting room too intimate. Despite the appeal of the library, the books there would distract them both. So she'd chosen the drawing room as the best place for them to speak.

Eleanor ascended the main staircase—muffling carpets rather than clattering wood at this level—to the royal apartments. Ordinarily she would take the service stairs, but she wanted to avoid the guards who stood at each landing. They'd have noticed Artur's arrival, and she didn't want to see their speculative expressions. However, she couldn't avoid the pink-clad figure bustling along the hallway towards her.

Martha beamed. "Good, I just took sandwiches through. I told Artur to help himself, the poor boy looks like he's been in the wars. Never met a man who didn't feel better with some food inside him."

In the wars? It was odd to hear that phrase, given that they'd never had any here. Seeing Martha's quizzical expression, Eleanor shut her mouth. "Ah, thank you. I was just thinking about something from earlier."

"Of course. Just ring the bell if you need anything." Martha bobbed her head and departed. Why did the elderly housekeeper never seem flustered? She could hardly have remained ignorant of secrets while working for Eleanor's parents, but she behaved as if she never noticed.

When Eleanor entered the drawing room, Artur was on the two-seater couch. A part-eaten sandwich lay on the plate beside him. He swallowed and rose to his feet, brushing crumbs off his faded cotton trousers.

"Never mind that, Artur." She plastered on a smile. He was only a couple of inches taller than her, and she could meet his gaze without cricking her neck. His earnest expression made her lose track of her thoughts. Pulse rapid, she plopped into a nearby armchair. "We don't need to be formal here."

"As you wish, uh, Eleanor." After abandoning his plate on the sideboard, he resumed his seat, fingers worrying the hem of his untucked shirt.

"Are you feeling better?"

"Somewhat. I can't believe I slept the night through after spending nearly the whole day asleep. Well, apart from dinnertime." His fair complexion took on a warm hue. "I'm sure I could have managed to eat it unassisted. I mean, I'm grateful for your help and all, but you didn't need to slice up—"

Don't remind me. She leaned over and briefly touched his arm. "I'm just glad you're improved. Did your parents say anything when you got home?"

"I could hardly avoid my mother's questions. She was very excited when I told her I'd been helping you with a project. Thankfully, she didn't push me further when I explained it was hush-hush. How was your morning?"

"Busy." She huffed, though it was a relief to discuss something less personal. "And Hastings seems to forget I'm not still ten years old."

Artur raised an eyebrow. "Well, my mother fusses, but at least she's *my* mother."

"There is that. Anyway, I'm starving." Over his protestations, Eleanor dragged a side table between them then poured tea for them both. She piled up their plates—his more than hers—with chicken sandwiches. "It's been a good morning. I spoke to the Council and a few other people about logistics. Things are moving along nicely." She summarised her plans.

"I don't envy you. It seems like a terrifying situation. I'm surprised you can be so calm about it." At Eleanor's enquiring look, he said, "I suppose your royal upbringing prepares you for all eventualities, even invasions."

"It does?" *Idiot, act like you believe it.* "I mean, yes, it's worrying. But I have so much on my mind, the thought of an invasion seems rather distant." That, at least, was honest.

He sipped his tea. "I hope I can help, but my experience is so limited. After all, I'm only a junior engineer."

"That's why you're perfect! You're not embedded in political factions. You're educated and not as set in your ways as the older engineers." She exchanged a conspiratorial glance with him. Artur's boss—Chief Blimp Engineer Haslett—was a prime example. "I want to improve communications with the settlements. That includes information sharing as well as physical travel on roads. Construction and so on. I think you might know Matthew Porter, the engineer? I'll be seeing him soon."

Perking up, Artur selected a sandwich. "That's excellent. His lectures were great, really got us thinking. I like your ideas though I wonder if many people will be keen to travel."

"It's a multi-pronged approach, with a new view of beasts. Better knowledge about them will be essential. A few weeks ago I had a visit from Silvers—obviously before all the stuff about his crimes came out. And I believe he made a valid point. He commented that beasts are quite small, and it's the curse that's the real issue, not the beasts themselves. Like, they're a... reservoir. So, if we could master the curse's benefits—powers—and ameliorate the negative aspects, we needn't be so frightened of attacks."

His eyes widened. "You're not thinking of cursing people deliberately?"

She stiffened. "Absolutely not, no matter what my father said." Or what Isabel claimed he said. Well, Staunton believed it too.

"Any word on Isabel?"

The sourness of betrayal eroded her appetite, and she dropped the sandwich on her plate. "No contact from her. Paton's investigations yielded nothing. I hope she's safe, but I also hope she doesn't do anything stupid." Surely all those years of support hadn't been a pretence.

"Sorry." Artur's brows drew together. "I shouldn't have asked."

"It's fine. The only reason I'm not deluged with enquiries about her is because people assume I sent her on a mission that went wrong." She poked her sandwich. Why did Martha insist on cucumber? "Oh, I'm sending you a visitor. Lester Black, a city captain. He's to visit the outlying settlements, and a blimp seems ideal."

"Always happy to meet potential travellers," said Artur. "It would be good to get opinions from new users. With our safe gases and propellors, we've come a long way from hot air balloons, haven't we?"

"At least hot air is easy to produce." Eleanor nearly snorted. Hastings could fill a balloon all by himself. The clock chimed. Drat. "I need to leave for my afternoon meetings. Always too much to do."

"I know that feeling," said Artur. "Er, are we still having dinner this evening? Or will you be too busy?"

Butterflies danced in her chest, and she suppressed a grin. He'd be much better company than a book. "Definitely yes to dinner. I'll need it. First meeting is with Hastings again. Made him commander-in-chief, but I don't want the position to go to his head." *So why did I give it to him? Oh, because he can't do much harm with it.* "After that, I'm going over my father's notes with Kenneth Staunton, in case he picks up something I haven't." Of course he wouldn't, but if she declined his offer it would make the Council suspicious.

Artur regarded the remains of his sandwich with a frown. "If it's about your father, do you need me to try—"

"No! I'm not asking you to use your power again. Takes too much out of you." Eleanor's gut churned. She had already learned more than she wanted to about his death.

"But I really want to help." He leaned forwards, face anxious, a hand outstretched. "I can't just sit by and let you make all the effort. If there's else anything I can do, to make things easier for you..."

Giving his hand a quick pat, she tried to smile. "I appreciate your offer, but will only take you up on it in dire need. We've not reached that stage yet." And they never would.

Susanna returned to her palace suite in the early evening and slumped on the chaise longue with an aching head. She envied Staunton his junior role. Despite Jonathan's heated defence of her earlier, this new job was nothing like being a captain.

The challenge of running the Keep was far more than dealing with the afflicted: training was maybe even the simplest aspect. Paperwork, personnel management, decision-making and research competed for her attention the whole afternoon. With an external threat to the realm—particularly one so intangible—she found herself paralysed over what to prioritise. A pang of shame struck her for previously doubting Eleanor's commitment. How did such a young queen manage an even larger set of problems? Well, if Eleanor could cope, it behoved Susanna to do so too.

Opting to start with something small, she'd assigned a couple of assistants to box up Lady Nelson's notes in date order. That would permit Susanna to move into her proper office. Additionally, she'd pre-empted Staunton and arranged for Silvers' papers to be delivered to her: both his official research logbooks and the papers seized from his house in the slums.

Why had a well-paid researcher like Silvers remained living in such an unsalubrious area? Kicking off her shoes, Susanna tucked her legs beneath her on the upholstered seat. Her finger traced its decorative stitching. Staying in the palace caused a different flavour of discomfort, even though Eleanor had invited her to use the suite for as long as she wanted. After Susanna's apology for installing Jonathan without prior permission, she had laughed and said there was plenty of space.

Eleanor seemed to be lonely. Her voice took on a wistful tone whenever Isabel's name was mentioned. So Susanna had agreed to stay for now. However, a protracted residence would lay her open to charges of currying royal favour. Luxury was all very well for a treat, but the longer they stayed, the more awkward she felt. She glanced down at her dress, a one-of-a-kind hand-embroidered creation that had probably last been worn by Eleanor's mother. Finding lodgings ought to be higher on her priority list, as should retrieving her belongings from the barracks.

Hmm. A house big enough for both her and Jonathan shouldn't be too hard to find. They were both used to living in modest quarters, never mind that Jonathan currently had no assets. It might be fun to take him on a shopping spree with his compensation money, once he received it. If she had anything to do with it, he'd soon be dressed to mingle with the gentry.

Where was he? She stood and looked out of the window as the streetlamps were lit, one by one. Was he still looking over Fellows' maps? Or perhaps he couldn't resist visiting Tabitha. Susanna had only *suggested* he restrict his visits, after all.

A knock sounded at the door.

Susanna opened it and smiled. "Oh, Jonathan. I was getting worried about you."

He offered her a bouquet of red roses. "May I come in?" He wore a red-striped cotton shirt under a patched blue corduroy jacket with sleeves that were too short. There was no sign of the sling.

"Of course." She stepped back, and he entered. After taking a moment to inhale the delicate scent, she arranged the flowers in a vase on the mantelpiece. Beautiful as they were, he couldn't have got them in the Royal Compound. "My favourite. Ah... did you get these from Bernice's Blooms?"

"I knew you'd like them." He regarded the toes of his

convoy boots poking out beneath dark trousers. "I had to give them a credit note."

"What happened to the sling? And the clothing? I can't help noticing you're wearing"—she tried not to wince—"something different compared to earlier."

He coughed. "I got my shoulder checked at the Keep infirmary. The chirurgeon with the unpronounceable name—the one with a power like mine—manipulated my shoulder internally. It still twinges, but he told me I wouldn't need the sling anymore. Then I went back to the barracks and spoke to Emily. She gave me her son's old clothing. I felt like everyone was laughing at me, wandering around in that fancy robe."

Susanna shook her head. He was a grown man with a right to go where he pleased and to wear what he wanted. *He* could take care of himself. "Actually, I'd been wondering about sending Tabitha to train with Kallistratos. She's getting restive, and it would be a positive use of her power while still living in the Keep. You didn't have problems getting through the checkpoint building?" There shouldn't have been, since Paton had cleared Jonathan with the guards, but given the now-cancelled price on his head he'd still potentially be taking a risk.

He snorted. "No, it was fine. A couple of folk did a double take when they saw me, but that was all. Listen, I'm sorry I made trouble for you earlier. Staunton really gets on my wick. When he had a go at you I, well, I lost my rag. But I know it's made things worse."

Her heart fluttered at his protectiveness, but she shouldn't encourage such behaviour. She pressed her lips together before speaking. "If you were more diplomatic, my job would be easier. I'd hoped to cover how you activate your power, but we didn't even get that far during the meeting."

"Well, I can tell you about it now..." Taking her hand, he pulled her towards the chaise longue, then he paused as his jacket rustled. He shrugged it off and pulled Fellows' map from a pocket. It was a bit crumpled, and he tossed it on the bureau.

After they sat, Jonathan explained how he'd gone through calling his power. Control wasn't a problem for him, of course, not after his years of practice. But due to his conditioning to suppress his power for every stimulus other than pain, it had been difficult. However, if the newly cursed weren't made to associate pain and powers, they wouldn't need to unlearn anything.

She nodded. "Tabitha managed something similar. And it might help that she's young and hasn't been doing this for long. Do you think, with training, any sensation or thought might serve as a trigger?"

He made a face. "For me, picturing Silvers worked the best, but I'm not suggesting people focus on people they want to kill."

Maybe Susanna could scribble insults over photographs of Staunton. Her lips quirked. "No, that wouldn't do as an official suggestion."

"Well," said Jonathan, "I didn't really have anyone else to think about while I was on the run."

"Really?"

"Of course I worried about Tabitha." His calloused fingers brushed her cheek. "And I thought about you, a lot. If only I'd courted you earlier, things mightn't have fallen out the way they did. But I always felt so uncultured when faced with your upper-class manner..."

Her cheek tingled, and she took a deep breath. "Poise can be learned. I wasn't born into an affluent household."

"But I always thought you were way above my class. The way you walk, speak, your air of sophistication. No?"

"Before I joined the guard, I was a deportment teacher. Twenty years ago, admittedly."

His eyebrows shot up, then he looked away and chuckled. "You certainly had me fooled. So why did you join the guard?"

"The regular salary. My teaching was paid by the session, and there wasn't much demand. Even tutored Isabel a few times when she was a teenager. Not Eleanor, though—I was already in the guard by then."

"Hmm." He straightened up. "They were both investigating beasts, weren't they? That reminds me..."

Susanna turned to face him, a frisson of disappointment in her chest. Tempting though it would be to snuggle against him, duty had to come first. "You're thinking about the beasts you saw while you were travelling in the wilds?"

His brow wrinkled. "Yes, there was something odd. Early on, a group of them approached my campfire, but they didn't attack. They just lay down for the night then left. And the really strange thing was..."

"Yes?" *Breathe in...* In the same situation, she'd have been terrified.

"One of them returned and dropped a dead animal near me."

"What? Why?"

"Yeah." He rubbed the back of his neck. "I don't know *why*, but I, uh, cooked it and ate it."

"Jonathan!"

"Well, I was hungry. And I got to thinking, why do we

eat chickens and fish, but not four-legged animals?"

She blinked. The answer was obvious. "Because chickens don't get cursed... Oh, you were safe because you're cursed already."

"That's what I thought too." He shrugged his good shoulder, then slid his arm around her. "And it was only the once."

"You're still alive, I suppose. And no further curses?" She leaned into his warmth. Duty might come first, but it needn't be everything.

"No." He smiled. "I'm sure I'd have noticed that."

"Makes sense. Eleanor had Isabel exploring cursed mounds on foot. I know she was bitten several times, and it didn't seem to affect her. We can't blame a curse for her actions."

"Really? About the mounds, I mean."

"I think she only went so she could kill beasts, but she didn't share information with me. Just dropped round on occasion so I could patch her up." Susanna's prior experience with needlework was an advantage. "She'd made it clear she wouldn't answer questions."

"I did see a cursed mound on my travels. One of the beasts took a liking to me. I'm pretty sure it was the one that brought the dead animal. Had a white spot on its nose. Anyway, it helped me out—Don't laugh! But it led me to a mound, and I saw a piece of cutlery and some rotten clothing. At the time, I thought someone had been killed by a pack of beasts. I didn't hang around. But there weren't any bones. Any ideas?"

Susanna rubbed her forehead. "Sorry, my brain's refusing to absorb any more information. At least tomorrow's meetings don't start until lunchtime."

"Maybe an evening off then?" He raised her hand to his lips. "A relaxing dinner and an early night?"

Smiling, she rested her head on his shoulder. "That sounds perfect."

Eleanor clung on to her temper by her fingernails as she regarded John Hastings across the expanse of her desk. He'd demanded the right to draft any able-bodied citizen he chose into his new army. If she gave him no powers at all, that would give the lie to her claims of an invasion. In an attempt to dampen his enthusiasm, she cited cost and the need to keep essential services running. But it had been hard going.

She crossed her ankles and resisted the temptation to kick him. "I'll send you a list of specialist occupations that *must* be exempted from recruitment. Even with those limitations, I'm sure you'll attract enough interest to get your thousand cadets without a compulsory draft."

"I hope so. If we don't, or if too few successfully complete training, might you reconsider?" Hastings tugged at his cravat, which had a boxing club motif. Paton wore a similar one on his rare days off.

"If you fall short, speak to me again." How much time would Eleanor have to waste dealing with the man and his demands? But if she allowed him too much independence here, who knew what essential services might be left understaffed? And at the end of the day, she bore ultimate responsibility. That was the burden of absolute power. And since a hereditary monarch couldn't be legally ousted... No wonder so much of her father's work had been carried out behind the scenes.

"There would also be the issue of leadership in combat..."

She narrowed her eyes. "In what sense?"

"Gauntlett's been checking the wartime laws in the archives. They date back centuries, but they've never been repealed." Hastings slid a paper across the table. "This is a duplicate. I can leave it with you if you don't have a copy in the royal library. Essentially, once active war is declared, the commander-in-chief takes on full command of the realm. On the monarch's order, of course, and temporarily. It means leadership isn't split between the monarch and military, and it allows for more efficient decisions."

Well, if it was in their laws already, it would be more trouble than it was worth to change. And in the hypothetical situation they did face war—actual physical combat—it would be a joke to have Eleanor in charge, absolute power or not. She certainly couldn't lead an army. "We're not at war, and I hope we won't ever be. However, the arrangement makes sense."

He glanced at the portrait of her father before clasping his hands on the desk. "I'm relieved you accept the need. Your determination to do what's best for everyone is admirable. However, I fear you're not hardened enough to come through trying times unscathed. Your father would have wanted me to look after you, which includes, ah, expressing opinions you might not agree with. For example, it might have been prudent to require Captain Hanlon to send you regular reports. Who knows where she's chosen to explore?"

His mention of Isabel made her chest ache, although he didn't know the truth. She twisted the end of her braid around a finger. "I shall carefully consider all your suggestions, given your years of experience."

"The thing is, I simply don't trust that new Chief Scientist's capabilities." Hastings frowned. "No doubt she's a perfectly respectable woman, but she's unused to the position. And she's associating with that unsavoury murder suspect."

She gritted her teeth. Not only was he casting doubts on Susanna's competence, he was indirectly questioning Eleanor's judgement in appointing her. It would be beneath Eleanor to retaliate in kind: her behaviour with him would have to be meticulous. "John, can I point out *again* that Captain Shelley has been exonerated. And with Kenneth Staunton being away"—admittedly for only a year—"he's lost touch with current science."

His jowls quivered. "And Susanna Longleaf knows all about such matters because...?"

"She's been working on a project of mine for some time, and I kept her up to date. I have no doubt that the Council meeting minutes you provided were a full and accurate record of significant information." There, he couldn't question that, although Susanna had only been helping her with Artur for about a week. A twinge of guilt struck her at landing the former captain with the role, tying her fortune to Eleanor's.

She glanced at the clock on the far wall. "You'll be pleased to know that I'm not ignoring Kenneth completely. In fact, he's my next appointment." He'd be early, maybe, or at least on time, trying to improve his standing with her. Hopefully she could keep the meeting short since her stomach was starting to rumble. "He spoke with my father several times about the possibility of an attack from elsewhere. I hope that Kenneth will be able to shed further light on my father's notes. Some phrases were very cryptic, and I'm sure my father wrote them for his personal use only." That was actually a bonus, since Eleanor could interpret them any way she wanted.

"But you're sure there will be an attack?"

"Obviously nobody can predict the future, but my father's notes were definite about that. Just not the details." She held her breath. If he asked to see that non-existent part of the notes, she'd have to fob him off until she could construct something suitable. Hopefully he wouldn't: fabricating evidence would be crossing a line, but she'd have no other choice.

"And there's also the matter of—"

There was a knock at the door.

Eleanor held up a hand. Excellent timing. "I'm terribly sorry, John. But my next appointment has arrived. We'll have to pick this up next time."

He goggled at her. "But I hadn't even reached—"

"You should have prioritised your list better." She bit back a giggle at his offended expression then called, "Come!"

Instead of the footman with Staunton, Paton strode into the room. His purposeful gait bore an element of urgency. He bowed. "Your Majesty. And Councillor Hastings."

Why was Staunton late? Unease wrapped around her gut. "Is something amiss?"

Paton's gaze slid over to Hastings, who stiffened and said, "If there's something significant going on, I should know about it."

"Go on," said Eleanor. It couldn't be that damaging, could it? If it was about Isabel, Paton would know not to—

Paton cleared his throat. "Kenneth Staunton has been found dead."

Chapter 5

Waving away a concerned gate guard, Lester sagged against a wall and groaned. *Why me?* He'd maintained a polite, attentive expression while Eleanor gave her final instructions. That was some comfort. But after he left the Royal Compound, the inner city's factories and warehouses had passed by in a blur.

Hopefully nobody had seen him. Despite the urge to hurry, he brushed some dust off his jacket and took measured steps into the outer city. It wasn't much further to the barracks if he cut through the city square. He just had to keep it together until then.

"Beast!" came a treble scream.

Lester yelped and landed in a defensive crouch, grabbing for the sabre he wasn't wearing. A quick scan of the area revealed two small boys poking sticks towards a statue of some old geezer. Half-hidden behind the plinth was a third boy.

The boy with the longer stick gave Lester a gap-toothed grin. "Did we scare ya, mister? We're playin' guards and beasts."

Heart still racing, he glanced around to see who else might have noticed him. An aproned waitress with a packed lunch sat on a nearby bench beside a plump grandmother scattering breadcrumbs for the birds. They watched him with amusement.

Only one way to play it. He clutched a hand to his chest

and thrust his other hand towards the sky. "Absolutely! I nearly died of fright. You lads will make fine guards when you grow up. No beasts would dare attack *you*."

He bowed to the two women and strolled away, wincing at the titters that followed him out of the city square.

Safely back in the barracks, Lester stumbled to the captains' lounge and grabbed a bottle of beer from the drinks cabinet, wiping the thick layer of dust off its neck. Captains being who—and what—they were, they rarely touched alcohol, but the staff kept the supply topped up as needed. By the time he'd finished it, his quaking insides had settled, and his power was still quiescent. At least he knew to limit his alcohol intake. He always had. Customers might enjoy company while boozing, but their escorts had to keep their wits about them.

He couldn't face going to his quarters just yet. Once he arrived there, he'd have to start planning. Not only had Eleanor assigned him to visit the settlements, she'd ordered him to take *Tabitha* along!

Maybe a brief diversion would settle his nerves. Although nobody was around for a card game, the lounge had a dartboard and a billiards table. He removed a dart from its case. Dealing with a besotted admirer was no challenge—he'd had plenty of practice—but this one was under protection. Jonathan had laid his life on the line to save her. The dart wobbled as Lester inspected its sharpened tip. Guts roiling, he replaced it and picked up a cue.

He was slouched over the billiards table, cursing softly, when David ambled in. "Lester, what's up? You'll rip the baize."

Lester focussed on his colleague—a convoy captain with cropped blond hair who boasted even more muscles than he did. "Yeah, can't get the right angle."

"Not just the angle, but if you keep bobbing your head up and down like that... Look, this is how you do it." David held out his hand for the cue then chalked it. He inspected the table, positioned himself—nearly whacking Lester when he pulled his elbow back—and pocketed the balls one after the other. "See? How about you have a go now?"

Lester slumped at the other captain's confidence. Because David had no cursed power, he could afford to be open in everything he did. Well, if he was helping with billiards, he might be willing to help with the bigger matter. "Actually, my problem's something else. Now the queen suspects an attack in the future, she's sending me out to the settlements. To inform them about her new infrastructure plans." He summarised the information as he understood it.

"So? Someone has to warn them. And the improvements sound like a great idea—leading the convoy along a proper road would be so much easier, take it from me." David took a few paces, thumping the cue on the floor like a walking stick. "What's the big deal?"

"I've never been out of the city."

"You'll survive. It'll do you good, and it's about time you learned there's more to life than Ascar. Plus, you can hardly get cursed again." After returning the cue to its rack, he swiped a bottle of beer. "Though... you know..." His voice grew grave. "You'll need to take enough hair gel. Rural markets don't sell that. Nor monogrammed silk handkerchiefs."

"Come on, it's Richard who uses fancy handkerchiefs, not me." Lester's shoulders tightened. "What if I mess things up?"

"Like what? All you need to do is tell them what you

told me. Anyway, if you can't answer their questions, refer them back to Ascar. Or flutter your eyelashes at the ladies." With a grin, David strode towards an armchair.

"Yeah. But that's not the only thing..." He swallowed. "She wants me to plant the idea of accepting curses. Like, tell them the afflicted can be treated so they're not dangerous anymore. Maybe even hint that powers could be useful if properly applied." Hmm. Since the queen already knew powers could be trained, she'd then be in a position to announce success. She'd certainly thought things through.

David's smile faded. "Well, I'd been wondering about that myself... When I escorted Jonathan back here for his trial, he told me about how you guys train. Seriously? Hit and miss experiments with the pain box until you get it right? No wonder it's so difficult." He took a swig. "I'd no idea the man was so sneaky. There was me, thinking he was going to act as straight as he always does, and he nearly got the better of Silvers immediately. Still, it worked out well. But yeah, I can see how bringing the ruralites round might be tricky."

"And the worst bit is, I have to take Tabitha with me!"

"Funny, I've heard a lot about that girl, but I've never met her. Spent an afternoon locked in her room—that skinny little herbalist tricked me. Annetta. What's the problem with taking Tabitha?"

"She's got a crush on me, and Jonathan will kill me if anything happens. I mean, nothing *will* happen, but if he gets that impression—"

"Like her, do you?" David raised an eyebrow.

"Hey, she's only a kid!"

"Bah, you're too easy to wind up. No challenge. Listen..." While Lester paced, David gave a succinct overview of the convoy arrangement and of captains' considerable discretionary powers. "So, settlements only expect a convoy visit every few months. Means they're mainly self-sufficient, and they have limited trade with Ascar..."

Slumping into an overstuffed chair, Lester unbuttoned his jacket's top button. "Blimp'll be good, yeah?"

"Sure." David uncapped a second beer bottle. "Faster, no beasts to avoid."

"Uh, what if a beast appears while we're in a settlement?"

"Psht. Run it through with your sabre. That'll make you a hero. Best to take a weapon with you—you'll look like you know what you're doing—even though you shouldn't need one when travelling by blimp. Oh..." He wagged a finger. "Official position is to eliminate any four-legged animal you come across. But the smaller ones usually run away. In my experience, they're harmless. No need to chase them unless some ruralite is watching. Got it?"

"Yep." Lester hoped he wouldn't encounter any beasts, no matter what size.

"Anyway, the blimp's definitely better than walking, even if you still can't carry much. Ha, if you're worried about Tabitha, the blimp operators will act as chaperones. I remember Isabel enthusing about blimps even a few years ago. Told me they'd be the next big thing. I guess she was right." David leaned forwards and put his bottle down. "Heard any news about her?"

He shook his head. "I know she's been absent for a while, and the queen's worried. Maybe some hush-hush mission? Something to do with the invasion?"

"I guess that makes sense. I hope she's alright."

"Me too."

Before Lester could think of any other questions, a messenger boy jogged into the room. "Captain Buchanan? Urgent message for you."

After giving the boy a penny, David unfolded the note and scowled. "Damn, I was expecting an evening off. Need to go. Good luck." He swung himself to his feet and departed with a wave.

Lester eased himself up more slowly and picked up David's untouched drink. He'd visit the blimp workshop tomorrow. No point seeing Tabitha until afterwards. But first, he'd make sure the beer wasn't wasted.

Someone thumped at the door. Susanna raised her head off Jonathan's chest and cracked open an eye towards the clock. Well past midnight. Decent folks—or even indecent ones—ought to be snug in bed. But in the palace it was unlikely to be a misplaced visitor. An emergency with someone newly cursed? She wriggled out of his lightly snoring embrace, pulled on a house robe and padded on bare feet into the sitting room.

While she was striking a match for the lamp, the knock came again, supplemented by low-pitched voices. Well, at least she hadn't dreamt the noise and got up for no reason.

She opened the door. Paton stood outside—not *hugely* surprising—but with David Buchanan. Hastings lurked behind them, his cravat casually draped around his neck. Surely it was past *his* bedtime too. He hadn't struck her as a man of action. Maybe that military appointment had gone to his head.

Susanna wrapped the robe more tightly around herself and raised her chin. "Yes?"

David cleared his throat. "Is Jonathan there?"

What business was it of theirs? But no, the men's grim expressions didn't suggest an interest in her sleeping habits. "He is, but he's asleep. What's so urgent that you need to disturb us at this hour?"

"Shelley will know perfectly well." Hastings folded his arms.

"Give us a few minutes to wake up." Pursing her lips, she shoved the door.

David stuck out his foot, preventing her from closing it. "Sorry. Now you're awake, one of us needs to secure the area." He stepped inside.

As she gaped, Hastings pushed past Paton but came up against David's outstretched arm.

David glanced over his shoulder. "I said, 'one' of us. You can wait outside. I'll ensure he doesn't escape." He faced Susanna. "I'm sure he won't try, but this has to be done."

Susanna recovered her wits. "Why would he—David, Jonathan's injured. Plus, we're *four floors up!* Do you believe he'll turn into a bird?"

"It's proper protocol." Hastings had stepped back, but his voice was sharp.

"Seems most *im*proper to me," grumbled Susanna. "What's going on?"

"Our business is with Jonathan. We need to speak with him downstairs." David closed the door behind him and stood by the mantelpiece. He gestured towards the bedroom. "Please leave the door ajar. I need to see you're not approaching the window."

If only she'd learned how to use her mind-reading power at will. Susanna retreated into the bedroom, where Jonathan was propped up on an elbow, eyeing her questioningly.

"Were you expecting visitors?" she asked. The visit had the odour of officialdom, but why would they seek him in the middle of the night? It wasn't as if he were still a fugitive. Surely it couldn't be a misapprehension lingering after his trial.

He whispered, "I've no idea what's going on. Who's there?"

"David's in the sitting room. Paton and Hastings want to speak with you downstairs. You need to dress." She tapped her temple, touched her ear then raised her voice. "But be careful of your injuries. I'll get ready too."

Principles be damned. After throwing on a turquoise dress, she yanked open the drawer where she stored her pain box and snapped the clip on her ear. She spun the knob, absorbing the pain until her power triggered, then dropped everything back in the drawer. Her lie-detection would remain active for a while, and it might give them an edge. Meanwhile, Jonathan took his time re-clothing himself, so they finished their preparations at the same time.

They left the bedroom together. Susanna retrieved Jonathan's borrowed corduroy jacket from the coat stand and helped him into it.

David frowned. "Ready?" At Susanna's nod, he opened the door to the hallway, where the other two waited.

Craning his neck, Hastings gazed around the room. He pointed a thick finger at the mantelpiece. "Nice flowers. Don't you agree, Paton?"

Paton's forehead crinkled, and no wonder. Hastings went from creeping around at night to making inane statements on blooms. Eleanor should have chosen someone else as commander-in-chief. The man wasn't up to the demands of the position, and that would jeopardise their chances in war.

Behind her, Jonathan said, "The most beautiful ones I could find. She deserves them."

Hastings inclined his head. "Bernice's Blooms, I suppose? I'm afraid you'll be deprived of the lady's company while we interrogate you."

"I'm coming with you." Narrowing her eyes at him, Susanna focussed on his truth strands: the wisps around him that would flicker if he lied. Little chance of full mind reading without physical contact, but she'd take what she could get.

"Best if you don't, Chief Scientist Longleaf," murmured Hastings. "It may be distressing for you to witness—"

It was more irritating than not that his expressed concern was genuine. "You rightly addressed me as *Chief Scientist* Longleaf. That means I'm responsible for Captain Shelley and his welfare. Our personal relationship is irrelevant. I'm coming with you."

A few minutes later, Susanna and the four men were walking briskly past the palace's detention rooms on the first floor. Susanna had spent some time there herself after being arrested, less than two weeks ago. She glared at Paton's red-clad back.

Paton ushered them into an interrogation room then stationed himself by the door while the others sat at the table. Positioning herself beside Jonathan, Susanna squinted with the brightness. The guest floor had traditional gas and oil lighting, but electrical lighting had been installed on this floor.

Hastings glowered at Jonathan's outfit, pointedly looking him up and down. Insufferable man. It was bad enough to drag Jonathan and her out of bed. He could hardly complain if victims of his petty tyranny clothed themselves in whatever came to hand.

David nodded at Paton. "You first."

The royal guard stepped forwards and tossed a sheet of paper on the table. "While making a delivery to the Keep earlier, I came across this."

It was a drawing in a childish hand. One of Samuel's visions. It depicted a figure in a red-striped shirt and too-small jacket, standing at a door with stained glass panels. There was no mistaking either the man or the location. *Staunton's house.*

"Oh, Jonathan!" Susanna could have given the idiot a clip round the ear. "Couldn't you have stayed away?"

Jonathan flinched. "I'd hoped we could settle our differences... but after I announced myself to his butler, I was told he wasn't receiving visitors."

"Well," said Susanna. *Phew.* "There's no law against trying to visit people. Staunton can't complain about—"

"Staunton's dead," said Hastings.

"What?" Ice crept down Susanna's spine while Jonathan's jaw dropped.

David pulled out handcuffs before addressing Jonathan. "You had a fight with him. You threatened him. Then you were seen outside his house shortly before his body was found. I'm taking you into custody, Shelley."

Hastings smirked. "Didn't think you'd been noticed?"

"I... I'm not denying my visit." Jonathan spread his hands. "But I didn't even speak to the man!"

Susanna's heart thrummed. Jonathan's truth strands were barely visible, and she couldn't tell if he spoke the truth. What had he done? A quick glance at Paton and David showed their strands distinct and honest.

"We know you can kill from a distance," said Hastings. "Like you did with Silvers."

"I never killed Silvers!" His truth strands remained stubbornly ambiguous. "You value powers like mine when they're convenient. And when it suits you, you blame us instead."

"I see what you mean," David murmured to Jonathan, ignoring Hastings' dirty look.

Susanna licked her lips, which had gone suddenly dry. She'd have to puzzle over the matter later. "Jonathan was with me the whole time after Silvers went into custody. He certainly couldn't have killed *him*."

"Be that as it may, we're now investigating Staunton's murder." Face serious, Hastings leaned on the table. "Chief Scientist Longleaf, I do sympathise with you, really. I can quite understand personal partiality. But you're too closely, ah, involved with the suspect to think clearly."

Temples throbbing, she quelled the urge to shout at him. She clenched her fists under the table. If she showed *any* reaction to his insinuations, he'd claim that as evidence of her irrationality. And he'd believe it too. "Please explain the circumstances."

David gave her a nod. "Staunton was found slumped over his study desk. Devoid of life but still warm. No injuries or nearby weapons. The door was locked and the window fastened shut."

"Her Majesty initially wished me to investigate on her behalf," said Paton. "Given Staunton's importance to the war effort, she had to agree that Hastings should be involved, especially because of his dual role as Chief Councillor. However, in light of previous accusations against Captain Shelley—now disproved—and the current unusual situation, Buchanan and I are representing our areas."

"Hence, I'm overseeing your arrest, Jonathan." David's gaze dropped to the handcuffs. "But you'll be a prisoner under Councillor Hastings' jurisdiction. Taken to the Council cells rather than the palace or the Keep. Of course, with your power, you wouldn't be held in a regular prison cell, no matter the charge."

Susanna couldn't really argue with their approach. Still... "Surely Jonathan isn't the only suspect? Staunton must have made other enemies." Her suggestion might be undiplomatic, but she was past caring.

Paton sighed. "Naturally we spoke with Fellows, what with him being a colleague. But he hadn't left the Royal Compound during the time window. The checkpoint building guard logged Shelley's time of departure and entry, and the timings fitted."

"Look," said Jonathan, "I'm not good enough to kill someone without being able to see them directly."

Hastings jerked his chin at Jonathan. "So? No doubt you circled the house, spied him through the window and did the dirty deed. That hardly needs subtle planning. Or maybe you even climbed through the window and fastened it behind you."

Susanna couldn't let this go without a fight. "Accusing Jonathan is a farce. I'm sure it was... someone else." She winced at her weak words, belatedly realising that she couldn't speak openly. Eleanor had requested silence on the topic of Isabel, and she and Jonathan should respect that plea. Frustrating, since it seemed more than likely that Isabel had killed Staunton as well as Silvers. If she'd gone after the psychopathic imprisoned ex-scientist, it would make perfect sense for her to go after the man who had manipulated him into that position. "It's almost certain that whoever killed Silvers—definitely *not* Jonathan—also killed Staunton."

"That's certainly possible." David's face cleared, and he dropped the handcuffs on the table. "And Silvers' killer is probably still at large."

Hastings tapped his chin. "Who do you suggest it was? And on what evidence?"

Damn. "I can't suggest a specific name, but I'm sure the investigators will find out the truth. Besides, the mind readers will be able to tell it wasn't Jonathan for either killing." Given the circumstantial evidence against him, Jonathan's defence would have to hinge on the mind readers unless Eleanor or Paton intervened. Ah, hadn't there been a mind-reading problem at his trial? With Annetta's drugs?

Hastings looked down his nose at her. "I'm sure they *would*, if I had access to any of them. It's such a pity you've reassigned all the mind readers to your new-fangled training methods in the Keep, and Her Majesty has agreed that takes top priority. Otherwise this matter could have been dealt with expediently. Shelley will just have to wait his proper turn, however long that takes. Of course, there's always the option of making an exception to the orders that you gave earlier today—I do beg your pardon, Chief Scientist Longleaf. Yesterday. It's not *quite* as recently as I recollect."

Why did he have to excel at being provocative? Susanna *had* to appear in control. But how she wanted to slap him, or even punch him in the nose. Swallowing her rage, she held back a growl.

... without a man to back her up...

That Hastings! Susanna's heart raced at the snippet of

his thoughts. Did he think she'd be easy pickings if he separated her from Jonathan? He'd soon learn his error, once she—*Damn*. But she couldn't confront him about it. Not here, and not when she shouldn't have been mind-reading him in the first place. At least he wouldn't dare do anything nasty to Jonathan, especially after the embarrassment of Silvers' death.

Sliding the handcuffs towards David, she spoke through gritted teeth. "I agree, Chief Councillor Hastings. It seems that the correct process will be for you to place Captain Shelley in custody. For the moment."

Chapter 6

Still in his chair, Jonathan struggled to hold in his temper while David put handcuffs on him. Again. He'd not seen the other convoy captain—assuming Jonathan still *was* a convoy captain—since the man had delivered him into Silvers' clutches. It had been with the best of intentions, and in the line of his duty, and with deliberate cooperation from Jonathan, but it still made things awkward. However, despite the sense of déjà vu, there was no psychopath after him this time, even if Hastings was trying to throw his weight around.

He lifted his chin and regarded the burly young captain. "Seen Annetta lately?"

The handcuffs snapped shut. "At least she only tricked me once."

Fair enough, she'd got the better of Jonathan at least twice and then capped it by rescuing Tabitha from Silvers. He owed her for that. "Touché."

Jonathan grinned, and David returned it, saying, "She'll go far. Never thought she had it in her."

"Are you two *quite* finished your friendly chat?" Hastings glowered as he stood.

Paton's grunt sounded like a stifled laugh. All very well for him. *He* wasn't the target of Hastings' attempt to bolster his authority, or whatever he was trying to do. The smarmy thug's condescension towards Susanna blinded him from seeking the real killer.

Well, Jonathan wouldn't let Hastings get away with that attitude. He opened his mouth, but Susanna's knee nudged his thigh. A sideways glance confirmed her stony expression.

Steady on, Shelley. Better not cause more trouble for her. He would be meek and cooperative until they freed him, and then he'd support her as best he could. This time, he had no fear about a guilty verdict. His shoulders tensed at the thought she might be vulnerable while he was in jail. But Paton and David would watch out for her. Unlike Hastings, they were both honourable men, and she was in the security of the Royal Compound.

Susanna stood. "Let's go."

Hastings loomed over her. "You're not allowed to accompany us."

"Sorry." David held up his hands. "He's right."

She planted her feet and folded her arms. Her determined stance was adorable. And on *Jonathan's* behalf! "Very well. Chief Councillor Hastings, while Captain Shelley is in your custody, you will ensure he comes to no harm. I expect you to look after him better than you did Silvers."

Paton raised an eyebrow at Hastings. "Her Majesty expects all the proprieties to be followed, naturally."

"Naturally." Hastings clenched his fists.

"Don't worry about me." Jonathan stood and grasped Susanna's hands in his cuffed ones. "You get on with what you have to. Once I've proved my innocence, I'll see you again. I'll be on my best behaviour. Promise. But before I go..."

He gave her a lingering kiss. When would he next inhale her honeysuckle scent? After rubbing his cheek against hers, he drew back. David inspected the floor and Paton readjusted his eyepatch while Hastings scowled.

Susanna's hand was sweaty and tremulous in his as she smiled. "Why, Jonathan, I'd no idea you were such an exhibitionist."

Me neither. But it was worth it to discomfit Hastings. Jonathan raised his head. "Lead on, gentlemen." *And Hastings.*

The three men escorted him downstairs and out of the palace. In the dim lamplight outside, Jonathan tried not to let the paving stones trip him up on the short walk to the Council building.

Of course, this being the middle of the night, the entry hall and reception were empty. Their footsteps echoed on the marble floor before they headed along a narrow corridor to the detention cells. The scent of roast chicken and parsnips wafted from a part-closed door on the way, as did the rattle of dice.

The guard manning the cells was hunched over a small table, playing solitaire. He jumped to attention and saluted Hastings. "Commander Hastings, sir!"

Hastings clapped him on the shoulder. "At ease. We have a guest for you."

Jonathan gazed around while the guard booked him in, logging his cursed power in a coded notebook. The area was rather cosy. Gas lamps flickered on the walls, and the three barred cell doors hung open. It was unsurprising there were no other prisoners. These cells were reserved for sensitive investigations and prisoners with knowledge of such matters, or those with powers. Such as himself.

The guard called for a colleague. Under Hastings' belligerent glare, the two ushered Jonathan into the middle cell, which lay in line of sight of the corridor. They locked the door behind him.

"See you soon," called David as he left. Paton muttered under his breath and followed.

Hastings gripped a bar on the door, his signet ring glinting. "Don't try any funny stuff."

Jonathan grinned. "Of course not. Can I be assured that *you* won't try any funny stuff either, Chief Councillor Hastings? Or since you're collecting titles like a schoolboy collects beetles, perhaps I should call you Commander—"

Turning on his heel, Hastings departed.

Formalities done and insults exchanged, Jonathan lay on the bunk; he'd not had much sleep since arriving back in Ascar. For comfort, the thin mattress ranked about the same as his old barracks quarters. He stared at the ceiling, wondering when he'd get used to sharing a suite with Susanna. The idea of growing older together held a lot of appeal...

When he awakened, it was still nighttime, and a couple of voices muttered outside. His gaze flicked to the barred door. The guards must be changing over. What an easy job this must be, guarding an area that was usually empty, getting cooked meals served up in their break room. They probably detained people once a year or something. Why, their last one must have been—

Silvers. He made a face. What if Silvers had occupied this very cell?

He swung himself upright. "Hello?"

A sleepy city guard shuffled into view. "Yeah?"

"Do you know who was in this cell previously?"

The guard scratched his head. "That scientist chappie. Big guy. Oh, Silvers."

Jonathan's gut twisted as he imagined blood splashed

on the floor. "And he died *in this cell?*"

"I guess so. I was off shift. Making the most of my free time." The man's voice bore a reproachful tone.

"Thank you. Sorry to have disturbed you." There, best to be polite to his captors. Susanna would approve.

The guard might be sleepy, but Jonathan now felt fully awake. He scrutinised every inch of the cell, sniffing for any hint of poison, tentatively touching the walls. Why did they have to pick this cell for him? He'd lain down on the same bunk as Silvers, regarded the same view outside. *Blech.* The barred windows only looked out on to the wall of the Royal Compound. There was barely room outside for anyone to—

He sucked in a breath, gazing at the windowsill in the dim moonlight. Caught on the rough stone was a shred of dark fabric. Sliding a hand through the bars, he pulled it loose. The texture was luxurious in his fingers. Silk, maybe? Jonathan carried the fabric towards the cell door, where the lighting was better. He squinted at his prize, seeking any distinguishing marks. The only thing of note was the colour. Dark brown. City captain brown. No other would wear that colour.

The hairs on the back of his neck prickled. And only one captain wore silk uniforms. *Isabel.*

As if the thought had called her, a whisper came through the window bars.

"Hello, Jonathan."

Standing at the window of her suite, Susanna stared out over the city. The twinkling lamp lights mocked her with their cheer. Of course Jonathan hadn't killed Staunton, but proving it to Hastings' satisfaction wouldn't be easy. If she pulled any mind readers from their assigned duties to demonstrate his innocence, Hastings would use that as evidence of her partiality.

Besides, the mind readers might not even be successful, given her own earlier failure to assess his truthfulness. Annetta had drugged Jonathan before his trial just a few days ago. In addition to neutralising his power for a full day, her drug had rendered him immune to mind reading. His power had recovered already, but who knew how long that extra effect lasted? Until they'd been disturbed tonight, Susanna hadn't attempted to access Jonathan's mind: it was only fair to him. In the interrogation room, when he kissed her, she'd wondered if he was trying to communicate. Apart from in the obvious sense, of course. Closing her eyes, she remembered the roughness of his cheek against hers.

But his thoughts hadn't come through. Insisting he be mind-read would likely achieve nothing: it would only give Hastings more ammunition against her.

Jonathan's behaviour made it clear he trusted her. He'd seemed unconcerned—although irritated—at his arrest. She'd trust him in return and not try to intervene while he was in prison.

She rubbed her arms in the breeze from the window, wishing he was there with his arms wrapped around her.

For all his temper, he was no rogue captain. He was as law-abiding as he could manage, even if restrictions chafed him. His attempt to kill Silvers arose from desperation, and if successful he'd have paid the penalty without complaint.

Isabel was a different matter. Until recently, her disregard of convention could have passed as an amusing foible of her noble background, maybe even a lesser degree of the Queen's Discretion Eleanor held. But that was before her confession of regicide. She had stopped the king's heart without leaving any marks. Now that Silvers and Staunton were dead—with no external signs—Isabel was an obvious suspect again.

The only other captain in Susanna's memory who'd committed crimes had been Denton. He'd abused his mind control abilities for personal gain, and murdered the powerful mind reader whom Susanna had replaced. Denton had met his end when the other captains united to take him down. They'd burned the sawmill where he was hiding.

Goosebumps rose on Susanna's arms. It was an extreme decision, but they hadn't dared approach him more closely. Nobody ever breathed the name of the captain who set the place alight. But there was only one city captain with a power over fire.

Isabel.

"Isabel!" Jonathan hastily looked around to check if the guard had noticed, but nobody was in sight. "What are you doing here?"

"I've come to break you out. Getting slow, Jonathan, that you need to be rescued?" There was a bubble of laughter in her voice.

She thought this was *amusing?* He crept back over to the window. "Uh, what if I don't want to be rescued?"

"Come on, you know perfectly well you didn't kill Staunton. Or Silvers." Tall and slender, Isabel bounced on the balls of her feet. She wore dark overalls and a scarf around her face, but her eyes shone.

Jonathan's jaw clenched as he noticed her earclip, its wire running to her messenger bag. "You killed them, didn't you?"

"Yeah. I don't plan to turn myself in, but it's not fair

that you're stuck in this cell."

"Only till the mind readers get here."

"You're always such a stickler for the rules. What's been happening? And why are you wearing that *ridiculous* outfit? Even though you're not into couture dressing—"

Footsteps sounded in the hallway.

"Hmm," said Isabel. "Don't want any witnesses." She opened her bag, revealing the calibrated stimulus generator inside.

Shit! What if she took it into her head to kill the guard? Jonathan hastily turned his back to the window and leaned against the bars. He was pretty sure Isabel wasn't trying to kill *him*, and hopefully blocking her view of the guard with his body would prevent her from violence.

The guard narrowed his eyes. "Not sleeping?"

"Just taking some air. It—" Jonathan tried not to squirm while Isabel prodded his ribs. "It's been a rather eventful evening, and I have a lot on my mind."

The guard walked away again, and Jonathan turned back to the bars. "Would you stop that!"

Her eyes crinkled. "Anyway, even if you don't want out, you can tell me what's going on."

Jonathan had seen Isabel's letter—her confession, really—to Eleanor and her stated position about deliberate cursing and the cruelty it entailed. He frowned, picking what information to share. Perhaps he could persuade her to give herself up.

He kept his voice as low as he could. "Nobody's after you. Eleanor's worried about the invasion her father suspected. She intends to go public about powers and emphasise their value. Susanna's working hard on a new training system for the cursed. She gives them mind-reading feedback, and they learn control more quickly. I'm helping too, after I learned a pain-free way of activating my power. So cursed powers really aren't as—"

Footsteps approached again, and a different guard peered into the cell.

Pressed uncomfortably against the window, Jonathan pretended to do shoulder and neck exercises until the man departed. "Look, this isn't working. Wait till I'm free again, then I'll share what I know with you. And why not contact Eleanor directly?"

She lifted an eyebrow. "Seriously? Regicide is a capital offence. No Queen's Discretion. I'm not chancing it, and it would break Eleanor's heart if she had to execute me. I wouldn't exactly enjoy it myself, either. But you're right. This isn't the place for a leisurely conversation."

"Agreed." If he could arrange to meet her once he was out, he might be able to apprehend her discreetly. Having her running around at large was dangerous for everyone.

Three guards arrived, looking suspiciously at Jonathan. The tallest said, "You're spending a lot of time by that window. You can't catch *us* off-guard with your power, and you're not escaping on our watch. Stand aside."

Two guards covered Jonathan with flechette guns while the tall one entered the cell and looked out of the window. Did they really think he'd try to escape that way rather than simply using his power to unlock the door? Best not to point that out, however. Best to keep his options open. Jonathan tensed and slipped the fabric scrap into his pocket. The guard tested each bar in turn before leaving with a final glare.

Every creak from the old building made Jonathan twitch, but Isabel didn't return. Hopefully she'd wait until he was out before contacting him again. Her years of work with the higher echelons of power should have taught her the value of patience. Hmm. To his knowledge she'd never lied. That was a strange trait in politics. She'd not had to go through the mind readers like the other captains and officials, but maybe she kept that immunity by always being demonstrably truthful. How ironic that this lack of scrutiny let her conceal that she'd murdered the king.

Sleep continued to elude him. He sat on the bunk, staring at nothing in particular and wondering if Susanna was comfortably tucked up in bed. When another guard looked in on him, he said, "Looks like both of us are having a sleepless—"

Behind the guard, a door swung open and a dark figure approached, a scarf around its face.

Jonathan leapt to his feet and pointed. "Look out! Behind you!"

The guard scoffed. "Don't try your cheap tricks on—"

A hand covered the man's sneer, and he sank to the floor with a sigh.

Of course it was Isabel. She wiped her hands on the guard's jacket, tied him up with his own belt, removed his keys and unlocked the cell.

Jonathan seethed. This was all going wrong. "What are you playing at?"

"Come on, we don't have much time. That knockout powder won't last forever."

"You expect me to go with you?"

She waved a hand at the unconscious guard. "Would you rather explain this guy and the others when the next shift shows up?"

The *others?* He gritted his teeth. He should be grateful

she hadn't killed them. They wouldn't have noticed Isabel entering, so Hastings would heap more blame on Jonathan's head, even if he stayed. Not something he wanted to sit through. "I promised Susanna I wouldn't cause trouble."

"Sweet. Unhelpful, but sweet. Tell you what, if you come with me, we can swap stories. Then you'll have something to report back to Susanna." Her gaze fell. "And Eleanor."

Persuasion wasn't one of Jonathan's strengths. But if he convinced Isabel that training could be painless, he might have a chance to bring her back, or at least to learn her plans. His shoulder-blades prickled. And if she turned out to offer an ongoing threat... Yes, he should accompany her. There would be less risk of innocents getting in the way, should he need to act. "You win."

He limped after her as she glided out of the cell, out of the Council building and along a narrow passageway to a door in the Royal Compound's wall. He expected it to lead to the inner city, or even the nobles' quarter, like the door she'd constructed to her house. To his surprise, it swung open to reveal rustling foliage. When he stepped forwards, his foot landed in a muddy puddle.

Isabel pulled down her scarf and grinned. "This is a really old door. Seems the Settlers weren't worried about security when they built Ascar." Her hand brushed a tarnished sign that read "Maintenance".

"Where are we going?"

"Somewhere we can talk."

Chapter 7

The following morning, bleary-eyed and nursing a sore head, Lester arrived at the gates of the inner city. Fortunately, the gate guards had changed over since yesterday: these ones hadn't witnessed his panicky daze. He gave them a careful nod before passing through.

From his previous work as a city guard, he knew the area well. Since this was the industrial district, crime investigations tended to relate to thefts: whether of money, items or blueprints. A time or two, he'd even visited the blimp workshop following reports of attempted break-ins. However, today's visit was his first as a potential passenger.

He entered the hangar and paused, head throbbing in time with the arrhythmic noise. Grubby workers at a nearby station applied strange tools to esoteric metal contraptions. The floor was gritty underfoot, and the scent of engine grease mixed with a chemical tang. This was no dream; he would soon be flying. Despite his trepidation and headache, a smile crept over his face.

A few workers—mainly the women—shot him curious glances. The closest one gaped and dropped her wrench. Fortunately, the implement clunked on the floor rather than her neighbour's foot. Ignoring her co-worker's scowl, she took a few steps towards him and went pink. "Can I help you, sir?"

With a shallow bow, Lester raised an eyebrow at her, holding her gaze until her blush deepened. *Damn, I should stop doing that!* He cleared his throat. "I'm here to see Artur Granville, please."

"Oh, sure. I'll just go and fetch him." She looked at him over her shoulder while she walked away, nearly tripping over a piece of tubing.

He sighed. Some people couldn't resist neatly pressed uniforms, but it wouldn't have done to turn up looking shoddy. Especially not when he was here at the queen's behest.

The woman walked past a deflated balloon and its attendant cluster of technicians. Approaching a platform by the wall, she called to the foreman then waved towards Lester.

The man climbed down and weaved his way past the work stations. He was around Lester's age—so not yet thirty—and compact rather than muscular, with sooty smears adorning his face and overalls. A tuft of sandy hair was plastered to his face. "Captain Black, good morning. I'm Artur. A pleasure to meet you at last." He extended a hand.

Lester shook it, trying not to recoil at the grime-coated palm. "Same to you, Artur. Lester's the name." A nearby resonating clang made his forehead crease. "Is there somewhere we can talk?"

"Sure." Artur led him to the back wall and a door which bore a nameplate:

Senior Research Blimp Engineer Artur Granville, B.Eng. (Merit), Dip. Blimp Eng. (Dist)

Lester's shoulders hunched. When Queen Eleanor had made her suggestion, he'd not anticipated the engineer's extensive credentials. He'd got off on the wrong foot already.

90

"I'm terribly sorry, sir, I'd no idea you were so senior—"

"Don't mind the nameplate." Senior Research Blimp Engineer Granville waved a hand in dismissal as he ushered Lester into a cramped room with walls covered in diagrams and charts. "It just went up yesterday, only because El—my sponsor wanted to make a point to Chief Blimp Engineer Haslett. He's my boss."

After the closing door muffled the clangour, Lester's urge to clutch his head eased. "But you're all those things it says? Uh, sir."

"Well, yeah. But I'm still Artur. The degree is a common one, and the diploma's something you do on the job. And my job title was created only recently. Have a seat." Artur gestured to the wooden chair by a rickety desk piled with sketches and notes. "I'm still settling into this office. The soundproofing is a huge advantage."

"Agreed." Lester perched on the chair.

Artur shoved some papers aside and propped himself on the desk. "I hear you're visiting the settlements, and it's time-sensitive. Blimp's a good choice. Can I run a few questions past you?"

"Sure." If he got out of here without looking stupid, he would be happy.

Scrunching up his face, Artur grabbed a pencil and paper. "Do you plan to return to Ascar after each settlement, or would you like to visit several settlements per trip?"

"What difference would it make?"

"How much do you know about blimps?"

"Close to nothing?" Lester's education on the job—in any of his jobs—hadn't covered blimps. Until today, he'd never even seen one up close. "Jonathan—Captain Shelley—mentioned using one on convoy, but he didn't go into detail."

Artur chuckled. "I'm sorry, I shouldn't laugh, but it was clear he really doesn't like them. Poor man. He's been through a lot, hasn't he? Just to be clear, I do know about... powers. And that you know about them too, being a captain."

"Ah!" Lester raised a finger. "Now I remember the queen mentioning your name after Jonathan's trial. I've only just made the connection. I think you were ill? Are you better now?"

"Oh, er, yes. Just a temporary indisposition." Eyelid twitching, Artur regarded his pencil and paper. "I'll give you a basic primer. How's your mathematical ability?"

"Bad." Mental calculations of hourly room rates probably didn't count for much here. "Is that a problem?"

"No. Just that the last person I discussed this with asked about the theoretical models. She—" He cleared his throat and waved a hand. "Anyway, I won't go into those details. A blimp can fly because it has a balloon that contains lighter-than-air gas. We need to balance the lifting from the gas with the weight of what it's carrying, aided by propellers. They're powered by electrical cells."

Lester nodded.

"In the old days, we used heated air in the balloons. Filling the balloons with air was easy, but we needed to carry heating equipment and fuel."

This didn't seem too difficult to understand. He leaned back in his seat. "I guess you'd have to take the weight of the fuel into account too."

"Exactly. You know how there are machines in the Keep basement that date back to the time of the Settlers? A few years ago, we—well, Chief Blimp Engineer Haslett—found a machine that can produce a lighter-than-air gas."

Lester gaped. This was like some children's story. "And it still worked?"

"Yep, pretty surprising." Artur grinned briefly. "The initial gas was flammable—an obvious problem, with hot air balloons using naked flames—but we now have levium, which is much safer. We haven't yet discovered how to make another machine, so the gases can only be produced in Ascar. To land the blimp, you discard levium from the balloon. So you have to take enough compressed gas in a canister to take off again."

"Ah." He could appreciate the problem. "So... visiting several settlements per trip isn't possible, because of having to carry extra gas?"

"If you'd asked me that a month or two ago, I'd have said you were absolutely right." Artur beamed. "However, the clever chaps working on the gas machine have persuaded it to produce a new type of gas. We're calling it 'versium' because it's versatile. It's the best of both worlds between hot air and levium."

"How so?" There were cleverer chaps than Artur?

"It's lighter-than-air under most conditions. When it's heated, the lighter-than-air property is greater, and when it cools, it's less so. That's the simplified version. We mix it with levium, proportion depending on the weight we want to carry. We then put the gas mix in a sealed balloon with a heating mechanism. With the heating on, it'll rise. Letting it cool down allows the blimp to land. But—and this is the important part—*without* losing any gas."

"And how's that different from just a hot-air balloon you can refill with air any time?" Lester waved his hand at the air surrounding them.

"Much less fuel needed."

"Ah." How amazing that someone could think all this up. He smiled. "This sounds ideal for our stuff."

"Test runs have worked really well, but this would be the first proper use. We'll start you with a single trip and tweak things if practical issues come up. And include a canister of levium, just in case. Are you travelling by yourself? We'd assign you a pair of blimp operators, of course."

If only. His smile withered. "Uh, no. I'll have one companion."

Artur eyed Lester. "Is he as heavy as you? No offence, but we need to consider weight."

"It's a girl. She's... small." At Artur's grin, he hastily added, "Queen Eleanor told me to take her! Her name's Tabitha, and—"

"Right, I heard about her. Sounds like she lived in the country until she... got taken to the Keep. Must have been difficult for her. I wonder if these blimp trips might help get her used to meeting regular people again."

Lester blinked. He hadn't considered *why* he'd been assigned this unwanted companion specifically. There was no reason for the queen to know of Tabitha's crush, never mind that he'd make a rotten counsellor. Could he find a pretext to leave her behind? "If I go by myself, might it make a difference to the blimp configuration?"

"No, not really."

Damn.

"Weight aside, taking one person less wouldn't make a difference because gondolas come in a limited range of sizes. We currently have two each of small, medium and large. The large one holds eight. We're even working on a single-person blimp, but I'm not sure whether it'll ever be used for real. It's a harness with a balloon, and the versium might have been ideal for it. The problem is not being able to carry the heating mechanism and fuel. Might as well just use the three-person gondola."

There was a knock at the door, and a small boy stuck his head into the office. "Engineer Granville?"

"Hey, Naj. What's up?"

The boy sidled in. "Promise you won't yell?"

Artur rolled his eyes. "Now what trouble have you got into?"

"Well, I was hiding in the back storage area after spilling Chief Blimp Engineer Haslett's tea..."

"And?"

"The single-person blimp isn't there."

Seated at her study desk, Eleanor massaged her neck. Absolute power shouldn't mean self-indulgence. She needed to make up for lost time, even though her father's notes had only granted her this opportunity recently. The job would be challenging—ensuring people stayed on track, nudging them to work in the right direction, and maintaining her fiction of a threat—but if it improved life for everyone, it would be worth it.

Her father's portrait was a reminder and a warning of what she stood to lose. If only she had paid more attention to him, she might have been able to sway his ideas towards more humane methods. But too late to worry about that now.

Her next visitor was Matthew Porter, the engineer. He was short, stocky and middle-aged, his stubbly chin contrasting with his gold-rimmed monocle. His hands were surprisingly fine.

"Delighted to help, Your Majesty," he said. "I wondered if it might be worth laying rail tracks in places other than the Ascar Tunnel and inner city. Although it's more difficult than road construction, which is difficult enough, it allows for faster transport. I approached Logistician Randall about it some months ago. But when he took it to the Council, they decided the convenience wasn't worth the investment, especially in the countryside."

"Yes, it is a shame," said Eleanor while berating herself for her absence from the Council. Even without the pretext of war, she could have supported his idea. "I'm glad you have thought this through, and you will certainly have your opportunity now. Unfortunately, circumstances dictate that you'll need to work fast. Moving on, do you have any ideas about rapid communications?"

His brow wrinkled. "I had an idea for sending electrical pulses along wires—maybe some coding that could be interpreted at the other end. But we haven't yet worked out how to lay long wires. To be honest, it's easier to shout or use a whistling message tube—such as you have in the Keep."

"I see." For distant communications, it looked like they'd continue relying on messenger birds. Maybe, once powers were accepted, people like Samuel could be stationed in settlements. Their far-viewing powers, suitably trained, would be invaluable. Were there many people with that power? Hopefully it was common. She'd have to check with Susanna. If there weren't enough of them—

"Your Majesty?" Porter's pen hovered over his notepad. "Have you had an idea about messaging?"

"Oh!" Eleanor's heart jumped. "No, my thoughts were heading in a different direction. Sorry, I won't take up more of your time."

While Porter took his leave, she tried to ignore the portraits surrounding her. She *wasn't* going to encourage deliberate cursing. If she did, she'd be as bad as her father.

Chapter 8

Lester's uniform jacket flapped as he pelted up the street after Artur. Who'd have imagined engineers were so impulsive? The pair of them must look ridiculous. Unlike the outer city, the inner city had straight, wide roads with good visibility, so he needn't worry about losing his quarry. On the downside, with the factory workers changing shifts, that meant more people to witness the spectacle.

By the time Artur arrived at the gateway to the Royal Compound, Lester was just a few yards behind him. He had him now. The guards on either side of the gate wouldn't allow a desperate chap in grubby overalls—

The guards bowed and stepped aside, and Artur plunged through the full-height turnstile into the cramped passageway beyond.

What the—Lester put on a final burst of speed then skidded to a halt as the guards blocked his way. "I'm with him. Captain Black."

They waved him through. He pushed into the checkpoint building, gulping air, relieved his hangover had settled. Throwing up over his shoes would really set off the morning.

Hand pressed against his side, Artur spoke breathlessly through the duty guard's hatch. "Let us in."

"Yes, sir."

Lester gaped. Even *Royal Compound* guards admitted him without their usual questions? Who was this guy?

With a click, the second gate opened, and Lester followed Artur through.

The engineer slowed to a walk as they approached the palace, Lester's eyebrows climbing with every step. But instead of approaching the grand entrance, Artur headed round the corner and knocked on a side door.

When the door cracked open, Artur muttered through the gap. There was a giggle, and the door swung wide.

Lester slipped in just behind Artur and found himself passing through a steam-filled kitchen to a set of back stairs. The scent of baking bread made his nose twitch. "Uh, where are we going?"

"Let's try the second floor. Sorry I didn't explain. If we don't find her there, you'd better wait—"

Her? The queen? Surely not that terrifying housekeeper.

A large figure wearing a red uniform stepped through the second floor doorway and paused. It was Paton. "Back already, lad? And with company?" He fixed Lester with his eye. "Morning, Black."

Standing below Artur on the stairs, Lester nodded back. Hopefully Paton wouldn't ask *why* he was here: he had no idea.

"Is she in her office?" Artur clutched the bannister and waved towards the doorway.

"What's wrong?" Paton's tone shifted from amused to concerned.

"Not *wrong*, but something odd came up when Lester was visiting. I think she'd like to know. Soon."

"Follow me."

Paton led them to the library, where the queen—*remember to call her Eleanor!*—sat across the table from a dark-haired city guard. Lester's brow wrinkled. Why would Hilary be in the queen's library? He was an odd fellow, more interested in historical research than sports. Despite his suspicious expertise at card games, nobody had ever managed to catch him cheating.

After a glance over her shoulder at them, Eleanor continued speaking. "Since we know the Settlers came from the south, I agree it's best to concentrate on information pertaining to that direction. Councillor Martek's already sent a squad to inspect the border. I'm sure your cross-referencing suggestion will prove invaluable."

Hilary's blush sat oddly on his usual po-faced demeanour. "I am gratified by your confidence, Your Majesty. The system is something I discovered to be of utility in the historical archives. Its main value was in tracking three generations of—"

Paton cleared his throat. "I apologise, Your Majesty, but Senior Blimp, uh, Big Engineer Artur requests a moment of your time. At your convenience."

She swivelled towards them. "Artur, what's the matter?"

Hilary stood and bowed, murmuring, "Perhaps this would be a good time for me to stretch my legs and secure an early lunch. I shall return in the afternoon."

After Hilary left, Eleanor waved Artur and Lester to sit opposite her as if such interruptions happened every day. Paton stationed himself beside the door.

"One day, Paton, you'll relax enough to take a seat along with everyone else." Her eyes twinkled. "And maybe to call me Eleanor."

Paton scowled. "It wouldn't be right, Your Majesty."

She leaned towards Artur. "You've whetted my curiosity. What happened?"

"Lester was visiting me after you suggested using a

blimp for settlement visits," said Artur. "I was explaining about our versium gas."

"It's a very exciting development, isn't it?" She beamed. "You get all the fun."

"And I mentioned our single person blimp, though it's currently impracticable—"

"Yes, I remember you had the problem of a heat source. Have you found a solution? Just this morning, I found a reference to purifying oil for a higher energy yield."

Lester sagged. Where had the urgency gone? Were they going to spend all morning talking about blimp research? If he'd known that, he'd not have tried so hard to keep up with Artur. Plus, he was starting to feel like a spare part in the conversation.

"It's something else." Artur licked his lips. "The blimp's been stolen."

"Not just mislaid? That storage area holds so many incomplete projects, it would be easy to lose track."

"It's definitely gone." Grasping Eleanor's hands, Artur gazed into her face. "And there's someone with a power who can use it!"

"Isabel," breathed Eleanor. "Of course." Her face fell.

Lester could understand Eleanor's distress. Isabel had mentored him when he became a captain, and she occasionally shared royal anecdotes. Nothing sensitive, but Isabel's affection for her younger cousin had been obvious. He hid a smile at Eleanor and Artur's entwined hands, but he wasn't here to ogle them. He'd better say something. "Just checking I understand. Isabel might operate that blimp with her heat power, but you think she stole it? Why not just ask for it? Does she need to get somewhere in a hurry?"

Eleanor slid away from Artur's grip and looked down,

clasping her hands together tightly. "I don't know. She disappeared a few weeks ago. We had a blimp accident. Near a cursed mound. Artur was injured."

Paton stomped forwards. "What were you thinking of, Your Majesty? Putting yourself in danger like that. You never said you had an accident—you told me she'd gone missing on her own. If you'd sent us out to look as soon as you—"

"I know, and I'm sorry I misled you. But she really didn't want people searching for her. And you know she's never come to harm on these trips before. So I assumed she'd be back in her own time."

Blimp accidents? Cursed mounds? And—Lester gaped at Artur. "You were injured by a beast?"

Artur wiped his brow with a grubby cloth, distributing his soot marks more evenly. "No, but being injured at a mound left its effect on me."

"Uh, and what sort of..." How could he ask?

"Nothing relevant here," said Eleanor firmly. "Anyway, Isabel stayed behind because the repaired blimp couldn't hold all three of us. When she didn't return, I thought she'd sacrificed herself. But it seems she was up to something more. I think she killed Silvers. And she may have killed Staunton."

"Staunton?" yelped Lester. "He's dead?"

"Just yesterday," said Paton. "Captain Shelley was taken into custody. Though I can't see that he did it. I wish you'd not allowed Hastings to take charge. Too driven by personal grudges. If he keeps digging..." He glanced at Lester. "There's a risk."

Jonathan in jail *again?* Lester opened his mouth then closed it again. What other news had he missed by sleeping in? This was completely nuts.

"If he hadn't been there when you told—" She shook her head. "I shouldn't override him with my Queen's Discretion after agreeing he should investigate. The more I use that power, the worse it looks. I can't afford to be regarded as a despot. I'm sorry for Captain Shelley, but I have other priorities."

She was sorry for the guy and believed *Isabel* was guilty? "Uh, why would Isabel kill Silvers and Staunton? I don't get it." Though that felt like Lester's usual state of mind, these days. Travelling with Tabitha was starting to look more attractive.

"She didn't want anyone else to be cursed." Eleanor paled. "And I believe she blamed those two for plotting to curse people deliberately."

Hmm. Isabel's seemingly casual attitude towards summary justice might not only apply to humans. "She'd be keen to wipe out beasts as well, wouldn't she?"

Nodding, Eleanor pulled a handkerchief from her pocket and dabbed at her eyes.

Lester persisted. "Maybe she stole the blimp so she could visit more mounds? Like you used a blimp to visit one."

"Maybe so." She dropped her handkerchief on the table.

"But why doesn't she make contact with you? I mean, she always struck me as someone who did what she thought was right. If she really did kill Silvers and Staunton, she'd be more likely to boast about it than to run away." Surely nobody would regret Silvers' death. "Presumably she thought she was justified. Even if the Council disagreed and charged her with unlawful killing, couldn't you pardon her? With that Queen's Discretion you were talking about? Can't you pardon everything other than regicide?"

Eleanor's shoulders went rigid.

Lester's collar felt too tight, like the noose they used for public executions. "You're not telling me that—"

"Classified information." Paton glared at him. "I mean it. If you dare even breathe a word—"

He held up his hands. "Sure, sure." Nobody would believe this crazy tale from him anyway, and he certainly didn't want Paton after his head.

Eleanor took a few deep breaths, winding a loose tendril of hair round her fingers. "If only we could track her movements."

Lester inspected the tabletop rather than look at her. An embroidered "ES" on the discarded handkerchief caught his eye. Monograms. "We might be able to. In fact, there's a captain who can locate items with his power. How about asking Richard Honeyman to track the blimp?"

Eleanor's face brightened, and she tucked her hair behind an ear. "He'd be ideal. He's the one who located my father's notes, although he... doesn't know the full details."

Paton dispatched a messenger to fetch Richard. Eleanor and Artur murmured to each other across the table. When she offered Artur a silk handkerchief to wipe his face, Lester excused himself to inspect the bookshelves. He ran his eye over shelves of tatty handwritten journals, his gaze pausing on a printed book: *Self-appraisal at the population level: an academic treatise.* He snorted. Sounded like the kind of mumbo-jumbo that could have been fashionable a generation ago.

Unfortunately, the messenger returned with the information that Richard was ill. "He apologises profusely and begs your forgiveness, Your Majesty, but he has a digestive upset and is unable to leave his quarters."

Eleanor sighed. "Well, I suppose a delay of a day or so won't make a difference, given how long Isabel's been gone. Can you please tell him to present himself at the palace as soon as he can?"

"I'll be very interested to see if this idea works," said Lester. The delay had the advantage of postponing his trip with Tabitha. For once, he was grateful to Richard for his fussy habits. All that rhubarb juice he drank, no doubt.

"Your suggestion is great." She smiled at him. "I'll be sure to keep you informed when you return from your trip with Tabitha. I think it would be best if you left tomorrow morning. Artur, would you mind facilitating that?"

"Of course I will," said Artur.

Shit.

After the others vacated the library, Eleanor slumped at the table, winding her braid round a wrist. Why was nothing straightforward? It was impossible to keep all her priorities in mind. She nearly laughed. Just as well there wasn't a *real* invasion coming up, or she would have completely gone to pieces.

She regarded the list in front of her. Martek's team would shortly return from the border after detecting nothing untoward. She'd find a plausible reason to dissuade him from setting up expensive permanent sentry posts. Infrastructure projects were with Porter, and Susanna was dealing with new training methods. Horrible though the thought was, Staunton's untimely death had a bright side: nobody else would challenge Eleanor's interpretation of the "evidence" in her father's notes. However, it also raised the spectre of Isabel running amuck, as did the presumed blimp theft.

If only she had someone to talk to. The people who knew about Isabel were busy elsewhere. Or dead, like Staunton. Susanna busy in the Keep, Jonathan—a frown tightened her forehead—*temporarily* in jail, and Artur dealing with Lester's trip. Although Richard had located the missing notes, he'd not been there when she'd read Isabel's letter. Despite her worries, Eleanor's lips twitched. The tone of Richard's apologetic message suggested he would be stuck in the privy for a while.

Of course. Paton. She reached for the bell pull.

After shutting the door behind him, Paton saluted. "How may I be of help, Your Majesty?"

"Please, sit down. I'll get a crick in my neck looking up at you."

His forehead creased. "Is that an order?"

She huffed. If she pressed him, he'd do it, but his unprotesting obedience would speak his disapproval louder than any words. "No, not if it makes you uncomfortable. When you were working with my father, what did he tell you of his plans? Surely he must have confided in you, as Royal Chief Guard."

He regarded the tabletop. "I'm sorry, Your Majesty. King Frederick really didn't tell me anything."

"If he trusted you with his safety, why not use you as a sounding board too? You've been in loyal service since I was a child, and you know the household and city."

"Your Majesty, I'm not an educated man." Paton's one-eyed gaze flicked across the library shelves. "He did start to talk about some ideas, in the early years. But when I couldn't follow his train of thought, he gave up. He never attempted it again."

"No memories of surveys or—" She regarded his pained expression. "Never mind." No, that would have been too easy. There was no point in inflicting more royal musings on him and then getting annoyed when he couldn't make sense of them. "Do you know who my father *did* confide in?"

He regarded a family portrait on the far wall. "Mainly Captain Hanlon, I believe."

Eleanor's fingernails dug into her palms. Everything led back to Isabel. "I see. Thank you."

He bowed. "Will that be all, Your Majesty?"

Idle curiosity got the better of her. "Why do you sometimes salute me and sometimes bow?"

His eyebrow lifted. "Sometimes one feels right, and sometimes the other. Which do you wish me to use, Your Majesty?"

She'd walked into that one. "Whatever suits you. I don't mind. Though a bow might be more appropriate since I'm not a guard or captain. Talking of which, could you please drop by the Council detention cells and check up on Captain Shelley's welfare?" Since Paton had escorted the man there last night, it wouldn't be *too* much interference if he dropped by for some follow-up.

"Shelley might demand to be mind-read, but Hastings will be obstructive. How much concern shall I express on your behalf?"

"It's best if I remain—Damn!" Breathing hard, she ran her hands through her hair. What a mess. "Jonathan knows about Isabel. If he's mind-read, she could be implicated. I'll have to side with Hastings, agree the mind readers have other priorities."

"As you wish." Paton's voice held a tinge of distaste.

"Sorry."

"You needn't apologise to *me*."

Eleanor squeezed her eyes shut. Letting others take the blame wasn't right, but she couldn't face revealing the truth. Not yet. What a coward she was, rationalising her decision as a desire to protect her cousin. "If you think things are going too far, let me know."

After Paton left, Eleanor frowned at the journal Hilary had been working on. Its cardboard cover was torn and discoloured, and the ink on the pages had run. Hilary had bookmarked a faded entry and transcribed a few words from the original Noble Ascarite:

... Checking up on the settlers...
making sure they're not... (chased? caused??) trouble...

Deep in thought, she returned to her study.

Her next major personal task would be to make a public announcement regarding the use of powers and their benefits. Careful preparation would be needed to forestall chaos. With his call for volunteers, Hastings had already primed the people regarding invasion and the need for defence. That was fine. He could give hot-headed recruits something to do and establish a culture of discipline. And it let her concentrate on the truly important issues. Once Lester had visited a settlement or two and reassured them about safety, she'd check with him about their reactions. That would let her decide what rumours could be planted. Say, tales of rescued children.

Better make a note of that before she forgot. Reaching for a pen, Eleanor paused. No. Even if she used Noble Ascarite—the written language of government and officials—she might inadvertently reveal too much on the paper. Her gut clenched. Had her father kept his most disturbing ideas in his head? Given what he *had* written down, that was an unpleasant thought.

Leaning back in her chair, she redid her braid. And then she would have to arrange the logistics of making her speech. It might take weeks or months for planted rumours to bed in, and picking the right time would be crucial. Steering a change in how the curse was viewed was a huge gamble. Given the unpredictability of a crowd's response, she'd need to have people like Lester and Franka available, in case of panic or negative reactions. Not really *manipulation*, more... *encouragement* to perceive things in the right way.

She pursed her lips. Was she being underhand or just pragmatic? Maybe she was a hypocrite, using cursed powers and maligning her father in the same breath.

Why had none of her ancestors pushed for such reforms that would benefit everyone? What was wrong with society, that they were so entrenched in custom and didn't think beyond today's limitations? Well, she would change all that or die trying. With a sigh, she picked up the engineers' new training curriculum.

Paton's returning tread sounded in the corridor with a second set of footsteps. Her eyebrows rose. Jonathan? Maybe Hastings had freed the man after seeing sense, and without the complications of mind-reading. She'd rather work with him than against him.

With a perfunctory rap on the door frame, Paton entered. Words of welcome died on Eleanor's lips at the sight of Hastings behind him. The man wore a disgruntled look.

She nodded at Hastings. "I take it you've freed Captain Shelley?"

Hastings' cheeks turned beetroot and quivered. "Er, no. He's escaped."

Eleanor crumpled the document she'd been reading. "You've lost *another* prisoner?"

Chapter 9

Jonathan stumbled behind Isabel into the dense vegetation outside the city walls. His feet sank into thick humus, with the occasional crack of a broken branch. At least he was wearing his own boots. He nearly laughed. How could he worry about footwear when he'd been dragged away from lawful captivity by a self-confessed regicide?

Twigs caught at his borrowed clothing, and he kept an arm up to protect his face. A glance at the moon suggested they were moving eastwards. Even though his previous convoy journeys traversed terrain without the benefit of paths, he'd never had to push through such thick undergrowth. Travellers departed Ascar through its southern gate or via the Armstrong Tunnel to the north, not sneaking around at the base of the Cleon Mountains like this. He supposed that nobody—bar Isabel—had set foot here for decades or maybe even centuries.

Sliding around obstacles ahead of him, Isabel barely disturbed her surroundings. Jonathan shook his head. *He* was the seasoned convoy captain, and here he was, blundering around as if on his first trip out of the city. When she glanced back and slowed her pace, he tried not to grit his teeth. After all, he was nearly two decades her senior.

By the time they stopped in a tiny clearing, the sun was rising. Jonathan squinted at his surroundings, blinked and had a second look. Almost perfectly concealed by the leafy shrubs stood a wooden shack.

Isabel tugged aside the foliage covering the door and gestured for him to precede her. "Welcome to my abode."

Ducking his head slightly—did the taller Isabel ever bang her head?—he slipped inside. Isabel followed him, her head not quite touching the roof when she stood up straight. A bedroll lay by the wall beside a pile of green fabric and ropes. On a squared-off chunk of log marred by singe marks sat a dented metal plate and spoon.

"Nice place you have here," he said. "When I was on the run, I was sleeping in piles of leaves and under bushes."

She lit a portable stove with a match. "When I built this, I wasn't on the run. I won't return here, obviously, now you know where it is. But I do have a few hidey-holes scattered around."

"Why? I hadn't thought of you as an explorer." This isolated shack was a far cry from palace receptions or implementing royal directives.

"I'd been investigating cursed mounds under Eleanor's instructions. Destroying most of them." Isabel glanced at him before rummaging in her satchel. "And hunting beasts."

"Including human ones?"

"Hey, it was only two of them!" She yanked out a loaf of bread. "Three, if you count King Frederick."

"Look, you can't just go round mur—" He bit his tongue. She probably could, and he didn't want to end up on that list. Conversely, if he updated her on the recent serious revelations about impending attack, he might convince her to refrain from further mayhem. "Uh, that's why you left?"

"Yeah." While she brewed them tea and sliced the bread—spreading it with duck paté, if his nose informed him right—she told him of her blimp trip with Eleanor and

Artur. "Seemed like a good time to disappear after that. I'd a feeling Eleanor would start making enquiries about her father. She's completely his opposite, tender-hearted rather than ruthless. I didn't want to be around when she realised I'd... well. I can work freely now, but it's a shame I had to leave her in the lurch." She chewed her lip. "Is she alright?"

"I think so, but the invasion threat has really been a shock to her. And everyone else. Or so I get from Susanna. You know she's Chief Scientist now?"

"Yep, good for her." Isabel blew on her steaming tea. "Did Eleanor say anything about me? Or did anyone else?"

"Not sure what assumptions people are making about your disappearance. Eleanor requested us to keep quiet about that and your confession note." He held back a growl. "That's why I ended up in jail."

"Ah. But at least I got you out again." She winked, then smirked at his glare. "How's Artur?"

"Cursed."

Her hand jerked, sloshing her tea. "What? How did he get bitten on the way home? I saw them off safely."

"Not bitten. Susanna thinks that there's something in mounds that causes the curse. Beasts carry it, but they're not the original source? When the mound exploded, Artur got hit by a piece. Something like that." He bit into the bread. Yep, duck paté. She must have pilfered it from the palace.

"My fault, I guess. Nice lad, and I'm sure Eleanor will see him right. They sleeping together?"

His eyes bulged, and he choked. "How should I know?"

"Poor Jonathan, now I've embarrassed you. But it would do Eleanor good to relax some." Her waggling eyebrows challenged him to say more.

"But isn't there a risk of passing the curse on?" His face warmed. "With, uh, person-to-person contact? I know Eleanor wants to be more open about powers, but if *she* became cursed she'd be open to accusations of bias. Even more than usual, I mean."

"Hmm. Do you know how I got cursed?"

"Well, no." Isabel had been cursed after him, but the particulars hadn't been bruited about. It did seem odd that a noble would be exposed.

"Like most people, you probably assume it's custom and history that keeps a certain family on the throne." She chewed and swallowed. "The 'family secret', not that it's much of one, is that those of royal blood are supposedly immune to the curse."

Jonathan gaped.

"That was the original belief." Isabel sipped from her mug. "With me being the tough one, and Eleanor immediately in line for the throne, Frederick figured I'd be a good person to investigate beasts. All very hush-hush. Accountable to him only." She frowned. "Clearly he was wrong in some respects. Though perhaps I was just too careless. It's not as if there are lots of royals to experiment on. And this was before I realised just how focussed he was on making more cursed. He *used* me. The idea of having a personal assassin—executioner, rather—amused him. I thought he wanted to eradicate beasts, but he really wanted them as a reservoir. Hence Staunton and Silvers. But Eleanor won't want to take that route." She looked at Jonathan meaningfully. "Nor will Susanna, I hope."

Shit. He wished he'd had longer to catch up with Susanna. "No, of course not. But Eleanor's in a real bind. After reading those notes you left, she's sure there will be an invasion. Hastings is raising and training an army." *When he's not arresting me.* "And Susanna's developing a feedback method so people can control their powers more easily."

Isabel's expression grew intent. "How does that work? With your help?"

"When I was on the run..." Jonathan explained how he'd learned—relearned, rather—how to activate his power without pain. "It still needs pain if I'm in a hurry, but otherwise it's more a case of adopting the right mental posture." He made a face. "That sounds pompous, but it's something like that."

"Interesting. So, being cursed isn't the ordeal it used to be?" She tapped the pain box still in her satchel.

"It shouldn't be. No more training and working in secret. Though it's early days yet. The public will need to be informed carefully. Susanna's working hard to improve things for everyone. I think, uh, it would be better if her research isn't *interrupted* by mysterious murders."

She chuckled. "Don't worry. Your beloved is safe from me."

His ears heated, even as he relaxed with her assurance. "Look, Staunton's death has thrown a real spanner in the works. And I say that as someone who didn't like him. But he was supposed to be helping Eleanor go over King Frederick's notes, to get better information about the invasion. His death might mean that she lacks some critical knowledge. It could be disastrous."

Isabel wrinkled her nose. "I guess I was a bit impulsive, but he was worse than Silvers. At least Silvers pitched in when needed. He even exposed himself to Terry's power, so Annetta could test her remedy. Bet you didn't know that."

Terry's power was that of inflicting pain. Jonathan had

accidentally fallen foul of it himself. He shuddered. "How did you find all this out?"

"I spoke to Silvers. Had a chat before I killed him."

His gorge rose and collided with the paté slithering down his throat.

Seeing his face, Isabel said, "Hey, I didn't torture him. What do you take me for? I spoke to him through the prison window, told him I was going to kill him. Said I'd do it so quickly he wouldn't even know it. He wanted to pass his knowledge on to someone. He lived for the science. And died for it too."

Jonathan gulped his tea. In a previous clash with Silvers, he'd used his power to give the man a nosebleed. And he'd taken satisfaction in doing so. Was he being a hypocrite? "He should have had a proper trial, not been murdered just because you felt like it."

"I didn't kill any of them for fun. If they'd lived, their ideas would have permeated society. Insidiously. Their deaths were for the greater good. I'm not talking about revenge or punishment or even justice—but damage limitation." She looked him in the eye. "Have you never been faced with such a decision?"

His gaze fell. He'd made exactly that decision previously, killing old Gerald and allowing Annetta to think it was her poor care. And his victim didn't even have ill intent. With Eleanor's reforms, the Council should no longer require such cover-ups. "I suppose you have a point."

"When you guys arrange accidents, the Council don't object, and then they pretend their hands are clean. I make my own decisions." Isabel offered him the last piece of bread, topped with a blob of jam. "Anyway, what's Eleanor done so far?"

"Got someone from the historians looking through their archives and her library. They're concentrating on lands to the south, since that's where the Settlers came from."

"South. I see." She looked thoughtful. "Well, we've both been up all night. You'd better get some sleep."

Jonathan regarded the dirt floor glumly. The prison bunk would have been more comfortable, although he was in no mood to be fussy. The night's activities were catching up with him. He stifled a yawn.

Isabel pointed at the bedroll. "You can use that. I'll just prop myself by the door. Don't want you getting ideas about wandering off. Besides, I want to think about how you activate your power. I'll try not to wake you with my practice." She grinned. "Or set the place on fire. I'll save that for beast mounds."

When Jonathan awoke, it was nearly dusk. His head was muzzy, and he was starving. Isabel was nowhere in sight. Damn her, sneaking off before he could ask her more. Had she drugged him, that he'd slept so long? At least she'd left a second loaf of bread, a tub of grain, and even a half-full pot of jam, along with the portable stove and a few matches. A luxurious dinner.

As the sun set, the patter of raindrops started on the roof. There wasn't any point in attempting to return to Ascar tonight. To be honest, he was in no hurry. He'd been through so much over the last week that taking a couple of days to collect himself wouldn't do any harm, would it? And picking up clues about Isabel would be more helpful than landing himself back in custody. He'd probably attract another dose of opprobrium from Hastings, but that would happen no matter how long he'd been missing.

A scratching on the door caught his attention. Maybe

Isabel hadn't abandoned him after all, or perhaps she'd forgotten something. Even her power might be challenged in this wet weather.

He cracked the door open and looked down.

A bedraggled beast whined at him. Its snout bore a white splotch, and there was a singed patch on its grey pelt.

Jonathan sighed. "Oh. It's you."

Chapter 10

Lester closed his eyes and turned his face to the sky, savouring the wind in his hair. Behind him, Annetta and Tabitha chattered to each other, punctuated by the ropes creaking against the gondola's side. This was the life. If travel to the settlements were always like this, why, everyone would want to do it! Well, everyone apart from Jonathan. Lester could believe Artur's words: the grouch probably preferred being in jail.

"Enjoying the ride?"

Lester glanced down at the petite operator next to him. Her eyes crinkled as she peered through her spyglass.

"It's grand," he said. "How long now?"

"It shouldn't be—Ah! I can see fields just past those trees. We'll start preparing for landing, sir." She brushed past him and called to her partner, "Time to cool the gas."

Dressed in beige overalls like Annetta's, Tabitha pressed herself against the handrail, her hair flying in all directions. She waved towards the trees. "Can I have the spyglass? I want to see if any birds take off."

"There you go." The operator handed the instrument over and said to Annetta, "Please move up a little, miss. Ben and I need to double-check the readings."

Annetta squeezed up beside Lester. "This is amazing! Just a few hours for a journey that took me a week on foot." She beamed. "I'd worried about running out of ingredients, but blimp travel will make life so much easier. Of course, I must keep good records of what grows where. And I'll need to contact my fellow herbalists, maybe collate a map. Perhaps Scientist Fellows could help..."

Lester held up a hand. Annetta had already mentioned how some of the Maldon folk knew of Jonathan's power, but she'd not mentioned how to behave. "Remember, this is my first time visiting a settlement. Are there any local customs I don't want to fall foul of?" This might have been a question to pose to Tabitha, her being his rural advisor and all. But he wanted to keep contact with her to a minimum. At least, as minimum as it could get in a blimp.

"Customs?" Annetta scrunched her face. "I don't think so. Ruralites are regular people too. Maybe they've less time for entertainments, but—" She stared up at him, and her cheeks reddened. "Oh."

"A problem?" Was his hair more mussed than was stylish? Next trip, he should tie it back like Annetta did, though his might not be long enough for that. He fumbled in his pocket for a comb.

Hands clutching the side rail, she looked away and mumbled something.

"Sorry?"

"You're male."

"You noticed? That's a relief."

She shot him an irritated glance. "Not many people travel between settlements and sometimes if the population's too isolated, there can be a risk of making diseases that run in the family worse. That is to say, it's best if people have children with partners who aren't too closely related to them. So, when visitors arrive at settlements, especially men who are young and fit, like convoy guards, they might be offered a... high level of hospitality from the womenfolk. I mean, no obligation or anything, but it's kind of doing them a favour." Her mouth slammed shut.

Lester's brow creased. What was she—"Visiting guards have *breeding potential?*"

She nodded and mumbled to her hands, "Even those who aren't as young or, um, physically attractive..."

Crap! Had Tabitha overheard them? He glanced towards her, but she was studying the trees through the spyglass. At least he'd learned of the custom from Annetta rather than Tabitha, but if it gave the girl ideas... *Jonathan'll kill me.*

"Because you're a captain, they might not ask. And it's not obligatory." Annetta's voice was barely audible, and she fanned her face despite the wind.

"I should think not!" Taking a deep breath, he told himself not to blame the messenger. "Sorry, I was just a bit shocked. Thank you for telling me." He forced a laugh through the tightness in his throat. "Though it's funny to think of someone like Jonathan being fought over by—"

"That's it!" Annetta's eyes widened, and she clapped a hand to her mouth.

"Are you ill?" *Oh, please don't let her throw up over me.* Their path took them over bare-branched trees towards a field that contained only a couple of chicken coops, so at least nobody would notice if she was sick.

She removed her hand. "I'm fine. Nothing important." Her colour deepened further.

He shook his head. The herbalist was a difficult woman to read.

"Ground's nice and flat for landing," called the operator. "Everyone ready?"

Lester checked that his sabre was safely sheathed while

the last of the trees disappeared beneath them. There was something almost hypnotic about how the barren field and ridged earth grew with the blimp's descent. He leaned over the gondola's side to watch the moment they landed.

"Down we go. Hang on!"

The floor shuddered beneath him. He threw an arm up, but mud still splashed his face. *Damn!* Tabitha giggled as he wiped his forehead with the back of his hand. Maybe he should emulate Richard and carry handkerchiefs.

The female operator grinned. "Not bad. I could get to like this versium."

Her chunkier partner nodded and picked up the tether rope. "Though we can probably cool less suddenly next time. That landing was a bit rough."

"I agree," muttered Lester. Still, as long as they didn't need to walk back, he should be satisfied.

The operators said they'd stay with the blimp until the balloon's gas cooled further, and then unload the baggage. Annetta led the way towards the town with Tabitha by her side, Lester wincing as his polished boots splashed through the muck.

The mud gave way to a vague dirt trail as they approached the outskirts. Between single-storey wooden houses with mismatched shutters, the trail turned into a street that Annetta explained was cobbled nearer to the town square.

Beside a two-storey building, she stopped, hands twisting the strap of her herbalist's bag. "If you don't mind, I'll just let Adrian know we're here. A friend. He probably hasn't noticed our arrival, and I think it would be useful to include him in the discussions." She pointed further down the street to an open square containing a cluster of townsfolk. "Are you alright to introduce yourselves?"

What could Lester say? *He* was supposed to be in charge of this trip. Annetta was only taking advantage of the blimp transport so she could gather her herbs or whatever. He glanced at his other companion. "Sure. Tabitha, let's go and chat with our hosts."

Tabitha grabbed his arm and whispered something.

"What?" He tilted his head towards her.

"So many people!" Her breath tickled his ear.

Patting her hand, he tried to muster some enthusiasm. "I'm sure they'll be glad to meet us. Come on."

At the front of the group of townsfolk stood a thin man in gaudy red robes, a golden chain around his neck. Painted for sure, not real. Not even a decent attempt with paste. Next to the man in red stood an authoritative woman in a black dress. A young woman in homespun stood behind them. She caught Lester's eye and winked then smoothed back her wavy red hair. Squirming inside, he looked away.

Fortunately, he spied a friendly face. A convoy guard called Opal stood to one side. Her grey jacket was unfastened, and her blue scarf provided an unofficial splash of colour. "Hey, Lester. Long time no see. Oops, I guess you're a captain now."

"That's right. Uh, why're you here?"

"Captain Shelley stationed me here after a beast incident. To keep an eye on things."

"Ah." A potential ally if he messed things up. He cleared his throat. "Good morning, everyone. I'm Captain Black from Ascar, and this is Miss Tabitha." Was that how he should refer to her? She wasn't a captain, but he wanted to give her some status. It would help if she let go of his arm.

Scuffing footsteps alerted him to Annetta's return. She

had company: a plump man—that would be Adrian?—wearing a canvas apron with a singed hem, and an equally plump blonde girl around Tabitha's age. Annetta and the man's faces were rather pink, and the girl was grinning.

Lester waved his free hand. "And I believe you know Annetta already."

With a glare at Annetta, the man in red stepped forward. "Welcome, Captain Black. I am Mayor Sutcliff. We are most honoured that you have chosen to grace our humble little town with your presence. The bird message said you'd be visiting about a possible hostile approach. Quite a shock, I must say. In all my time as leader of this community, of looking after its inhabitants and interacting at the highest levels with royal representatives... I am extremely shocked. To think of my people being captured and driven away in chains, forced to end their miserable lives as prisoners..." He puffed out his scrawny chest. "And what is Ascar doing about this, eh?"

Lester stared. What lurid fiction had the man been reading? Did they have penny dreadfuls out here too? The woman in black folded her arms and raised an eyebrow while the redhead smirked.

It was a comfort that the other townsfolk didn't seem nearly so concerned. "The queen would value your thoughts—the thoughts of all the townsfolk—on various matters related to the *possible* threat." He disengaged his arm from Tabitha's and waved behind him. "But before I start, our two blimp operators are still with the craft outside town. Could someone help them with our bags?"

"Of course!" Sutcliff flapped his hands, his shoulders hunching. "We must of course facilitate everything to do with blimp travel."

Opal stepped forwards. "Shall I deal with it, Mayor Sutcliff?"

At his nod, she walked off, a couple of young boys trotting along behind her.

"Now," said Sutcliff, "what are these matters?"

The black-clad woman's lips pursed. "I see no reason to remain in the square as if we're gossiping on market day. Perhaps Captain Black and Miss Tabitha would like a seat and some refreshments. And I'm sure Annetta would like to catch up with her friends. The guesthouse is ready for visitors if the blimp operators would like to rest."

A short while later, Lester and his two travelling companions were sitting in the mayor's meeting room with Adrian and the black-garbed woman, whose name was Giselle. Oozing servility, the mayor had indicated that Lester was to occupy the chair behind the polished desk. Tabitha perched on a chair beside him, although thankfully the chairs' arms kept her from getting too close.

"A road system?" Adrian raised his eyebrows. "It would be fantastic for shifting resources in bulk. Maybe even regular trade with the other settlements. We have plenty of wood here, but stone for buildings is more of a problem." He pulled out his notebook and studied it. "Though I'm not sure about how to communicate over distances other than birds..."

Sutcliff's nose wrinkled. "But if we don't provoke anyone, I think potential attackers would leave us alone. It seems dangerous to make roads that just anyone could travel along. Who knows what kind of riffraff might arrive?"

Giselle sniffed. "And what if attackers *don't* leave us alone? And we have no rapid way to alert anyone?"

Lester held back a groan. "I am simply conveying Her

Majesty's wishes." Eleanor hadn't given him the impression that improvements were *optional*, but it didn't seem that Sutcliff was the right person to approach. Protocol was all very well, but the man was clueless.

After a frustrating circular discussion, Giselle glanced out of the window. "It's getting late, and I think our guests may be tired after their journey. How about continuing with an open discussion in the town square tomorrow morning?"

At last! Surely sensible people would attend. Lester nodded at the mayor. "Mayor Sutcliff, thank you for your time. I think Giselle's suggestion is excellent."

She extended a hand towards him. "Would you like to use my spare room rather than the guesthouse?"

Damn! Her too?

Sutcliff's fists clenched. "Given the significance of Captain Black's visit, it would be more appropriate for him to avail himself of the guest accommodation in my official residence. Though I'm afraid I only have a single room..."

Lester leapt at the chance. "That sounds good, Mayor Sutcliff, uh, thanks for the offer."

"In that case," said Giselle, "Tabitha can stay with me." She glanced at the others. "Adrian, I suppose you'll want to look after Annetta?"

Sutcliff scowled while Annetta hid a giggle behind her hand.

Adrian tugged at his collar. "If it's not a problem—"

"Thought you might. Send Lisa over, and she can keep Tabitha company." Giselle nodded at Lester. "Lisa's been living with her father since we divorced, but she helps me when we have visitors. Make sense?"

"Sure," said Lester faintly. Ruralites were certainly open about such things. None of the sneaking around he usually witnessed.

Splashing into another puddle between two bushes, Jonathan cursed at the beast's disappearing tail. Why was he doing this? Because he'd deluded himself that he could help Susanna by obtaining information about beasts. It had nothing to do with his hunch they might not always be hostile. Now he'd come this far, he might as well carry on.

The beast had stayed in Isabel's shack overnight—the irony! Once morning came, it licked a spoonful of gruel from Jonathan's hand, then gripped his sleeve in its jaws and tugged. The meaning was clear. Before following it, he detached the bedroll's waterproof outer layer, which could double as a cape. Isabel hadn't stinted on quality. But then, she never did.

It led him through the morning drizzle and past a cursed mound that bore signs of a recent blaze. Jonathan's nose wrinkled at the lingering smell of smoke. Obviously Isabel's work. Every so often the beast would stop, its tongue hanging out, and wait for him to catch up.

His foot squelched into another puddle. He was too old for this.

A mile further on, two more beasts huddled beneath an evergreen thicket. The larger one—with rough black fur—snarled as he approached, but Jonathan's beast touched its nose with its own, and the black beast subsided. The third beast lay on its side, panting.

Jonathan's hand twitched. His power thrummed. His training would demand he dispatch these beasts, by whatever means he could. But...

His beast whined, then it sat on its haunches, watching him expectantly.

"What?"

It nudged the smaller beast's side. Jonathan stepped forward cautiously, taking in a mottled pelt that covered a bulging belly and protruding ribs.

"Pregnant?"

His beast's head bobbed up and down. He *wouldn't* think of it as a nod.

"And hungry too? I guess you want me to help?"

A whine. Eyes wide and liquid, it held his gaze until he sighed and looked down.

Assisting a beast to birth wasn't on, but there were practical things he could offer. A portion of Isabel's cape went towards a water collector. With his odd companion continually getting underfoot—every time he turned round its splotched nose was nudging his ankles—he spent the rest of the day rigging fish traps in a nearby stream. Luck was with him, and soon he could show the beasts a sample catch. His beast licked his hand before he left. No doubt he smelled of fish.

The beasts hadn't seemed aggressive, other than the large one's initial snarl. It had seemed more warning than imminent threat—the back of his neck heated. It was similar to his intimidation of Lester that time they'd both visited Susanna. Of course Susanna wasn't his property, and Lester wasn't even competition—he'd learned that embarrassingly late—but Jonathan had had an overwhelming desire to see the young captain off. Perhaps it would be possible to learn something from beasts. They could be cursed, but they weren't the true enemy. Not anymore. Maybe they hadn't ever been.

Lester knocked on Giselle's door the next morning, then

yawned and eased a crick in his neck. The mayor's drafty spare room and lumpy mattress hadn't been conducive to sleep. Plus, last night's meagre plate of stringy chicken and limp green vegetables barely satisfied his hunger. It would be discourteous to complain about Sutcliff's hospitality, however. No doubt rural resources were limited compared to Ascar's, and he shouldn't expect city comforts here.

When the door creaked open, he straightened.

A sweet scent wafted past Giselle while she dried her hands on a small towel. "Good morning, Captain Black."

Lester's stomach rumbled. "Wow, that smells wonderful." Damn. Where had his manners gone? "Good morning, Giselle."

"Lisa's teaching Tabitha to make pancakes. Have you eaten? Would you like some breakfast?"

"No. I mean, yes, I'd love some breakfast. Please." His mouth watered.

"Thought you might." With a sniff, Giselle led him to her sitting room table and fetched him a plate of pancakes and honey. "So. Why're you really here?"

He took his time chewing. The runny floral-scented honey and open-textured pancakes made a wonderful combination. Could he ask for some to take home? "Queen Eleanor's desire is to make cursed powers more acceptable, so it won't be necessary to lock people up. Of course, it'll need to be done carefully."

She nodded. "After what happened with Samuel, we'd wondered... I was glad Captain Shelley was found innocent. Was this something he initiated?"

"I don't know. He does seem to have set events in motion, but I get the impression the queen had been considering this for some time." It seemed insensitive to mention

Jonathan's recent re-arrest, and Lester well knew the damage that careless gossip could cause.

"I dare say her hand has been forced after discovering this threat. Very sensible decision. What's she like?"

"The queen? Oh, young, earnest... nice?" Lester eyed Giselle's curious expression and swallowed. "I've only met her a few times. Uh, how soon are we going to meet everyone else?"

She placed a mug of tea before him. "Annetta's out collecting herbs. Once she's back, we'll ring the bell to summon everyone to the meeting. Will you need Tabitha there too?"

"No! I mean, she's advising me about rural customs, but there's no need for her to attend the meeting."

"I see. She can help Lisa make bread."

"Sounds great." He gulped his tea. "Before I speak to everyone, I'll need a few minutes alone to gather my thoughts." Although he was getting better at calling his power without the pain box, it would be best to use one for this first visit. Just in case.

"Of course." She raised an eyebrow. "My bedroom has a mirror and the best lighting at this time of day."

Damn! Though she probably thought vanity drove his desire for privacy. That was a good thing.

The scent of baking bread filled the house before Giselle escorted Lester into the town square. Sutcliff rang his bell, and the locals gathered. At Sutcliff's direction, Lester climbed on top of a rickety bench. Slats bending, it creaked under his weight. Standing beside Annetta at the front of the crowd, Adrian frowned at Lester's feet in concern. Great, the man would probably blame him if he broke it.

The crowd hushed.

"Pray be quiet and allow Captain Black to speak!" bawled Sutcliff into the silence. "Quiet, everyone!"

The dratted man was the only one making any noise. "Thank you for ensuring order, Mayor Sutcliff." Lester scanned the crowd. "The reason I'm visiting..."

He started with the concern about an attack from outside forces then reassured them that they had a few years for defence preparations. After that, he moved on to the curse and powers.

"Annetta here has made huge advances with her research. Her remedies are helping the afflicted so their cursed powers don't endanger others. The queen hopes that some day it will be possible for them to return to society safely..."

The herbalist's face went pink while Adrian beamed. Lester scanned the other faces in the crowd. As Annetta had said, ruries weren't much different from city folk, and their expressions weren't difficult to read. The townsfolk were mainly thoughtful, occasionally murmuring to their neighbours. Calling his power in advance might have been overkill, but best to be cautious.

"Any questions?" When Opal mouthed something and rolled her eyes, he tried to keep his expression straight.

Sutcliff made a sour face. "Herbal mumbo-jumbo is all very well, but how do we know such things are safe?" His voice grew louder. "What if the remedies fail at a critical moment and then we decent normal people are left vulnerable? We might even be murdered in our beds or overrun by—"

"Thank you for your comments, Mayor Sutcliff." Lester smiled at the idiot, gathered his power and *pushed*. "Be reassured that all remedies generated by research in Ascar will be rigorously tested before wider release. Formal written feedback will carry most weight with the scientists. I'm sure you'll agree."

Sutcliff smiled vaguely, his voice slurring. "Quite right. Submit my feedback in writing."

Oops. He'd overdone the mind control, but he hadn't dared be more subtle. Better disperse the crowd before the man started to whine again. "I'll wind up this meeting now. If anyone else has any questions, come and find me before we leave." He hopped off the bench as Sutcliff slumped on to it.

After throwing a sharp glance at Lester, Annetta approached Sutcliff. "Mayor Sutcliff, I've warned you before about over-exerting yourself. You'd be well advised to spend the rest of today at home, resting quietly…"

Lester's brow wrinkled. Her words were solicitous, but there had been a certain gleam in her eye. Anyway, not his problem.

When he returned to Giselle's house, Tabitha met him. Her hair was neatly braided, but floury patches decorated her overalls. She held up a cup of breadcrumbs. "That was fun! Lisa says there's a posthouse. Can we go see the birds?"

Lester's shoulders sagged, but he'd done what he needed to. Might as well help Tabitha get some enjoyment out of her trip. "Sure, for a short while. We want to fly back while it's still light."

At the posthouse, the postmaster led Tabitha and Lester up external stairs to the room where the birds were kept. Lester's nose twitched at the dust, and he brushed feathers off his jacket.

While Tabitha fed crumbs to the messenger birds, she said, "Don't you think they're really clever?"

The postmaster's face grew rounder as he laughed. "You're quite right, young lady. You know we train them to recognise symbols for each settlement? I'm trying to expand their use, by showing them sketches of distinctive buildings as well."

She beamed. "And they like my breadcrumbs! I love feeding birds, but I've never made my own bread before. Messenger birds visit me in Ascar too. I think it's because my room's in the—"

Shit! "Sorry to interrupt." Lester held up a hand. She had nearly let slip about being cursed. "But we must go now."

Tabitha lagged behind in sullen silence while the postmaster escorted them to the blimp.

Annetta was already waiting in the gondola, barely visible behind cotton bags filled with bundles of cuttings. She flapped a hand at Lester as he climbed in. "Careful where you tread. These plants are delicate, and I don't want accidents."

"Don't worry, I'll be careful." Where had he got the idea she was timid?

She eyed him through the foliage. "Like you were with the mayor?"

He cleared his throat. "I've no idea what you're talking about."

Was that a snicker from behind the leaves?

"Why couldn't we stay longer?" Tabitha pouted. "You spoiled it."

"Me? If *you* hadn't started talking about—Never mind." Lester leaned against the side. The last thing he needed was a tantrum. "Just be careful what you say. Best not to mention the Keep at all."

"I guess you're right." Her hands clenched the handrail. "But one day I'll leave."

Seated at the table in the royal library, Eleanor watched Susanna and Richard set up their calibrated stimulus generators. A muscle in her cheek twitched, and she fiddled with the end of her braid. Beside her, Artur flipped through his blimp schematics. A square of green fabric lay by his hand.

Richard smoothed out the map of Numoeath before him. He touched the clip on his ear. "I'm ready when you are, Susanna."

Susanna took his hand, and they both reached for their controls.

Eleanor let go of her braid and tried not to fidget. With Richard recovered from his indisposition, she hoped he'd manage to locate the missing blimp. For once, she didn't care about the blimp itself. Its value was in leading her to Isabel. Most likely, Isabel had purloined it so she could target more cursed mounds, and the map on the table included those Eleanor had identified. However, that was probably only a small proportion of the total number. Now that Isabel had access to air transport, she could be anywhere in the realm.

Richard stared at the map. He murmured, "Fabric consistency?"

Artur placed the fabric into Richard's hand. "This is an offcut from the sheet used to make the balloon."

Despite the serious situation, a smile tugged at her lips. Surplus blimp fabric had many uses. Artur's mother had even turned some into overalls, which they'd ruined when patching a blimp. Eleanor's amusement faded. They might owe their lives to that.

Richard's gaze intensified. "Composition of the other parts?"

"Silk ropes, canvas harness."

"Just that?" He rubbed the square between his slender fingers.

"There's gas inside, with a texture you might find odd."

"Right." After dropping the fabric on the table, Richard leaned over the map. "Let's see..."

Wrinkles deepened around Susanna's eyes as she closed them, and her face looked haggard. It hadn't been an easy decision to put more pressure on Susanna, but she was the most experienced at this technique of giving feedback to increase the effectiveness of powers. Eleanor chewed her lip. With Jonathan's abscondment, the poor woman had been under a lot of strain. Yet her diligence in her scientific work hadn't abated. Eleanor was tempted to confide in her, to tell her there wasn't *really* an invasion to prepare for and that she could ease up on her efforts. However, the burden of that lie should remain Eleanor's alone.

Richard touched a spot on the map a few miles east of the city. "It was here... but no longer. Maybe a couple of days ago? Hmm..."

"Your focus is wobbling," murmured Susanna. "Ease up, and back again. That's better. Eleanor, any ideas at all which way it might have gone? Your historian assistant is looking towards the south, isn't he?"

"True, but that's not relevant here." The young ex-guard Hilary was researching the Settlers' original homeland. Since it was the likeliest source of an invasion, she didn't have a plausible excuse to reassign him elsewhere. A pity, since he'd have been helpful with other projects—even origins of mounds. "If only we knew where the other cursed mounds—"

"Ah!" Richard clucked his tongue. "That's why I'm having problems."

Eleanor leaned forwards, and her shoulder rubbed Artur's. Richard's hand wavered over the map, his fingers stroking its surface.

"What sort of problems?" asked Eleanor.

"It's moving."

"Walking pace?" asked Artur.

Richard shook his head. "Much faster, I think. It's..." He pointed. "Heading in that direction."

Artur drew in a sharp breath.

Susanna let go of Richard's hand and opened her eyes. "Where is it?"

Eleanor stared. It couldn't be true. Heart racing, she tapped the map. "South. She's nearly reached the border."

Chapter 11

Jonathan brushed at his filthy clothing as he walked through Ascar's southern fields, past toiling workers with hoes and spades or those stopped for an afternoon break. The busy surroundings felt peculiar after nearly a week alone in the wilds.

That pregnant beast hadn't needed further help. So he'd spent the next couple of days poking around the remains of the cursed mound, trying to find anything informative. Among the fire-blackened stones, he found pieces of metal resembling cogs and rusty springs, plus shards of broken glass. There were even a few bones, though thankfully smaller than he'd expect for a human. Presumably remains of animals that beasts ate.

Slim pickings for the time spent, but the best he could do without tools. And the scraps in his pocket were better than returning with nothing, now that Isabel had vanished again. If Susanna decreed it useful, she could send out a properly equipped team to investigate more thoroughly.

He snorted. Here he was, returning to civilisation with a story nobody would believe. And yet another murder charge to face. Damn Isabel for dragging him into this. And then she swanned off, who knew where? Well, if she was on a one-woman mission to destroy cursed mounds, she'd be safely away from the city.

A nearby worker leaned on his spade and watched Jonathan's progress up the road. Neck prickling, he gave the man a cheery wave. He was hardly inconspicuous. It would have been tempting to sneak back into the Royal Compound via that maintenance gate in the wall, just to avoid all the stares. However, that would have been asking for trouble, and he'd risk being shot full of flechettes. Damn Isabel. He'd honour Eleanor's order for secrecy about the regicide, but Isabel couldn't complain if he reported back about everything else she'd shared.

And damn Hastings too. Over the last year, when the man had been leading Council meetings, he hadn't struck Jonathan as short-sighted. In fact, he'd been organised and competent. So why this unbudgeable assumption that Jonathan had killed Silvers and Staunton? Even without knowledge of Isabel's confession, Hastings should have a more open mind.

Politics, obviously. Hastings' new position as comman-der-in-chief was a powerful one, but with a more restricted scope than his previous role. Reluctant to give up that power, he'd be testing his limitations and trying to expand them into his former territory. As if he didn't have enough to do already.

Jonathan trudged on, his eyes on the ever-open gates interrupting the city's grey stone walls. Had his arrest—his current one—been publicised, along with his escape? If not, it was another sign that Hastings didn't really believe the charges against him. The man might even try to save face by keeping quiet about the whole business.

When Jonathan approached, the two brown-clad gate guards straightened, a vaguely familiar one frowning. No doubt wondering why Captain Shelley was running around in a grubby cast-off jacket with a lurid stripy shirt. Still, better that than the velvet robe from the palace.

The guard who recognised him swallowed. "Please state your name, uh, sir?"

How should he answer the routine question? He couldn't call himself a captain, not really. Wouldn't look good. What might a civilian say? He grinned. "The name's Shelley. Jonathan Shelley."

"And your business?" The guard's forehead wrinkled.

His grin widened. "I'm an escaped prisoner. I've come to hand myself in to the authorities. Can you please inform Captain Buchanan I'm here?"

"Erp. What's the charge?"

Murder? Breaking out of the Royal Compound? Discretion got the better of him. "Never you mind that, lad. Just send someone to fetch him."

"Yes, sir." Mouth open, the guard started to salute, then he dropped his arm and backed away towards the barracks.

Shaking his head, Jonathan addressed the remaining guard, a red-nosed lad with watery eyes. "I'll just stand here quietly while your colleague fetches my colleague. Right?"

The boy nodded, hand gripping his truncheon. "Right. Sir."

Jonathan's gaze fell on a mass of people milling around just up the street. Given the time of day, it seemed odd that so many were of working age. He pointed. "Is there some event? With all those people?"

"They're signing up for the new army."

"Ah." Jonathan's lip curled. Finally Hastings was being sensible.

A few minutes later, David arrived at a trot. His jaw dropped. "Jonathan! What are you playing at?"

"I'll save that for when I'm safely back in custody. Assuming I *am* still in custody?"

David started walking towards the Royal Compound, indicating that Jonathan should follow him. "Yes, you are. Hast—Commander-in-Chief Hastings was adamant you be placed in *very* secure confinement this time and monitored around the clock. He was thoroughly embarrassed in front of the queen."

"I see." Being kidnapped by Isabel had a silver lining. Jonathan lengthened his stride to keep up with the larger man. "Seems he's busy with recruitment. Anything else interesting happen while I was out of contact?"

"I've only heard bits and pieces. The queen requested Richard's presence at the palace. Maybe she lost something?" David glanced at the shuffling queue of would-be recruits and lowered his voice. "She's planning to make an announcement. About the value of powers. I'm part of the security detail there. So's Franka. And Lester."

"Lester? Why—Oh." Lester might be a conceited twit, but his mind-control power could be useful when making such an important announcement. And Franka, in addition to being tough and competent, had the power to instil fear in people. Not something one should use lightly, but perhaps helpful in the circumstances.

"He's really having to earn his keep these days. Been touring the settlements in a blimp with Tabitha."

With Tabitha! Pulse pounding in his ears, Jonathan grabbed David's sleeve. "The bastard! To think I'd started to trust him. If he's put his hands on—"

"Hey, hey. It wasn't his choice. Queen Eleanor directed him to."

Jonathan's grip eased, and his face warmed. *Snarling a bit, are we?* "Oh."

David smirked. "Lester was horrified. Does that make

140

you feel better?"

Jonathan's head hurt. Well, at least he was returning with good news for Eleanor, that Isabel was definitely still alive. And reasonably harmlessly occupied with destroying cursed mounds and beast dens. He felt a touch guilty on thinking of that pregnant beast. They weren't the enemy in the way an invading force was. That needed to be the priority. Maybe Isabel would think over Jonathan's warning and return to help. If she killed anyone else—His breath hitched, and a chill slithered into his chest. He would forever regret that he hadn't attempted to stop her.

Once in the Royal Compound, David led him to the Council building and back to the detention area. The guards placed him in a different cell from previously. With their flechette guns pointed towards him, two of them kept watch until Hastings arrived.

No longer was Hastings wearing a suit in the suave style he favoured. Instead, he was kitted in a neatly pressed uniform, in green rather than the grey, brown or red used by current guards. He scowled at Jonathan and David. "So, the miscreant returns to the scene of his crime."

"I did announce myself and request Captain Buchanan to escort me here," said Jonathan. "Hardly sneaking back." It was just as well he'd resisted the temptation.

David saluted. "And I knew that you would be pleased at Shelley's return. Sir."

Hastings' glower deepened. "Captain Buchanan, you may leave."

"I'll arrange for some fresh clothing to be sent over." David winked at Jonathan before walking away.

Hastings gestured at the guards to back off. He then approached Jonathan's barred cell door and fixed him with a gimlet glare. "What excuses do you bring back this time?"

Jonathan grinned. "I was kidnapped by Captain Hanlon. She told me she'd killed Silvers and Staunton. No doubt you're aware her power's even more dangerous than mine..."

Hastings' eyes nearly popped out of his head, and his face grew purple while Jonathan spoke.

"So she's going round hunting beasts and destroying cursed mounds. Be thankful she doesn't see *you* as a target." Jonathan proffered the fabric scrap he'd had in his pocket when he escaped. They hadn't even searched him on the way in. He'd keep the metal fragments for Susanna.

The man wrinkled his nose in disgust. "That's your proof?"

"Sure, it's silk." Though admittedly the worse for wear after Jonathan's week in the wilds. "Like the cravats and bow ties you used to wear. You know most people can't afford it. Want to feel it?"

"What an idiotic story. Do you really think we'll believe a big girl did it and ran away? You can cool your heels here for now."

"At least let Susanna know I'm back. I have the right to send a message."

"You have the right for one message to be sent on your behalf. Chief Scientist Longleaf will be informed of your recapture, but that's all. No need to confuse her further with the misinformation you're trying to spread. I've no idea how you've managed to cloud the poor woman's judgement so she believes you're worth associating with."

Hastings stalked off. Jonathan chuckled softly. Once the mind readers confirmed he was telling the truth, the former Council chief would have to eat his words. That would be a sweet moment for Susanna, making up for any worry Jonathan had caused her.

Susanna's grip tightened on her pen while she tried to concentrate on her visitor's words. But Jonathan's abscondment haunted her thoughts. Had he panicked after being imprisoned yet again? In retrospect, that seemed the likeliest answer. And she'd not even noticed his distress. If she had, she'd have insisted on a mind reading, and damn the consequences. Guilt settled on her shoulders. She didn't deserve him. *Breathe in...*

"The Maldon trip was very useful." Annetta fiddled with her hair tie and tucked a greying strand behind her ear. "Even though it's early in the season, I managed to collect a good range of herbs. I've planted some in the rooftop garden, the rest in greenhouses in the southern fields. If they survive, I should be able to reliably produce remedies to suppress powers. Talking of which, did you learn more about how long the side-effects lasted?"

Susanna swallowed. She couldn't share *all* her information, but she ought to give the woman feedback on her recipes. "As you'd predicted, Jonathan's power returned the day after you'd administered your suppressant. However, I still couldn't mind-read him even three days later. That was my last chance to assess him since he's, ah, left the city for a while. I checked with Terry shortly after attempting Jonathan and had no problem."

The tip of Annetta's nose reddened. "I tested the drug on Terry the day before I gave it to Jonathan. So we might guess the extra effect has worn off by now?"

"I do hope so."

"Me too." She squinted at her notebook. "I can't see

how to formulate a suppressant without that effect. Oh, I've found a booster recipe that looks promising."

"Excellent. One of the clerks Silvers experimented on"—by injecting him with an extract from Jonathan's flesh—"has gained a power similar to Samuel's. That could be useful for reconnaissance. He's keen to work on it further, but understandably reluctant to use the pain boxes."

Annetta shook her head. "The booster needs several rare ingredients, never mind all the rounds of distillation. I'm producing it in tiny amounts, so it should be for emergency use only."

Susanna sighed. It was too much to hope that powers could be pharmacologically manipulated as standard. "Well, it's something. And I'm pleased that Samuel coped by himself while you were away. It helped that Franka was next door to keep an eye on him." Not to mention, the extra guards assigned in the corridor. It wasn't that Samuel was *more* accident-prone than other boys, but his sense of timing was impeccable. Or dreadful.

"Yes, Samuel." Annetta squirmed.

"Is there a problem?"

"Not exactly a problem. The room's comfortable and he loves the food, and I think he's enjoying his stay..."

Despite practising in her brief free moments, Susanna still couldn't call her power at will. She pressed the pointed end of the pen against her wrist, hard. *Pain.* Her power rose, and she gazed at Annetta, viewing the wisps that would inform her whether the herbalist spoke the truth.

A frown of confusion appeared on Annetta's face. "Is something wrong with your arm?"

Drat. She relaxed her grip. "Ah, no. Just got plenty on my mind. You were saying something about Samuel?"

"Um, his drawings."

"Yes?" *Get on with it, woman.*

"If he sees people—I mean, with his power—Jonathan's always in the picture." Annetta chewed her lip.

Jonathan. Samuel certainly hadn't drawn him during Annetta's absence. Fortunately Hastings hadn't publicised his arrest and escape, or else Annetta might be even more anxious. "What are you thinking?"

"When I was on that trip with Lester, I had to warn him about, um, convoy trysts, because it wouldn't have been fair to land him in it, and I guess Jonathan used to be a regular convoy guard before he became a captain, and I remember him visiting my old village the year before I delivered..." Annetta took a deep breath. "Might he be Samuel's father?"

Susanna's jaw dropped.

Annetta regarded her clasped hands. "I'm sorry, I shouldn't have said it, especially with you two being... It's not like there's a physical resemblance. I just know his father wasn't anyone from the village. His mother never mentioned a name."

Jonathan hadn't said anything. But then, why would he? In their brief time together, they'd not talked about their convoy days. And Susanna had always politely ignored such arrangements when she travelled with the convoy: as a female guard, she'd no reason to avail herself of the custom. *Breathe in... Speak calmly...* "I suppose in theory... How old is Samuel?"

"He'll be eleven in a few months."

If Jonathan had fathered the boy, the timing fitted. It would have been just before he was cursed, and he wouldn't have learned of the pregnancy after being detained in the Keep. For the span of three deep breaths, Susanna clenched her fists and stared at the boxes of Lady Nelson's notes. "Can you remind me, just how common are such, ah, temporary pairings?"

"Didn't happen much in my old village of Keighley since it was so small. In Maldon, there are dozens of unattached women the right age, and they take what opportunities they can get." Annetta's expression was earnest. "It's really quite practical. Maybe you city types find it odd, but if the town's population dwindles too much, or even worse, if some inherited disease became common, it could jeopardise the entire settlement. After all, reproduction is a biological imperative."

"I've not always worked in the city, you know. I was a convoy captain for many years. Though it's different for captains." Captains simply didn't.

Annetta looked down. "I think that's why Giselle in Maldon offers captains her spare room rather than expecting them to share the guesthouse with the regular guards." A smile quirked her lips. "The captains needn't witness anything they don't want to."

Biological imperative. Susanna was overreacting. Annetta was right to be pragmatic about the matter, and Jonathan had probably viewed it as one of his duties. "We can't be certain. Even Jonathan isn't likely to know. I'm not sure it would be a good idea to tell him, especially in the absence of proof. You know how ferociously protective he is about Tabitha."

Annetta nodded.

"And we might say he was a different person in those days. Probably best to keep it quiet." Was she being cowardly, not wanting to openly acknowledge the possibility?

After Annetta left, Susanna closed her eyes against a developing headache. Of course Samuel's father wasn't of current relevance. And whatever Jonathan had done over a decade ago was none of her business. But now she had an overwhelming desire to be certain, yet at the same time she didn't really want to know. She tugged her hair in frustration.

"Ma'am? Message from Chief Hastings."

She opened her eyes. A gaping messenger boy stood in the doorway. *Blast.* Giving him a hefty tip, she accepted the sealed paper, dismissing him before she opened it.

She groaned. Jonathan had reappeared at the city gate, and Hastings had stuck him back in jail.

> *... Shelley was most uncooperative when I spoke with him. If you wished to request an exception to the Council's "No Personal Visitors" policy, I would be delighted to receive your written request. JH.*

Still, in view of Susanna's inner turmoil about what to say to Jonathan... If he'd panicked over his previous confinement, his return indicated that he'd now calmed down. It might be a slight relief for him to remain incommunicado in prison for the moment. He shouldn't come to any harm there.

After leaving her office, she headed back to her palace suite. Tomorrow, she'd be assisting Eleanor when she made her public announcement. Better get an early night.

Chapter 12

Sweating under a black full-length dress and cape, the royal circlet topping her head, Eleanor stood rigidly on the stone stage. Her scalp twinged under her formal bun, and she clenched her fists against the urge to rip out the pins.

The mass of citizens in the square below her represented businesses, families and communities. Bespectacled clerks stood shoulder-to-shoulder with sturdy farmers and parlour maids. Franka and Lester would be concealed in the crowd, although she hoped not to call on their powers. There were even off-duty soldiers in green uniforms: the results of Hastings' recruitment efforts, and a reminder of her assertions to the Council.

Never had she wanted so much to flee.

She tried to slow her breathing. It was unworthy to think of escape. She straightened her shoulders and regarded the far extent of the square, where the crowded buildings continued until they met the outer city walls. *She* had initiated this. This was her big gamble, her transition point, her chance to make life better for everyone.

At least she wasn't completely alone. Paton stood just behind her. Hastings was positioned to her right, his solid physical presence oddly reassuring. Maybe it was his transformation from dapper politician to soldier, reflected by his green uniform and alert posture. On Eleanor's left stood Susanna in a blue trouser suit. The woman's tranquil expression was belied by the sweat beading her forehead.

At the rear of the stage stood a dozen royal guards. She'd balked at bringing them, since their presence might suggest she feared for her own safety. In a rare display of agreement, Paton and Hastings had both recommended she keep them. A row of guards would signal serious business.

And serious business it was, albeit sprung on her with unwelcome abruptness. She'd expected to have months to compose this speech. But Isabel's southwards travel had forced an earlier announcement. Her cousin's motivations grew more suspect each time another piece of evidence came to light.

However, even when dodging topics for discussion, Isabel had never lied, not to Eleanor. And here was Eleanor about to deliver the biggest lie of all. Not only had she previously assured the Council that her father's notes contained firm evidence; not only had she planted rumours about potential invaders; she would now mislead the entire realm by concocting a tale to explain the curse and use of powers. She wasn't nearly as honest as Isabel.

Approaching footsteps made her flinch, but it was only a *techne* worker with a free-standing amplification device. The amplifier ran on power cells and had been brought out of storage for this occasion. The last time it had been used was over a year ago: on the day of her coronation. According to Hastings, the last time before *that* was the announcement when she was born.

While the technician positioned the device at the front of the stage, Eleanor's gaze fell on a statue near the platform's edge. Commemorating the arrival of the Settlers, it had allegedly been placed when they laid foundations for their first permanent building—the Keep at her back. The statue depicted a couple sitting by a campfire with a small child. By tradition, the fire was kept fuelled and lit on cold nights so that the destitute had somewhere warm to gather. The motto on the plinth was nearly worn through, but appeared to say, "We have thrown off the shackles of expectations. We will prevail." What might those long-gone Settlers think of her today?

The clock chimed midday. The technician bowed and stood aside. Eleanor stepped forwards, flanked by her companions.

Hastings indicated the chattering crowd. "May I?" he murmured.

When Eleanor licked her dry lips and nodded, he inclined his head towards her then bent down and spoke into the amplifier. "Ascarites, pray be silent that Her Majesty may speak."

His voice reverberated round the square, and the crowd hushed.

Why couldn't Eleanor produce a commanding tone like that? She cleared her throat, wincing at the squawk from the speakers. "Thank you for coming. I have important news for you. You already know of our concern that we may be approached by another nation, possibly a hostile one. We have always been peaceful, but fortunately we have historical accounts to guide us through these uncertain times. I am grateful that Commander-in-Chief Hastings has stepped up to the challenge. He is recruiting and training an army."

A bonneted elderly woman in the front row patted an adjacent soldier's arm. He grinned. Good. Eleanor's introduction, which shouldn't be news, was striking the right balance between raising concern and keeping everyone calm. The next part of her speech would stretch their acceptance further.

"What you don't know is that my father"—she bowed her head—"a man of great insight, had foreseen this situation. He understood that we might eventually face an enemy with more advanced *techne* than we have. In a leap of inspiration, he realised that we might benefit from cursed powers if it were possible to harness them. He pioneered a system to help the unfortunate afflicted come to terms with those self-same powers, enabling them to help the rest of society. Because he was unsure his system would work, he opted to introduce his system secretly. He... died before he saw the results of his studies."

The crowd stilled. The weight of their myriad gazes made Eleanor's sweat-dampened sleeves cling to her arms.

A plump bird flew across the overcast sky. As it vanished into a cloud, she pictured it as a blimp with her at the controls. That would be so much simpler. She faced the crowd again. "You'll have heard that the afflicted are no longer a danger. I am pleased to say that there have been even more promising results. In some cases, more every day, they have learned to control their powers and use them for the benefit of us all. For example, they can locate missing people or handle dangerous objects safely."

After scanning the expressionless faces before her, she raised her chin. "Therefore, I have a new decree. Curse victims who can demonstrate they are safe need no longer remain confined. Your loved ones may return home to you." She forced a regal smile on to her face, mentally rehearsing her assurances about safety.

There was a buzz of conversation in the crowd, and then someone called, "So people have been given special powers for years? Nobody else got to acquire one? That's unfair!"

The sweat on Eleanor's neck chilled. She hadn't expected this reaction, of all things. None of her pre-prepared responses would cover it. "Er, could you come to the front, please? Your questions are important, and I wish to address you properly."

The crowd parted, and a young man with a bushy red beard stepped forwards. It was perhaps no surprise he wore a green uniform. He made a sketchy bow. "Just saying, Your Majesty, seems odd to think this has been happening behind our backs. How long's it been going on?"

She glanced at Hastings, who had a poker face, before she replied. "To be honest, I don't know. The researchers involved were sworn to secrecy. My father didn't confide in anyone else, and it was only recently that I came across his notes."

"Seems like some of us mightn't have minded volunteering for the experiments, like. Who decided who got to be the special test subjects?"

"People weren't selected." The speakers whined, and she pitched her voice lower. "The scientists worked with victims of beast attacks, who were quarantined in the Keep, as you already know. Since the outcome wasn't clear, he wouldn't have deliberately exposed people."

He folded his arms. "So some people get nice powers and a cushy life, and the rest of us had no idea?"

"Hardly a cushy—" It was too late to mention the pain. What could she say? She shot a desperate glance at Susanna.

The scientist, Settlers bless her, stepped up to the amplifier as if she'd planned it. "Although I've only recently become Chief Scientist, I've read my predecessor's notes, including her accounts of curse victims. I wouldn't recommend trying to get yourself cursed. The entire process, from conversion to learning control, is highly unpleasant. Some victims don't survive."

The soldier's beard bristled. "I see. But why are you telling us just now? It seems suspicious that just when there's a threat, you come up with a solution. I'm surprised you didn't make use of the powers secretly."

Eleanor was tempted to confess that he was right. But if she did, it would be another opportunity for accusations. "I admit it's the sort of thing that *could* have been kept secret under other circumstances. However, I feel it only right to keep the public informed. You now know as much as I do." *I'm such a liar.*

He scratched the back of his neck. "And how do we know the invasion is for real? Maybe you're just claiming it in order to increase taxes."

Her dress felt too tight for comfortable breathing. Even she didn't know whether her claim was true or not. As her throat closed up, her voice came out a breathy whisper. "I'm sorry, I can't offer you certainty either way, but—"

"Of course Queen Eleanor has compelling proof." Hastings' calm voice carried around the square as he raised his hands and bowed towards Eleanor. "She assured the Council it was so. However, this is not the right venue. Perhaps this afternoon, some of you good citizens could attend an audience with the queen in the Council Hall. Ideally, she would summon witnesses to speak to her claims. Unfortunately, those witnesses are now deceased, including Scientist Staunton and discredited Scientist Silvers." He shook his head sadly. "So far the culprit remains a mystery."

Damn. Hastings had put a burden on her she couldn't

meet, in addition to raising suspicion about the deaths. Had he planted that soldier with his questions? Her absolute power set against royal falsehoods was a recipe for chaos.

Hastings continued, "Even though there are no surviving witnesses, I'm sure the queen can provide her objective evidence that there will be an invasion. We can't demand complete certainty, of course. Queen Eleanor, perhaps you could say a few brief words about your sources? Your father's notes, I believe you told us?"

Eleanor's mouth dried up. Her story would collapse as soon as someone dug into it. She'd created a tale for the Council out of whole cloth. Her father's reputation might have placated the Council, but the public would demand more evidence. For her sceptical audience, he was only a distant symbol. Like Eleanor, now. What a fool she was, playing at being democratic. She should have remained a figurehead and not become involved in government.

"You wouldn't mislead the people, of course." Hastings raised an eyebrow at her, his voice still carrying over the speakers. "That wouldn't be an action worthy of a true monarch."

The soldier took two paces towards her, placing a foot on the bottom step. Behind him, the crowd moved forwards, confused frowns appearing on the nearest faces. The man opened his mouth and raised a hand towards Eleanor as if in appeal.

Waiting for him to pronounce the words that would damn her, she flinched and stepped back. She collided with Paton. He steadied her with a hand on her elbow. His touch assured her of his loyalty, but she couldn't expect him to contribute a satisfactory answer.

The man's mouth stayed open, and he froze. The people standing behind him gaped, heads tilting upwards. Heart hammering, Eleanor chanced a glance behind her, but Paton's red-clad figure obscured her view. His fist clenched, and he glowered at the crowd.

The spokesman's hand moved. He pointed, but not at Eleanor—

Paton's head whipped round. With a speed that belied his bulk, he tackled Eleanor to the ground.

The breath whooshed out of her. She gasped, but Paton wouldn't let her move. When his weight shifted and his knee dug into her thigh, she squeaked.

"Protect your queen!" His shout vibrated in her chest.

A cry came from the crowd. Paton tensed while she tried not to squirm.

Feet scuffed on the stone slabs close by. Eleanor tried to shrink under Paton's protective body. He was exposing himself to harm. Because of her. She should face the assassin herself and accept the consequences of her misjudgements.

"Why, Paton, I didn't know you had a thing for our dear queen." The voice was amused... and familiar.

Isabel.

Chapter 13

Uneven flagstones digging into her back, Eleanor twisted her head round as she wriggled under Paton's suffocating weight. Spots danced in front of her eyes, and she wheezed, "Let me up!"

"Captain Hanlon?" Paton had never sounded so surprised before. He scrambled up and offered Eleanor a hand, his face nearly as red as his uniform.

Paton's grip was firm, but his hand was slick with sweat as he hauled her to her feet. Behind him, Susanna muttered an epithet and elbowed her way out of Hastings' embrace. It seemed his protective instincts had also kicked in, although not to the same extent as Paton's. Royal guards ringed their little group, hands on sabre hilts and faces bewildered.

Eleanor couldn't keep a smile off her face. "Stand back." She tugged her hand out of Paton's and stepped around him. He scowled.

Isabel stood harnessed to to a collapsed green balloon only an arm span wide. She dusted off her sleeves, wearing her tattered black jumpsuit with amused panache. "That was fun. I must try dropping in on you again some other time." She surveyed the crowd, who had retreated a little, leaving the gaping problematic soldier at the front, arm still upraised. "Looks like people are confused."

Eleanor relaxed. Isabel would help, somehow. "I was just explaining..."

"Sure, your voice came through the amplifier loud and clear, with only a couple of squawks. I even heard you from the Keep roof." She addressed the crowd. "Your queen speaks the truth. She sent me on a secret reconnaissance to the south, to the lands the Settlers came from. I can confirm that there are military preparations under way."

Chill shards ran through Eleanor's chest. Why would Isabel be lying? Or had Eleanor inadvertently told the truth, setting the right plans in motion despite her own disbelief? Maybe some long-gone Settler was watching over her. She swallowed. "I appreciate your timely return, Captain Hanlon. Commander-in-Chief Hastings was just bemoaning the practical difficulty of presenting my father's written evidence to everyone at this gathering."

Isabel glanced at Hastings. "I agree that would be challenging, but I've witnessed the preparations with my own eyes. I've even taken photographs." She patted her pocket then stared at the soldier. "Any questions? Or doubts about my veracity?"

Face pale behind his bushy beard—was it a fake, maybe?—he bowed. "Can you tell us whether it's true about King Frederick experimenting on cursed people? Like, special treatment? Uh... if you don't mind. Ma'am." He made a second, wobblier bow.

Eleanor managed to keep her face neutral. However, gratitude at being bailed out fought with rancour that people trusted Isabel's word over her own. And that was without knowledge of Isabel's lethal power.

Isabel shook her head. "You poor ignorant sod. I was one of his first test subjects. Queen Eleanor was trying to protect you from knowledge of how nasty those experiments were. She is a gentle soul. I, on the other hand, am

157

not." She grinned. "Just as well I'm here to educate you now, eh?"

The soldier gulped. "Yes, ma'am."

"It's true enough that powers can be controlled. But the learning process involves pain for the practitioners. Lots of it. Administered using *techne* that leaves no scars, but we're talking red-hot pokers, needles into eyeballs-type pain. Got it, kiddo?"

"Yes?" The soldier's eyes were round, and Eleanor winced.

"To make things worse, a couple of the scientists recently decided it would be fun to inflict the curse on poor unsuspecting innocents." Isabel scowled. "Abusing people they should have been protecting. You know the official protocol tells us to 'neutralise' any afflicted who're a danger to those around them?"

The soldier nodded mutely.

"Well, those two scientists—Silvers and Staunton—were more of a danger than any number of afflicted. Left unchecked, they'd have carried on indefinitely. So they had to go. Make sense?"

As the soldier and his neighbours nodded again, Eleanor shut her mouth. What was it about Isabel that she could express her decision to kill someone and have everyone agree it was justified?

"Good. Any further questions?"

The soldier shook his head, but the bonneted elderly woman near him raised her hand. "Ma'am, did you actually gain a power?"

"Nearly forgot to mention that. I did indeed." Isabel turned towards the Settlers' statue and pointed at the campfire on its plinth, the wood already laid out for this evening's fire. A flame kindled at her fingertips and she set the wood alight.

Apart from a couple of gasps, the only sound was the pop and crackle of the fire.

The soldier's eyes rolled up in his head, and he collapsed into the arms of the people behind him.

"Show's over for the day," called Isabel. "Now, go home and be calm. I need to report to the Council. You will be kept informed. But rest assured we have the good of the realm at the heart of our concerns."

"Do you wish me to apprehend that soldier?" murmured Paton.

Eleanor shook her head. Isabel's revelations had put paid to any doubts Hastings might want to raise. Even if he *had* planted the soldier, neither he nor Eleanor would benefit from closer public scrutiny. Best to focus on more important matters. If war preparations required her to step down, so be it.

A couple of other soldiers lifted their comrade, and the crowd dispersed rapidly.

Isabel unbuckled her harness, letting the equipment fall to the ground. "Can we head back to the palace?"

"Of course. Paton, can you tidy up?"

With a few curt words, Paton ordered one of his guards to return the blimp's remnants to the workshop. He then offered Isabel his arm.

"Don't mind if I do." Isabel's face was pale as she started to walk. "I'm starving. Wouldn't mind a drink and a bite to eat while I catch you up on what happened after I left Jonathan."

"Jonathan? What's he got to do with this?" Eleanor glanced at Susanna, whose forehead creased.

"Didn't he tell you about meeting me? I thought you'd have received his report at least a few days ago."

Hastings cleared his throat. He wouldn't look at any of them. "I questioned him when he arrived back in custody. But he told such a tale I assumed he was lying. Captain Hanlon's speech in the square has fully confirmed his statements. I, ah, deeply regret that I didn't take his words seriously."

"You idiot!" Isabel pointed a shaky finger at him. "All that time wasted—"

Susanna grabbed her arm and pushed it down. "Hush. Jonathan only returned yesterday."

"How come? I broke him out"—she staggered, and Paton put an arm around her—"a week ago."

Eleanor eyed Isabel's sweat-sheened face with concern. "Look, we'll sort things out in private. But my physician will attend to you first." She lowered her voice. "I don't want to lose you again."

Crouching by the cell door, Jonathan laid his empty plate on the serving tray. The chicken sausage, runner beans and mashed potatoes had been decent fare, especially compared to foraging and Isabel's eclectic scraps. But it might get monotonous if his imprisonment lasted more than a few days. After the three guards who watched him around the clock had provided old copies of the *Informer*, catching up with recent events hadn't taken much time.

Going by Hastings' parting words and his preoccupation with raising an army, it seemed like he'd draw out Jonathan's captivity as long as he could. Still, the longer Jonathan remained in prison, the greater Hastings' embarrassment when the truth came out. It was just a matter of outwaiting him.

Jonathan lay on the bunk, enjoying the smoothness of clean clothing, even if it was a shabby exercise suit delivered courtesy of David. And they'd provided a bucket of water so he could sponge off the worst of the grime.

Footsteps sounded in the corridor, and a guard left to investigate. He returned in short order with a familiar red-uniformed figure.

Paton carried a canvas bag. "Captain Shelley's to be freed," he told the guards. "Queen's orders."

As the guards opened the cell, Jonathan stood up with a frown. "That was quick. What's happening?"

"You're needed at a meeting." Paton handed him the bag. "You might want to change into this first, but don't keep Her Majesty waiting."

To Jonathan's relief, the bag contained a grey captain's uniform. He never felt quite right without it. Paton refused to answer any questions while Jonathan was changing, merely commenting that everything would be made clear on arrival.

They arrived in the palace as a messenger boy was delivering a bulky envelope. Paton took the package and gave the boy a couple of pennies.

When Jonathan raised an eyebrow, Paton muttered, "Photographic prints. Let's go."

In Eleanor's drawing room, Isabel lay on the couch. Her hand trembled when she waved hello. Eleanor sat beside her, occasionally dabbing her face with a damp cloth. Disquiet trickled down Jonathan's spine. In all the years he'd known her—

"Jonathan!" Standing in front of the window with Artur, Susanna beamed. She took a dozen rapid paces across the room, grabbed his hands and kissed him on either cheek. "I'm so glad you're back."

"I missed you." Stomach fluttering, he squeezed her fingers. Was everyone watching them? It was one thing to wind Hastings up, but this meeting included *the queen!*

By the fireplace, Hastings coughed. He stepped forwards and met Jonathan's glare. "Captain Shelley, I owe you an apology. I, er, let personal prejudices sway my judgement. I should have believed you and not been so keen to act based on the rest of the evidence."

That was all the man offered? Jonathan opened his mouth to deliver a blistering retort, but Susanna's fingers twitched. He paused. There were more important matters afoot. "I'm here now. Let's get to business." Susanna's dimple reassured him he'd made the right response.

Eleanor stood, hands tightly clasped. "While we're on the topic of apologies, I owe you all one. I hadn't found my father's notes about an invasion as convincing as I'd claimed, not until Isabel returned with her evidence. I was more interested in using an invasion as a pretext, so I could persuade the public to accept open use of powers."

Jonathan's eyes narrowed, and his jaw clenched. "You lied to us."

Susanna's grip on his hand tightened.

"I believe I had good reason for my actions." Eleanor's voice grew stronger. "It isn't right that powers were kept secret, with practitioners suffering because of it. Invasion or not, that chicken's out of the egg now." She gave a weak laugh and held out a hand towards Hastings. "It was a real stroke of luck that John has proven such a capable commander-in-chief. I'm glad I chose him."

Hastings' gape and bulging eyes brought to mind the

fish Jonathan had recently trapped. Clearing his throat, the man fumbled with his collar then raised his chin. "So... no change in my appointment?"

"Definitely not. You've been a real credit to the position."

"I'm glad to be of help." He bowed towards her. "Perhaps it's not necessary to mention your, ah, ruse to the rest of the Council. We have enough to be concerned about."

She returned his smile. "Thank you for being so understanding."

Jonathan exhaled slowly. If Hastings could accept matters, so could he. Susanna pulled him over to sit on the other couch.

Artur had been watching the exchange with wide eyes. He turned to Jonathan. "Isabel's been giving me information on the blimp's operation, so you've not missed anything relevant to you."

That was a relief. He tried to ignore Susanna's deepening dimple, but the swish of her blue silk suit was a distraction.

Eleanor resumed her seat. "Now that Jonathan's here, we can discuss the threat from the south. Isabel, I appreciate your rescuing me in the square. Just to be sure, I trust you weren't exaggerating your claims for effect? Other than giving the impression I assigned you to that investigation."

Isabel chuckled. "I only went rushing off to the south in that balloon because Jonathan told me you believed an invasion would arrive from there. So in a sense you *did* send me on the mission. Even if you didn't know it."

Eleanor patted her hand. "We've been incredibly lucky."

"Right, time to reveal all." Isabel swung herself upright,

swaying a little. The sallowness of her face was worrying. "I stopped overnight just south of Holmbeath."

Jonathan consulted his mental map. Holmbeath was the southernmost settlement, maybe three days' walk from the wastelands. Not that anyone was mad enough to venture that far south, other than Isabel.

She sagged against the sofa back. "I took off at dawn. At first the terrain was much as you'd expect—hills, grass, bushes—but then the greenery disappeared. The ground became barren, dry, grey and then rusty-looking. Rocks, soil, nothing moving. A few watercourses, but I didn't see any signs of plants or animals. That said, I didn't have much time to look. Was concentrating more on not hitting the ground than sightseeing. Had a decent wind, fortunately."

How could Isabel sound so relaxed about the risk of crashing? Jonathan swallowed. "I take it something attracted your attention."

She nodded. "After about half a day, I saw... Paton?"

While Paton passed round the photographs, Jonathan asked, "Half a day for you might be a week on foot, maybe? If we didn't have civilians slowing us down?"

"I guess so."

Artur's brow wrinkled as he inspected his photograph. "How far away were you when you took these? Ah, hang on..." He pulled a ruler from his pocket while Eleanor handed him a pencil and paper. "We can probably calculate by the length of shadows on the ground, allowing for Isabel's altitude. And..."

Jonathan stared at the photograph he held. The monochrome image—clearer than regular daguerreotypes—depicted cracked earth punctuated by sharp rocks. On the horizon, a humanoid figure stood with a broad stance.

Light glinted off a spear-like weapon angled towards the sky. Jonathan's nostrils flared.

Beside him, Susanna put a shaky hand to her mouth.

"It's holding a pole," said Isabel. "You'll see from the pictures I took that the, uh, giant pointed it to one side and then the other, like it was following a target. The movement was quite slow. I only noticed because winding the film on took a few seconds each time."

Twisting the end of her braid, Eleanor gasped. "And it pointed towards you as well?"

Isabel winced slightly. "Yeah, well, when it aimed in my direction, I decided it was time to make tracks. Gusts. Whatever. I backed off and moved directly west. There was another, and then another. Like, lined up at intervals. After that, I scooted back here as fast as I could."

Eleanor chewed her lip. "That was incredibly brave of you. Or foolish."

"Time will tell. But at least you now know."

"That's not right," muttered Artur to his pencil. "I must have miscalculated. Eleanor?"

After perusing his paper, Eleanor frowned. "I can't see any obvious errors in your calculations."

"But *fifty feet* tall?"

"The—" Clammy dread squeezed Jonathan's gut. "The giants?"

"Why don't they fall over?" asked Hastings while he loosened his collar.

"Dunno," said Isabel. "They weren't actually walking around. Could they be guarding something? Resting? I can't add anything. But I worry what will happen when they decide to walk in our direction."

Face sober, Eleanor gazed around the room. "And there

you have it. Fortunately we'd already started to prepare, even if for the wrong reasons. I hope we still have enough time. John, sorry again about misleading you. Let me know if you need more resources for your troops."

"Thank you." Hastings saluted. "I will contribute as best I can. Martek's border survey may have found nothing, but I should send out more squads as a matter of urgency. And I need to rethink and check some of the older records." After placing his photograph on a side table, he left the room.

Eleanor regarded Jonathan. "I'm sorry about all the trouble with your arrest, but I'd been worried about Isabel."

"Not to worry," he mumbled, standing and pulling Susanna to her feet. "I'll help you however I can. And help the scientists too, of course."

As they walked back towards their suite, Susanna slipped an arm about his waist. "I'm glad to have you back."

"Me too." The brush of her thigh against his sent tingles up his spine. And it had only taken a little jail time for her to become so affectionate. Maybe he should get jailed more often.

"I've been... looking into buying a house. I hope I'm not too forward in hoping you'd be happy to share it with me?"

His heart sang. "I would be honoured."

Eleanor suppressed a giggle when Susanna and Jonathan left. Not that they were a demonstrative couple, but they were sweet even in their restraint. And at their age too! On catching Artur's curious eye, her humour faded and her pulse increased. Unless she was discussing blimps or *techne*, her mind went blank when speaking with him. It must be her guilt over his curse.

Paton straightened the abandoned chairs and took up his habitual position by the door while Eleanor and Artur moved their seats closer to Isabel.

Gazing at the carpet, Isabel gave a wry smile. "Eleanor, I owe you a huge apology too, regarding your father. It was obvious he believed in the invasion, but I didn't take his concerns seriously. I can understand why he became so desperate to generate more cursed. Even if he sent me into situations where I risked being cursed, if I'd been more careful it needn't have happened. It wasn't completely his fault, although I trust you to be more humane than he was. I now agree powers will be part of the solution."

"But you'd been working for him for years," said Eleanor. "What changed?"

"We argued."

Artur pulled his chair closer. "Yes, that's the impression I got. Not a premeditated attempt."

Isabel's eyebrows shot up. "Impression?"

Eleanor swallowed. "Artur was cursed."

Isabel sagged. "Sorry. I heard. What kind of curse?"

He leaned back. "I can sense people's last moments. Or so we think. It's not easy to test."

"I guess it's not something you could practise," said Isabel. "Short of hanging round execution sites or hospital wards..."

Artur shuddered. "I'd rather not, if you don't mind. I could *feel* what they went through as if it was happening to me. Even afterwards it left me ill."

Poor Artur. Eleanor wouldn't have wished that power on her worst enemy, never mind—She pushed the thought away. "You were saying, about my father?"

"Well," said Isabel, "we drank together and talked, the

way we often did. Policy, strategy and all that. The alcohol loosened both his tongue and my hold over my power. And when he started going on that every household would have a cursed member, I lost my temper. He'd shifted from concern about an invasion to grandiose plans about using the cursed as glorified slaves." She bared her teeth. "Unforgivable."

Eleanor reached out but paused. "Until I read his notes, I couldn't fathom why you would kill him." Not wanting to see Isabel and Artur's faces, she stood and paced to the window. The Keep's implacable stone walls provided no inspiration. "Now I understand your reasons, and also why you kept refusing the throne. There could have been a better way, but... Outside of this room, only Susanna and Jonathan know. I don't intend the information to spread."

"I can't say I regret killing Silvers, even though he was being manipulated by Staunton. But killing Staunton made things worse. I messed up your best chance of getting decent information."

A band of guilt tightened around Eleanor's head, like a phantom crown. "If I'd done my duties properly and spent more time with my father, it mightn't have come to this. So I'm partly responsible too."

Isabel closed her eyes. "Only very indirectly. When it comes down to it, Eleanor—"

The door swung open, and Paton jerked to the side with a muttered curse.

"—I was the one who killed your father—"

Hastings stood gaping in the doorway.

Chapter 14

Folding her clammy hands so they wouldn't shake, Eleanor regarded the expanded Council seated around the table. Captain David Buchanan and Engineer Matthew Porter had joined their ranks. For once, the established members hadn't objected. Rather, they regarded her with fearful hope, as if she were the one to save the realm. Their wide eyes and tight lips made her guts writhe. How she wished she could turn the clock back and once more be a figurehead facing indulgent, patronising glances.

But no. Ignorance would be worse for everyone.

She didn't dare look at Hastings in the seat beside her, but his presence pervaded her thoughts. He *must* have heard Isabel's confession yesterday. But he'd merely apologised for the intrusion and picked up his photograph. This morning he'd greeted her politely, a neutral expression on his face. Was he offering a tacit truce?

In fact, he'd even withdrawn his objections to Eleanor chairing all Council meetings in person. He'd agreed his new responsibilities—he was answerable to her only—would keep him fully occupied. Now that she'd taken on his previous duties, Eleanor was busier than ever despite her Queen's Discretion cutting through artificial barriers. Once she had time, she'd choose an otherwise uncommitted deputy to assist her. Isabel had worked with Eleanor's father and might be amenable, but she still wasn't fully recovered. That hasty return to deliver her findings must have overtaxed her stamina.

Hastings waved at Isabel's photographs, scattered across the table. "As a temporary measure, I've despatched guards to the south. We'll need to push recruitment and training. And make more weapons."

"We must also maintain the welfare of the civilians." Eleanor glanced at his face. His sober expression, rather than the knowing smirk she dreaded, was perversely reassuring. "Fortunately, the settlements are widely spaced and we've used relatively little in the way of raw materials, even in Ascar. We can accelerate extraction processes and manufacturing. The main issue will be time to build roads. Establishing a southwards travel route towards Holmbeath is a priority. Even rudimentary trails would give us something to work with. Logistician Randall?"

Randall shook his head. "We're trying our hardest, but carving out roads through nearly untouched terrain is slow going." He nodded at Porter. "It's very helpful having input from the engineers."

"I appreciate all your efforts," said Eleanor. "I've assigned someone to translate our old documents from Noble Ascarite. Hopefully she'll find something you can apply. And from now on, we will communicate in regular Ascarite only. It's ridiculous to keep official records in a language so few people understand."

"Very sensible," said Gauntlett. "After working with our historical records for many decades, I don't think it's a boast to claim I have a high facility with the language. Some concepts don't translate easily, but I see no reason to continue using Noble Ascarite now."

That was an easy change. Dealing with other issues might be more tricky. "Currently, I have a captain visiting the settlements by blimp to address any concerns. He's not needed his mind-control power, and the ruralites are accepting things quite well. Captain Buchanan, from now on the regular convoy captains can visit the settlements on foot again. That way, they can bring back new recruits."

"I'll set up a schedule, Your Majesty," said David.

Susanna looked amused. She wore a sober grey jacket—one of her own, presumably—but set off with a filigree butterfly. "I suspect Captain Black would appreciate being reassigned to city duties. He's more comfortable when surrounded by buildings, and he can help me with training. Could his helper apprentice in the infirmary?"

"Good idea," said Eleanor. Tabitha's telekinetic power was too valuable to leave unused. "Now, weapons. Engineer Porter, any progress on production?"

After adjusting his monocle, Porter peered at his notes. "The factories have capacity to manufacture more flechette guns, though there are still issues of how to power them. Increasing power cell storage capacity isn't too difficult, but the river-powered generators already run at full efficiency. I can't think of a way to produce electricity faster. As a separate thought, we could maybe convert phosphorus-containing compounds to incendiary devices, although there might be some risk in implementation."

Gauntlett pushed his glasses up his nose. "How about human-powered weapons? Our archives contain descriptions of how to construct crossbows."

Hastings frowned. "While we could keep them in reserve, I doubt they'd work against those armoured opponents. Porter, your proposed explosives might be worth concentrating on."

Eleanor's hand crept towards her braid, and she stilled

it. She'd rechecked Artur's calculations with him, and his fears of giant opponents had been correct. Time for a note of hope, no matter how tenuous. "Maybe we'll find something in the old records. I'm also allowing library access to anyone who might help. That includes requesting material from the royal library. What other concerns do we have right now?"

Hastings glanced at her. "In the event of significant overwhelming force, we may need to evacuate Holmbeath and... leave the enemy with no resources."

His serious expression made her shoulders tighten. Even if she didn't want to consider his implication, best to be open about it. "In what way?"

"Ah..." He coughed. "Demolish the buildings, burn the fields..."

Her fists clenched. Destroying her subjects' livelihood. But better that than allowing them to be slaughtered. "Only as a last-ditch measure, when the village faces being overrun. The strategy may buy us some time, but I hope it doesn't come to that."

"I also. But our best resource will be cursed powers. I believe that we should—"

"No." Eleanor thumped the table. "We've been through this previously, and I am *not* sanctioning deliberate cursing."

"But it might make the difference between winning and losing—"

"If we force the curse on people, we have already lost the war."

Lester leaned over the side of the gondola, focussing his spyglass on a bird's nest in the trees below them. The scarf around his face didn't fully protect him from the elements, and his wind-chapped cheeks smarted. Once they landed, he'd apply some moisturiser. He wrinkled his nose. Better to wait until he was unobserved. David would have a field day if he found out.

With the queen's dramatic announcement a few days ago, not to mention Isabel's spectacular return, Lester's remit had changed. This trip to Holmbeath should be his final one. Ruralites were pragmatic, and urgency over defence preparations made cursed powers almost an afterthought. He hadn't yet needed his mind control to sway anyone. Well, other than the Maldon mayor, but that idiot didn't count.

Tabitha joined him, leaning into him as the gondola swayed. He put the spyglass away with an internal sigh. Because Annetta was occupied in her laboratory, they'd been provided with a smaller blimp. He could have done without the cosiness.

She tilted her head to watch a flock of birds, somehow snuggling even closer. "Do you think Jonathan's been here before?"

"Probably," he muttered, glad that Jonathan wasn't also in the blimp. *He'd kill me.* "He trekked around as a convoy captain for a good ten years. Plus however many years before that as a guard."

"I wonder if they'll remember him."

"Probably. There aren't that many captains. If the convoy only visits a few times a year, it would be quite an event. Do you remember convoys from when you were younger?" Oh, crap. When would he learn to keep his mouth shut?

Her head swung towards him, and he flinched at her dark-eyed glare. "*Of course* I do! My parents threw me away when we were travelling with the convoy." Lip quivering, she dropped her gaze. "And Jonathan rescued me."

Lester tentatively smiled. "He cares about you a lot." Her upset was understandable. Even though Jonathan had no choice about sending Tabitha to the Keep after she was cursed, her parents' rejection must have poured salt into her mental wounds. Lester shouldn't resent her for her clinginess. There were worse things. Like being caught up in an invasion.

"Holmbeath coming up," called an operator.

His shoulders relaxed. Hopefully this would be a quick meeting—squads of guards would have passed through previously while investigating the border—and then he could head back to Ascar and offload Tabitha before the day was over. Pulling out his spyglass again, he noted they were approaching a bare field, a cluster of houses nearby. A couple of dozen people waited at the edge of the field, some shading their eyes with their hands. He grinned. The blimp must be quite a sight.

The gondola lurched when they landed, and Lester instinctively put out a hand to steady Tabitha. She fell into his arms and giggled.

Sweat prickled his neck. "Can you let go of me and hold on to the rail, please? I'll disembark first."

After climbing out, he helped her down. She thanked him with a smile before releasing his hand. Then he helped the two operators. The female one winked, but he was used to her by now. Because of his height and strength, they'd lost their shyness over asking him for assistance.

"Need a hand?" came a rough male voice. "I'm Tony, Holmbeath's headman."

A young man in a well-worn canvas apron stood before

him, muscular arms bulging under linen sleeves. No pompous red-robed mayor, here. This boded well.

"Thanks," said Lester after a glance at the operators, "but we're managing the blimp. I take it you received the message about our visit? I'm Captain Black, and this is Miss Tabi—"

Tabitha's fingers dug painfully into his arm.

Lester jumped and stared at her. "Wassup? Er, what seems to be the problem?"

A weary-faced, middle-aged woman pushed her way through the crowd, eyes fixed on Tabitha. A weedy man followed her, tugging her knitted shawl with mumbles of, "But, dear..."

Tabitha's grip tightened. "Ma? Pa?" She turned her back on them and buried her face in Lester's chest. "They didn't want me! They threw me away!"

Shit, what do I do? He held up his free hand. "No interruptions, please."

The couple paused, and the woman lifted her hands to cover her mouth.

The man's face crinkled. "But that's our Tabitha, that is. What's she doing riding around in a blimp?"

Lester gulped. Being an orphan was easier. But he had a job to do, and his priorities didn't lie with the girl's parents. He patted Tabitha's shoulder and raised his voice. "As I was saying, this is Miss Tabitha. *Personal ward* of Her Majesty Queen Eleanor."

A sickly smile crossed the man's face. "I knew you always had it in you, my girl."

Tabitha's head whipped round, and she scowled. "Not *your* girl. I'm *Lester's* girl."

Gah, she wasn't helping! At the headman's disapproving expression, Lester's bowels quivered. "Uh, what she means is that I'm responsible for her safety. As per the queen's instructions." He glanced round for help, but the blimp operators had their backs turned. The younger one's shoulders shook as if in silent laughter. "Can we move on to the purpose of this visit?"

"Of course," said Tony. He nodded at the couple. "Go home. I'll speak with you later."

The woman's mouth opened, but the man murmured in her ear. With his arm around her shoulder, they slunk off.

Lester watched their departing backs with relief. How ironic he felt more at ease talking about a possible invasion than dealing with a teenager's hangups about her parents. He gently disengaged from Tabitha and cleared his throat. "Explorations to the south have yielded evidence that there are people there..."

He delivered the spiel about the possibility of an attack from the south and Queen Eleanor's strategy of using cursed powers. Since this town lay in a vulnerable position, he'd been directed not to seek army recruits here. "As a temporary measure, Commander-in-Chief Hastings has already assigned you three dozen guards who should arrive here within two days. They'll help you prepare for defence or evacuation, and they'll be replaced by trained soldiers in due course. Commander Hastings will also arrange a rotation with the troops watching the border."

After he scanned the crowd, his lips twitched. The two youngest women—a blonde and a redhead—wore speculative expressions. He'd seen such looks before. Even in wartime, it seemed, they were thinking of future generations. And what better time to think about preserving the population? "Any questions?"

Frowning, Tony waved a hand at the houses behind him. "Protection is welcome, but we might have difficulty housing them all. I expect they'll have bedrolls, but are they carrying tents?"

What did foot travel require? Lester had no idea. "Commander Hastings emphasised speed, so I guess they're travelling light? Which means..." His mind went blank.

Tabitha sniffled, tugged his sleeve and whispered, "No handcarts."

"Uh, no handcarts."

Tony nodded. "That figures. No equipment or materials. We'll need to double up until we can build more huts." When the blonde woman giggled, he snorted. "Yes, when they arrive, you can ask."

Lester gaped. He'd never understand ruries. "Any other questions?"

Tony shook his head, but the redhead lifted an eyebrow. "Will you be staying overnight, Captain Black?"

Argh! "No, sorry. Got plenty of things to catch up on back in Ascar. You know how it is, and we really must be—"

Turning to the blimp operators, Lester glimpsed Tabitha's sullen face. Although it was tempting to ignore the issue and escape, he should clear things up between her and her parents. Was this also part of Eleanor's plan? Her actions—such as intervening at Jonathan's trial—showed that she cared for people as individuals.

"Tony?" he said. "Just one more thing."

"Yes, Captain Black?"

Lester swallowed. "Before we leave, can we speak with Tabitha's parents? Privately?"

"What? No!" Tabitha hissed in his ear. "I don't want to see them again!"

"Excuse us a moment." Lester gave Tony a weak smile before pulling Tabitha to the other side of the gondola and several paces into the field. Hardly true privacy, but he could pretend it was. At least there was no mud today. "Listen, I know you're upset. But since we're here, speaking to them is the right thing to do."

She pouted. "Why should I?"

"Look, it's just the once."

"No." She folded her arms and turned her back on him.

He clenched his jaw against an urge to shout at her. "You don't need to see them again after this."

"Don't wanna."

The locals were peering at them from the other side of the blimp. They wouldn't stay at a polite distance for long. "Tabitha, you're fifteen now. Grow up."

She spun round with a scowl. "I bet you wouldn't do it, if it was *your* parents."

"I would have done. But I never got the chance. My mother died when I was a child."

"Oh?" Her eyes widened, and she put a hand to her lips. "And your pa?"

"I don't know who he was. But that's not relevant." He cleared his throat. Time to play his trump card. "Jonathan would want you to speak to them."

She looked down. "I guess he would."

Lester eased out a breath. Jonathan was hardly a close friend, but the man's determination to do what was right stood out like a beacon. "It'll be fine. I'll be with you."

"But what should I say?"

"Well, how about I tell them the queen asked you to look after me? You can tell them about your nice rooms in the Keep. Come on, let's go meet them."

In a cramped cottage with rough wooden floors, Lester carefully sat beside Tabitha and across the table from her parents. "They've made a lot of progress in the Keep since Tabitha went there."

Tabitha's mother wiped her eyes with a linen cloth. "It was obvious when Tabitha became cursed. She didn't even recognise us. She was wild, fevered, flinging rocks and sticks around the campsite."

Tabitha's father patted his wife's arm. "Captain Shelley calmed everyone down. He said he'd need to send her to Ascar."

Tabitha glowered. "You threw me away!"

The woman extended a hand, then glanced at Lester and dropped it. "We had no choice. Really."

"They really didn't," muttered Lester. He could imagine the terror of a new power manifesting. Not just for the victim, but for those around her. Just as well Jonathan had been there. "It's a shame such extreme measures were needed, but with the queen's reforms, things shouldn't be so bad in future."

Tabitha's mother sniffed. "You've got taller since spring. I can see they're feeding you well. Have you seen any new birds in Ascar?" Giving Tabitha a wavery smile, she stood and rummaged in a cupboard. She returned with a wooden box. "Honey cake? I remember you used to like these."

Tabitha's lip trembled, then she picked up a cake and bit into it.

Back in the ascending blimp, Tabitha sobbed into Lester's shoulder while he gazed unseeingly at the ground. She wasn't angry anymore, but her tearfulness was nearly worse. As his jacket grew soggier, his blood ran cold. What if *Jonathan* decided to welcome Tabitha home? And blamed Lester for upsetting her? "Uh, Tabitha?"

"What!"

He pointed. "Isn't that the flock of birds you noticed on the way here?"

She squinted up past the balloon and huffed. "That's a cloud, Lester."

"Oh, I see. Er... I wonder what kind of trees we're passing over. The ones that are... all in a row?" He fumbled for his spyglass. "And what's that ugly hill?"

"Well spotted, sir," said the young operator. "It's a cursed mound. Better update our maps."

Lester frowned. "Isn't there something odd?" Maybe he was just being stupid again. "But I could have sworn the trees line up towards it and—Look! The grass is a different colour, like in a straight band."

Tabitha held out an imperious hand. "Give me the spyglass."

Thankful for her changed mood, he handed it over.

After turning the focus knob, she said, "Yes, like the grass started growing at a different time."

It was weird how the bands were so straight. Almost like roads. Jonathan had mentioned visiting a cursed mound and finding human artifacts there. Might the two have been related? When they returned, he'd speak with Artur. If someone were to make the crazy suggestion that the Settlers had once built roads leading to cursed mounds, he'd rather it not be Captain Lester Black. Far better the matter be raised with the queen by Senior Research Blimp Engineer Granville. Besides, even if it was nothing, it would give those two something new to talk about.

Eleanor straightened her braid and knocked at the door to Isabel's suite.

"Come!" When she opened the door, Isabel grinned from her desk. "Hey, cuz. How'd the meeting go?"

"Tricky, but that's no surprise." She wandered over and peered at Isabel's notes. "How're you getting on with those translations?"

"It's kinda boring." Isabel dropped the quill into the inkwell. "Pompous old gits waffling about irrelevant topics. Pretty typical for Council minutes. But I won't complain. You have me doing penance, and quite right too."

"I'm not punishing—" She swallowed. "Well, maybe a tiny bit. But I really believe it will be beneficial in the long term."

Isabel scrunched her nose. "I get your point, but I'd still dispute the value of minutes. The Council only discuss what's in front of them, and of course the stuff to the south is new. How about me looking at, say, inspection reports from convoy captains? Or theories from the historians? *Techne* experiments?"

"You win. I'll let you pick what to translate next."

"Yay! Don't worry, I'll choose something that looks useful." She winked and ran a hand through her hair. She'd had it cut short since her return. "Pure coincidence it'll be more fun to read. So, what did you talk about at the meeting?"

"Well..." While Isabel stood and rolled her neck, Eleanor gave a brief recap of the topics they'd covered at the Council meeting. "I'm sure Hastings is being pragmatic—"

"Hastings? Did he, y'know, *say* anything?"

Eleanor's breath caught. "No. Nothing."

Isabel raised an eyebrow. "I could speak with him."

"No! Just... don't." Her hands trembled. Surely Isabel wasn't proposing to kill him for something that was Eleanor's fault?

"I was just trying to spare you an argument, silly. Not offering to send him to Settlers' Rest."

Heat built in Eleanor's chest, but she forced herself to meet Isabel's gaze. "Sorry."

"You're a good queen. You care for everyone." Isabel's serious expression vanished after a moment. "Hey, how about we take a walk?"

"A walk? I don't have time to—"

"I don't know what it was about that trip, but I was really whacked afterwards. I need to get into better condition. So you might as well tag along, like you used to as a kiddi-winkle with little stubby legs. We can chat along the way." She waggled a finger. "Assuming you're not too out of breath."

Eleanor glanced out of the window. It *was* tempting to take a break. "I'm not sure..."

"How quickly can you walk a mile?"

"I don't know—"

"My point exactly! Your royal amble is elegant and dignified, very queenly and all that. But if you needed to run for your life, I bet you'd have problems. Imagine if the blimp had been irreparable when we had that accident?"

Eleanor winced. "You and Artur would have outpaced me easily."

"Nah, Artur wouldn't have left you behind. And neither would I. If I'd been at your level of fitness—unfitness, I should say—I'd never have made it back from the waste-lands."

"You're right. I shouldn't endanger other people because I'm reluctant to exercise."

Isabel slugged her arm. "And we can take over the barracks gymnasium. How about it?"

She had to laugh. "You'll finally get your wish. But this won't get you out of doing those translations."

Chapter 15

"Another one?" Susanna rubbed her temples while she ran her eye over the details on their latest resident's booking-in sheet. The rural victim had stumbled on a beast den and stuck his hand inside, with predictable consequences. "That's the third one this week!"

She spared a guilty glance at Lady Nelson's old notes, still boxed up in the corner of her office. Maybe her noble predecessor hadn't been so disorganised after all, if she'd needed to document every incident. That said, the influx of "willing cursed" had only been a problem since Eleanor's proclamation last month. Isabel's graphic description of training had been no deterrent.

Her assistant tapped his stubbled chin with a pen. "At least we have access to more blimps these days, and there are always Annetta's remedies in case of emergencies during travel."

But how were they going to handle the newly cursed? Where were they going to put them, even? The Keep had only two dozen suites, half already housing the long-term residents. Susanna had already cut corners with the observation period for potential curse victims, but the system was becoming overwhelmed. How could people act so stupidly? Because they believed the advantages were worth the risk. It didn't help that Hastings offered a bonus to trained "practitioners" if they joined his army.

Her lips firmed. "They'll just have to stay put. Send out

word that even if people are cursed, they're not to be moved unless there is *significant* danger to others. We'll send a pain box to them—the way we used to train here. They'll have to cope on their own."

He scribbled a note. "And keep us informed of what powers they develop?"

"Of course. It's not ideal, but there's only so much we can do. We can't support them all."

Susanna returned to Hastings' latest request and the reply she was composing. She'd point out *again* that few powers—such as Isabel's and Jonathan's—offered immediate practical applications. Tabitha's apprenticeship in the Keep would hopefully leave her beneath Hastings' notice. Since Samuel only drew Jonathan, there was little point in mentioning him either. The other televisualiser, the one from Silvers' experiments, had a power so weak as to be useless. Using it to watch the border wasn't an option.

As the weeks went by, the incoming flow of afflicted dwindled. Instead, sporadic reports arrived from the settlements, usually hand-delivered by new army recruits. Susanna remained in the Keep to oversee training. Sometimes Jonathan helped. But they discovered that without the oppression of the old system, new practitioners rarely had a problem with activation.

Initial results from Susanna's training system were promising, with rapid acquisition of control. But the resulting powers seemed weaker than those of practitioners like her who had undergone traditional, pain-fuelled training. She had a theory about that, even though she couldn't ethically test it. With the old system, only the most determined practitioners succeeded, and their mental fortitude was somehow related to strength of power. Anyone who thought of powers as an effortless route to success would be disappointed.

She scheduled settlement visits by blimp for her mind-reading colleagues: both to lend help in training and to assess the motivations of those with powers. The few who showed potentially useful powers and a responsible attitude were invited to Ascar for intensive training. As for the others? If Hastings wanted them, he could have them, and good luck to him. What use was the ability to discern if something was alive or dead by touching it? Or to tell how many people had handled an item within the last day?

Groups of foolhardy people—Ascarites more than ruralites—would head off into the country in search of cursed mounds. The city folk often didn't even prepare with protection from the elements. An occasional "lucky" individual might get bitten by a beast, but even beast sightings were rare these days. Susanna shook her head at the most egregious incident reports:

> *... subject N. deliberately slashed himself with a metal fragment from a cursed mound. Unfortunately, the resultant gangrene spread...*
> *... subject T.'s autopsy examination revealed large amounts of grit in his gullet and windpipe. I suspect attempted ingestion of "cursed soil"...*

After a few deaths, including some from hypothermia or gangrene—stupidity, given the circumstances—the rush died down.

To be fair, Hastings set guard camps at the more accessible cursed mounds. As far as Susanna could tell, their discipline and performance seemed reasonable. It would be fruitless to complain if an occasional soldier became cursed.

When Jonathan strolled into the Keep, the boy at the reception desk stood and saluted him. "Good morning, Captain Shelley."

Technically, Jonathan was now one of Susanna's assistants rather than a working captain, but the honorific remained. Additionally, Emily indulged him with uniforms from the barracks. He returned the salute. "Morning, Euan. I'm taking Tabitha out to lunch."

"Very good, sir." Euan picked up the speaking tube. "I'll let her know you're here."

As Jonathan walked towards the stairs, Euan called, "Captain Shelley?"

He stopped. "What?"

"She told me she'd meet you here when you arrived. No need for you to go up."

He waved a hand. "It's no problem." It wasn't as if he were an invalid, and he was up and down these stairs daily.

"Sir? She was quite insistent. Could you wait here, please? If you don't mind..."

Eyeing his anxious expression, Jonathan sighed. Tabitha wasn't a detainee anymore, although she still lived upstairs. He should respect her wishes.

Still, the matter was odd. A suspicion reared its head. "Does she have a visitor already?"

Euan shook his head. "Not that I'm aware of."

Jonathan's brow wrinkled. "So why can't I go up to her suite?"

Gazing at the floor, Euan cleared his throat. "Permission to speak, sir?"

"Go on." What advice could this pimple-faced boy provide?

"I have two younger sisters. And sometimes they get kinda sensitive about me or Pa going into their rooms." He winced. "Janny threw a shoe at me once. So, uh, it might be something like that."

Jonathan stared. This was completely unfamiliar territory to him. "You're suggesting she's... more aware of privacy now?"

"Could be."

"I see." Frowning, he retreated from the stairwell. Why was it such a big deal? When he returned home, he'd ask— the back of his neck heated. Susanna's knowing smile arose in his memory, that time she'd admitted him to her rooms while dressed in a bathrobe. How many other clues, or even cues, had he missed? "Yes, I see. Thank you."

"Jonathan!" Tabitha waved at him from the stairs. Dressed in beige infirmier's overalls, she held a backpack. "Where are we going?"

His gaze softened as she skipped down the last few steps. "I thought we could have lunch at the Granville, then go wherever you want." Even without her movements being restricted, she'd had limited opportunity to explore the city. He hoped she wouldn't find the experience too stressful.

"Sounds good, I'm starving." She took his sleeve and tugged him towards the entrance. "What are we waiting for?"

After polishing off the last of her apple crumble, Tabitha sat back and patted her belly. "The Keep food's nice, but it gets kind of samey after a while."

"I know." He'd spent six months there himself, and the

catering probably hadn't changed much over the last decade.

"Though I'll miss those fancy rooms when I move in with the other staff."

"With new practitioners coming in for training, the space will be needed for someone else." It was only Susanna's intervention that had let Tabitha stay in her suite for so long, although Annetta and Samuel would remain there for now. Franka had returned to the barracks a fortnight ago. "If you don't like your new accommodation, Susanna would be happy for you to stay with us." He held his breath. When he'd suggested it to Susanna, she raised an eyebrow before hugging him with a laugh.

"We'll see." She wrinkled her nose. "She told me about your new house. It sounds really big. And it's just the two of you?"

"Yes. We have hired help, but nobody living in. Now that the queen wants me investigating"—he lowered his voice—"mounds and beasts, I'll be away for a few days at a time. She might welcome some company."

"Can I come with you? Exploring?"

"What?" He closed his mouth. Of course she couldn't, for a whole host of reasons. "Best not to. You're needed in the infirmary."

"I guess. I know my plants and things, and all the warning signs, but tramping around the countryside is no picnic. Hey, remember the first picnic you took me on?"

"How could I forget?" It had been when she was a detainee. Handcuffed together, they'd crossed that terrifying bridge between the Keep and Eleanor's rooftop garden. That was when Jonathan had determined to protect her, no matter the cost. But no point getting maudlin or wondering what else could have happened. He must be getting soft with age. Tabitha was now safe, and that was what mattered. He pushed away the memory and signalled a waiter. "Ready for a stroll?"

"We'll need one after eating so much." She giggled, then snatched the bill from the waiter before Jonathan could accept it. "My treat."

He blinked. "No, that's not right—"

"Hey, I got my first pay! Time to spend it."

Faced with such enthusiasm, what could he do? "As you wish. Where do you want to go now? There's a museum—"

"I want a dress." She frowned at her overalls. "Can't be wearing these all the time."

"What's wrong with them?" Clothing provided for Keep use was practical and sturdy.

"They're ugly. I want something pretty."

The child was as bad as Susanna. Still, hadn't he thought Susanna more attractive in a dress than in her uniform? Of course she was dear to him no matter her clothing, but still... "Who's going to see you in a dress?"

"Oh, nobody." Her cheeks grew pink. "I just want one."

He shook his head. "I've no idea where you might get one, but I'm sure we can find somewhere that sells them."

As Tabitha twirled before the full-length mirror in the fitting room, the shop assistant nodded approvingly. "The young lady looks very sophisticated and elegant."

Hovering just inside the brocade privacy curtain, Jonathan winced. The maroon fabric clung to Tabitha's curves and the whole construction threatened to collapse any moment. "Isn't it a bit, uh, lightweight?"

"Not at all, sir. This is current fashion, and your daughter will be the envy of the other debutantes."

"She's not my daughter." At the woman's raised eyebrow, he hastily added, "I'm responsible for her welfare, a sort of guardian, but she's not actually, biologically, my daughter. I'm not her father. Really." *Shut up, Shelley, before you make things worse.*

"Of course matters are as sir states. I completely understand." She inclined her head while he gritted his teeth.

"He's not my father." Tabitha beamed at the assistant. "But he's a lot nicer."

"I'm sure he is," came the reply.

Jonathan's shoulders hunched as the room grew stifling. What was he doing here?

Tabitha tossed her hair back and placed a hand on her hip, shooting her reflection a coy smile. "Jonathan, I like this one best. Do you like it too?"

"Uh..." He didn't want to puncture her exuberance, but it behoved him to insert a note of caution. "It's very pretty. But I wonder if it's more adult than you might want?"

While the assistant smiled tolerantly, Tabitha straightened and clasped her hands. "That's the whole point!"

His shoulders sagged. His little girl—and she wasn't even *his* little girl—was growing up. He should accept it with grace.

"I'm impressed," said Susanna, treading carefully on a loose cobblestone. Even though court shoes were elegant, some days she missed wearing sturdy captain's boots. She and Hastings were returning to the Royal Compound after a shooting demonstration at the barracks.

"I was quite pleased with the results myself." Hastings paused to return a small boy's salute, nodding at the child's wide-eyed mother. "You're far too modest about your training system. You've really proven yourself in the Keep."

"Kind of you to say so. But the new practitioners still have weaker powers than they used to. Even the ones who went on to try the pain boxes." Her shoulders tensed beneath her velvet jacket. It had been three months since Eleanor's announcement. Would Hastings now suggest they revert to the old methods?

"I don't think that's a problem, actually." At her quizzical glance, he waved a hand in the direction of the barracks. "I wouldn't *mind* having someone who could watch the border from here, but it's not been a problem to station sentries with conventional equipment, as long as they have blimp access too. Previously, there were few captains, and they had strong powers. Now, we have a much larger number of soldiers with weak powers, and they're not reluctant to use them. They're also good at following orders. Tactically speaking, I believe that's better."

"I see." She pursed her lips. Older captains might challenge orders they weren't happy with. Something didn't feel right about unquestioning obedience, especially from those with powers. Still, he was probably correct, given the situation. "It's good they've found practical uses for their abilities."

Several soldiers had weak televisualisation. They could barely see half a mile away, which was no better than a cheap spyglass. However, Hastings' demonstration had shown improved accuracy with flechette guns, and fair success in striking concealed targets. It was an application Susanna hadn't previously considered.

She stepped to the side to avoid a handcart. "Any more thoughts on practice for the fire starters?"

"That's a trickier challenge. Captain Hanlon very sensibly suggested we wait until it rains and use a tiny pinch of phosphoric compound."

"Or make a paper boat and float it on the river?"

"Maybe." Hastings' shoulders shook with his laughter. "If we damage the hydroelectric generators, Engineer Porter will have my head."

After parting from Hastings, Susanna returned to her perusal of Lady Nelson's notes. The old woman had seemingly cherry-picked her data, dwelling on the risks that powers posed to the unafflicted. Her habit of cross-referencing everything tempted the unwary reader to go round in circles.

An entire box was dedicated to the Denton incident, including official statements from all involved. Out of morbid curiosity about the event she'd completely missed, Susanna flipped through the accounts. Isabel's furious words left her in no doubt the situation had been desperate enough to merit burning the building where the criminal was hiding. Jonathan's account was sober and factual, just like the man himself. Lady Nelson had scribbled copious acerbic annotations beside each report.

Susanna's attention drifted to the photograph she kept on her desk. Jonathan's long-suffering blue-eyed gaze tempted her to smile. Wearing his usual grey uniform, positioned in a stance of readiness, the backpack at his feet, he looked prepared for anything.

That photograph was from the day Jonathan departed for his first solo mission. Eleanor had requested him to explore cursed mounds and document beast behaviour while minimising disturbance to the animals. It was little surprise he'd agreed. He and Isabel had *debated* one evening as to whether all beasts should really be killed on sight. Jonathan took the side of the beasts. Among other things, he argued that since beasts were a subset of four-legged animals, *dangerous* beasts might be an even smaller subset. Maybe his vehemence was no surprise: he had experience of being unfairly hunted. There hadn't been a clear winner, but afterwards Isabel had looked thoughtful.

Reaching for a file, Susanna pulled out a photograph of Samuel. She held it up beside Jonathan's. They both had blue eyes and slight builds, but she could see no other obvious similarities. She huffed in frustration. There had to be a better way of determining—No. If she asked Jonathan, he wouldn't know. Even a tentative question would make him feel guilty. There was no point in causing him upset or worry. Not in the absence of certainty.

Breathe in... And she shouldn't pry. What happened then didn't matter now. But the question itched at her out of proportion to its importance. *Breathe out...* Probably because she was tired. Time to call it a day. She'd have a light dinner and an early night—Jonathan was away—and her sense of proportion would return after a decent sleep.

As she stacked up the Denton notes, the marginalia beside Jonathan's report caught her eye:

Inheritance project - cross-reference file 32.

A clue, or just a tantalising irrelevance? Lady Nelson's comments had yielded nothing so far.

She crouched by the boxes, yanking them open and scattering files on the floor, coughing at the dust she disturbed. It was silly, really—the old records wouldn't disappear overnight—but the urge to know was overwhelming.

Finally, she found the right file. She returned to her desk and opened it with trembling fingers. Carbon-copied extracts from settlement census reports lay atop a few papers bearing Lady Nelson's spidery hand.

The three yellowing sheets listed all the cursed captains spanning a period of some thirty years, in order of appointment. Beside some names were further names and locations. Her gaze landed on her own name, near the top of the final page. She scanned the list, and her eyebrows rose as she learned more than she liked regarding her erstwhile colleagues.

Jonathan's name was a few lines beneath hers. Unlike hers, the space beside it wasn't blank:

Shelley, Jonathan (m) - Keighley Village - ???, Lynette (f) - male progeny highly likely

A date from eleven years ago was scribbled by the note. Susanna seized the bell pull. When the on-duty messenger boy arrived, she snapped, "Fetch Annetta."

"At once, ma'am." He departed at a run.

She closed her eyes and buried her head in her hands. Why was she summoning the herbalist? Because she would burst if she didn't confide in someone.

Once Annetta provided the name of Samuel's mother, Susanna could finally confirm the name of Samuel's father.

Eleanor clasped her hands and leaned back in her chair, regarding the other Council members with a smile. "I am proud how everyone has set aside their differences for the good of the realm. John Hastings' efforts have been invaluable, considering we've never faced this type of threat before." Hastings' speed in educating himself about martial history and tactics had been impressive. If—when—the realm approached active battle, she'd hand over leadership with confidence in his abilities. "John, could you expand a touch, please?"

"We've trained six hundred soldiers. Four hundred regular guards are in the reserves. Joint exercises had been going quite well, but then we had an unscheduled one." Hastings gave a modest laugh. His chin was stubbled, and he'd rolled up his green uniform sleeves at the start of the meeting. "After the *Informer* published one of Captain Hanlon's photographs, some ill-informed citizens panicked that we were going to be invaded by giants. Fortunately, the guards and soldiers cooperated to disperse the resulting near-riot peacefully. David Buchanan and I agreed it was best to make no arrests."

"Indeed, at least we're not facing giants," said Porter.

Working together, the *techne* folk and item-sensing practitioners had gleaned further information from Isabel's images. After finding the structures to be predominantly metal, they'd gone on to make initial suggestions about function. Perhaps the giants were exoskeletons that people—regular people—could use for travel and fighting, or they were controllable automatons, maybe patrolling the area. They'd tentatively suggested calling them "sentries" or "sentinels." Not to be discounted, but Eleanor was still dealing with people and not some completely alien society. Still, she didn't know how Hastings' troops would fare against an opponent with access to such advanced *techne*. Were the people to the south somehow monitoring the realm and laughing at Ascar's feeble preparations? Just because their own patrols detected nothing... the converse might not hold.

Eleanor's gaze strayed towards the end of the table where Artur sat. His eyes met hers and he blushed, tugging at the collar of his ill-fitting suit. Her own face warming, she hastily spoke. "We've been incredibly lucky. Aerial surveys revealed that there used to be roads between the settlements and leading to Ascar. Matthew Porter and his teams have cleared and repaired those roads far faster than we could have built new ones. The agricultural workers living close by helped too. Hauling a load from Ascar to a settlement now takes a day rather than a week. Yes, the roads run close to cursed mounds, but we can take precautions when travelling in those areas. John set up permanent guard stations there to reduce the risk of, ah, accidents."

She nodded towards Susanna. "The improved training system has reduced the number of permanent residents in the Keep. We now have practitioners who can..." She consulted her list. "Set fire to things, locate people and several who can see items at a distance. This last will be of use not just for combat and reconnaissance but for communication. Unfortunately, Matthew hasn't yet got his telecommunications working, but if we station someone who can 'televisualise' in each town, they could write messages to each other." The boy Samuel seemed to have the strongest power when it came to people, but Susanna had decided not to pressure him in view of his young age. She'd seemed uncomfortable, almost distressed, when Eleanor asked her about it.

"How powerful are they?" asked Martek.

"It's not so much a case of strength." Susanna's voice was subdued, and her jacket needed ironing. "For some practitioners, their powers seem to manifest at random times. For others, distance from their targets is highly significant. Application and practice count too."

"The best results have been with the marksmen." Hastings winced. "Although igniting explosives is too unpredictable for safety. I don't think we should take that application of powers further."

"It's still progress," said Eleanor. "Added to the new training system, Research Apothecary Annetta is producing pharmacological agents which can temporarily suppress or boost powers. They are only available in limited amounts. We should keep them in reserve for emergencies."

"I agree," said Susanna, and Hastings also nodded.

Thank the Settlers, the routine part of the meeting had gone smoothly. "What we desperately need is more knowledge about the threat that lies to the south. On the one hand, they may have been there all the time and are in no hurry. On the other, if I hadn't sent Isabel to explore, they might have caught us unawares." Hastings knew of the accidental reasons for that trip, and the other Council members probably suspected. But it wasn't in their interests to tell anyone. Certainly, Isabel's revelations had boosted Eleanor's reputation, although it was Isabel whose name was included in tavern songs. No doubt she relished her notoriety.

"What have we tried?" asked Martek.

"We attached identity rings to messenger birds and sent them south using Isabel's photographs for orientation. They didn't come back, and the rings have moved out of detection range. We've tried powers—but as Susanna said, distance is quite a limitation." She twirled a strand of hair around a finger. "Given our lack of success with remote investigation attempts, I am forced to conclude that we need to send an exploratory team across the wastelands. The people on the other side might even be friendly. Maybe that's why they haven't yet approached our lands, and we've spent all this time fretting for no reason."

Gauntlett repositioned his thick glasses on his nose. "I don't remember any records of civilisations leaving each other alone, once one became aware of the other. The oldest reference is an account of two seafaring groups who met on a small island."

Hastings waved a finger at him. "The one where they destroyed each other's boats, and all starved to death? I'd always thought of that as a cautionary tale rather than a real event, since there was no one left to relate the story."

Gauntlett shrugged. "That's a possibility, admittedly. Could we opt to wait and see?"

The historian's concerned expression didn't give Eleanor confidence. But it wasn't his decision to make. She licked her lips. "I'm not convinced that's a good idea. Are there any engineering developments in the pipeline it would be worth waiting for?"

Porter shook his head. "Possibly small improvements in efficiency, such as with the hydroelectric generators, but nothing major."

"I suppose..." Hastings frowned. "We're about as well prepared as we can be, in the absence of concrete information. An exploration is the next logical step. But although the sentinels weren't overtly hostile towards Captain Hanlon's small blimp, a larger force might provoke the very attack we're trying to avoid. After all, neither we nor they have yet crossed into the other's territory, assuming the wastelands don't truly count. I advise that when you send your team, the army move to the border. We will then be prepared in case of retaliation against our peaceful approach."

He had a point. And his support of the exploration reassured her she wasn't making an unreasonable decision. "I agree. Lesser preparation would be too risky."

After the meeting broke up, Eleanor remained by herself at the Council table, mulling over candidates for the exploration team. They'd need to be prepared for any outcome and willing to risk their lives.

With a leaden weight in her chest, she left the meeting room. As usual, Paton awaited her in the hallway.

Maps in hand, Artur stood awkwardly beside him. "Can I help?"

She tried to smile. "Thank you for the offer, Artur, but I feel I need to think things over by myself." She swallowed. "I'll be in touch, soon."

Chapter 16

Jonathan adjusted his backpack as he walked past Ascar's southern fields towards the city gates, a smile touching his lips. What was that old saying? Absence made the heart grow fonder? He'd never really appreciated what it meant. How odd to find out at his age. When out on these assignments in the wilds, thoughts of Susanna kept him warm at night. He missed snuggling by the fire with her, or chatting while she embroidered, but his work was useful and kept him from under her feet.

On his first such outing, he'd walked a good distance away from the new roads, pencilling in his progress on Fellows' map. The small group of beasts he found ignored him, other than scavenging food scraps he dropped. They hadn't even reacted to the clicks and whirring noises when he took photographs. His impression was that they'd be happy to leave him alone as long as he returned the favour. When he reported his observations to the others, Isabel grew rather quiet. Previously she'd argued with him over whether killing *all* beasts was necessary, and she'd shaken her head when he mentioned the pregnant beast he'd helped. Maybe she'd come round to his way of thinking as he made further observations. Fortunately, he didn't need to deal with her in the field: Eleanor gave her plenty to do in the palace.

However, Jonathan's last few trips had yielded little new information, confirming Eleanor's suspicions that beast populations were relatively few. Hmm. Maybe she wouldn't send him out again, and he could usefully occupy himself in the city. Susanna was perfectly capable of looking after herself, but Jonathan didn't completely trust Hastings to behave. At least the man's army preparations gave him less time to act like a pompous boor.

The industriousness of the field workers gave no clue that war was looming. A slender girl perched up a ladder, dropping fruit into her partner's basket. She paused to wave at him. Jonathan waved back, taking comfort in the familiar sight.

Other workers pedalled cultivation equipment in the fields, lumps of soil flying behind them. Of course food production still needed to continue. With so many young and able-bodied now drafted into the army, the engineers had adapted equipment to provide agricultural assistance to those who remained at home.

As Jonathan entered the city, he returned the gate guard's salute. By now, everyone knew he reported to the queen. It was funny how that had become more significant than his curse—his *power*—and it further raised his status. "Anything new happening?"

"Not that we've been told, sir. But Queen Eleanor requested your presence at the palace as soon as you returned." The guard signalled a messenger boy, who jogged off.

He sighed. Eleanor wasn't usually in such a hurry for his reports. "I see. Send a message to Chief Scientist Longleaf, telling her I'll be back for dinner." His self-consciousness at such requests had ceased.

Ignoring the frisson of worry in his chest, Jonathan ambled towards the palace. His previously injured leg and shoulder were fully functional, although with weather-related aches, but he wasn't going to strain himself.

He approached the palace library to the sound of hushed voices. When he reached the doorway, his eyes widened.

Eleanor sat on the couch beside Artur. The engineer had an arm around her shoulders.

Fumbling in the pocket of her purple silk dress, Eleanor pulled out a handkerchief. "I can't come up with any way around it."

Jonathan cleared his throat. "You wanted to see me? I can come back another time..."

Artur looked up and rose to his feet while Eleanor dabbed her reddened eyes. The damp patch on the shoulder of his overalls suggested that she had been crying for a while. "Jonathan, good morning."

"Good morning, Eleanor, Artur." He slid off his backpack and placed it by a bookcase. With the youngsters' murmurs in his ears, he pretended to make a close study of the shelves. They weren't so crammed with dusty volumes as previously.

Jaunty whistling sounded in the corridor, and Isabel strolled in. She wore a maroon velvet lounging robe and matching slippers. "Wotcha. Is this all of us?"

"Just one more." Eleanor's voice was hoarse.

When Artur resumed his seat and patted Eleanor's hand, Jonathan again averted his gaze. It was a relief when footsteps approached.

Annetta trotted along the corridor after the messenger boy, trying unsuccessfully to wipe stains off her beige overalls. The pungent odour made Jonathan's nose wrinkle. "Um, sorry. I couldn't leave the batch until it was ready."

Eleanor coughed. "Let's sit round the table."

After they were seated, Isabel unrolled a map.

Nodding at Jonathan and Annetta, Eleanor said, "I apologise for being so reticent, but it was only fair to speak with you privately at first. Just in case—"

Isabel snorted. "Say it without faffing around, will you? You're making it sound worse than it is."

"Right." Eleanor straightened. "Hastings' military preparations have gone well, and he tells me we're as prepared as we can be in the absence of further information. We still don't know what—who—we face, or even if they have hostile intentions. We can't remain on alert indefinitely since that can risk unrest and either falling into complacency or jeopardising the realm's stability. Because of all this, I've decided to send a blimp expedition team to the south. The army will march to the border as well, so there is backup. I would like the four of you to go in the blimp." She gazed around their faces. "I'm not ordering you, but you are the best people."

Blimp. Jonathan's innards quivered at the memory of Ascar's grey buildings shrinking beneath his feet. Battling enemies on the ground would be easier.

"Why me?" squeaked Annetta.

"Because of your pharmacological knowledge, especially about powers. We must depend on powers to have any chance. Your preparations and written recipes are invaluable, but it might be necessary to improvise. Only you can do that. If there was more time for you to train them, I'd pick one of your assistants instead, someone who is less..."

"Timid?" Isabel smirked while both Eleanor and Annetta glared.

"Less difficult to replace." Eleanor's gaze dropped. "And it may be necessary to perform, ah, sabotage of any hostile forces."

Annetta gaped. "You want me to *poison* people?"

"Only as a last resort, if the situation is desperate. Remember, the worst-case situation for *us* is being overrun and obliterated by advanced forces."

"This wasn't what I trained for," Annetta mumbled. "But *if* there is dire need, I would know what to do. I remember the old protocols about 'neutralising' afflicted who are dangerous, but I've never faced that situation." With a glance at Jonathan, she ducked her head. "I would have to make the decision. For myself."

"Of course," said Eleanor. "I don't want you to act against your conscience. And nobody will pressure you into it."

Isabel said, "I need to go. I'm the only one who's travelled that way previously. Plus, my power will be needed for the blimp. And I have the political savvy. My life's forfeit anyway, so I might as well be useful."

Annetta's eyes widened. "Forfeit? What do you mean?"

Isabel waved her hand. "Private joke."

Before Annetta could enquire further, Jonathan hastily asked, "And why me?"

Eleanor said, "Firstly, your power is versatile and well controlled. You can even use it to help steer the blimp, although lifting it really needs heat. Also, you're experienced with dealing with people, and you're canny and innovative. And you're sensible."

He blinked. Nobody had ever praised him so fulsomely.

"And for some reason," continued Eleanor, "Samuel's drawings always feature you. Even though his power doesn't manifest often, we hope he might draw you while you're on your travels. Could give us useful information."

"Really?" His brow creased. When Silvers kidnapped Tabitha, one of Samuel's drawings had led to her rescue: plus Jonathan's exoneration at his trial. And in the more distant past, a drawing had led Jonathan to realise Samuel was cursed. But surely he'd done other drawings? "I don't remember anyone mentioning a *tendency* for him to draw me. Annetta, I suppose it was you who noticed this? Any ideas why?"

The herbalist's face had turned scarlet, and she wouldn't meet his eye as she shook her head.

Jonathan tried not to scowl. Did she really find him that intimidating? Or maybe it was just embarrassment that she'd inadvertently aided Silvers. Well, no point in making the poor woman squirm. "Never mind. Annetta, please know that I won't hold anything against you if you want to express an honest opinion. I know we've had our awkward moments and misunderstandings"—that drew a weak smile—"but we need to work as a team."

She fanned her face, wafting an acrid scent in his direction. "I understand."

"And that," said Eleanor, "is why I'd like you to lead the group, Jonathan. You don't let personal issues get in the way of doing what's needed. Am I clear on that, *Isabel*?"

"Yeah, yeah." Isabel waved a hand.

Jonathan refrained from a sigh. If Isabel took off on her own or went on a rampage, he could hardly stop her. "And Artur?"

Artur reached out towards Eleanor, then glanced at the others and let his hand drop. "Of course you need a blimp engineer. And I already know the background. I've spent time with Eleanor discussing her surveys and research findings."

Isabel grinned and winked at Eleanor. "Sure, that's why you spend hours in the library together."

Eleanor blushed, then she slumped. "I'm not forcing any of you to agree. If you decline, nobody will ever be told."

"But we're your best hope." Jonathan's voice was harsh. Did Eleanor really think she was offering them a free choice?

"Yes. I have other candidates who might be willing..."

Tabitha. If Eleanor needed to assign a different telekinetic to the trip, it would be Tabitha. The only other telekinetic—the infirmier—would be needed for the army. Jonathan's absence would leave Isabel in charge of the expedition, which was altogether too much of a gamble. "I'll go," he said. "But on one condition. Tabitha is to be kept away from the front line. She's doing good work in the infirmary, and there's no reason to move her."

"Agreed," said Eleanor.

Annetta squirmed. "And I'll go."

Jonathan exchanged a glance with Isabel, and she nodded slightly. They would protect the two civilians.

"What's our remit?" he asked.

Eleanor rubbed her forehead. "Travel south by blimp, assess the situation and do whatever is necessary. It may be a very minor trip, other than the travel."

Or it might be a suicide mission.

In the mansion she shared with Jonathan, Susanna nodded in satisfaction at the dishes she'd laid on the table. She rarely had the chance to prepare a proper meal, but Jonathan's note had allowed her to stop at the market on the way home and pick up some treats. They'd start dinner with duck, followed by steamed trout with a mixed salad and freshly baked bread. With luck, he'd return with foraged blueberries to finish. Last time it had been strawberries.

A decanter of red wine stood on the sideboard. With the widespread acceptance of powers these days, slips in control didn't need to be concealed. Drinking alcohol didn't carry the risk it used to. Each time Jonathan returned from a mission, they'd celebrate with a glass. That was too small an amount to activate either of their powers, but it symbolised the trust they had in each other.

Over the couple of days since her discovery that Jonathan was Samuel's father, confirmed by information from Annetta, Susanna had recovered her equanimity. After all, the past was past. Such services from convoy guards were more or less encouraged. Besides, it was too late for them to start a family now. No reason to be jealous of a long-dead woman.

So, she'd treat Jonathan to a nice dinner. Once he was relaxed and well-fed, she'd raise the issue of Samuel. Carefully, of course: and in the spirit of acceptance and support. Jonathan was keeping no secrets from her, and it was only right to reciprocate. Whatever the future held, they'd face it together.

The front door opened, and Susanna went into the hallway, a welcoming smile on her face.

Looking down, Jonathan wiped his feet on the doormat, then he dropped his backpack on the floor. When he met her gaze, he didn't smile.

"What's wrong?" she asked.

He shook his head. "We'll talk after dinner."

The duck confit was lacking its usual savour. Or rather,

she couldn't appreciate it for the anxiety building in her throat. As for Jonathan, he ate as if he couldn't taste it.

At length, he put his fork down.

Breathe in... "What's wrong?" she asked again. It couldn't be too urgent, could it? Or else he'd have been in more of a hurry. Or not returned home.

He met her gaze, his eyes glistening in the candlelight. "She's sending me south, across the wastelands."

Breathe out... It had been too good to last. No need to ask who "she" was. "To explore?"

He shrugged. "Or maybe more. Depends on what we find."

"When? And who else is going?" Pride warred with regret that Eleanor had chosen him. Of course she had. Was it selfish to wish him less capable?

"The army leaves first, so we'll go in a couple of days. Isabel, of course. Artur, as we're travelling by blimp. Annetta, even."

"Annetta?" Susanna nearly dropped her knife.

He snorted. "I know, she's so timid. I was surprised she agreed, but—" His mouth remained open as he stared at her.

"What?" Had Annetta already said something to him about Samuel? How would Jonathan cope if he learned of a child, only to be wrenched away soon afterwards? This wasn't the right time to mention it.

He picked up his fork again and stabbed a tomato. "Sorry, I was thinking this is depriving you of your innovative herbalist. But she's written down her recipes for posterity."

"I see. Fortunate, that." Susanna licked her lips. "Did she say anything else of significance?"

"Not that I recollect. I've underestimated her before,

and I suspect I did so again at that meeting." He regarded his plate. "Susanna..."

"Don't say it." Why acknowledge that he might not come back? "Do you want me to tell Tabitha?"

"Please. Eleanor's agreed to keep her in the city rather than with the army. Probably better for her if I simply disappear and let her get on with the rest of her life. Who am I fooling? I don't feel brave enough to talk to her."

"Oh, Jonathan. You're the bravest man I've ever met."

Chapter 17

Because the army would set off before the blimp, Jonathan had a couple of days to prepare. He visited the infirmary—when Tabitha was elsewhere—and the resident bonesetter confirmed his shoulder was back to normal. *As good as it'll get, at your age.* Jonathan had asked him to ensure Tabitha would stay in Ascar, even if the army needed more medics. *Stop fussing,* the man had said. *It'll ruin your digestion.*

Susanna rearranged her schedule, and they spent a morning walking around Ascar, hand in hand. Children and white-haired elders queued outside confectioners to buy "sweet survival packs" for relatives and friends in the army. The couturier where Tabitha had bought her dress now offered uniform repairs and adjustments for free.

At Bernice's Blooms, Jonathan bought the last white orchid in the shop. Trying to ignore the florist's tolerant smile, he presented it to Susanna.

With trembling fingers, she pinned it to her jacket. "Lucky I still have my flower press. I'll keep this with the first bouquet you brought me."

"You kept that? I learn something new about you every day."

"Of course I kept it. Memories are always worth keeping."

In the city square, they stood in front of the Settlers' statue. Jonathan squinted at the child's hand, positioned so it almost touched the fire. Odd how he'd never noticed that before, but then he'd never had reason to pay attention. This might be his last opportunity.

"We will prevail." Rubbing a hand over her face, Susanna heaved a sigh. "I wonder who they prevailed over."

"I'll try my best to find out." As she started to walk off, he tugged her towards him and added, "I'm not good at fancy speeches, but know this: I will do all I can in my power to return to you."

Then he held her and stroked her hair while she wept.

That evening, they took Lester and Franka out for dinner at the Gilded Pigeon. The raucous crowd in the tavern's main area seemed determined to drink the place dry. With so many people marching off in the army, Jonathan couldn't blame folk for trying to ease the pain of separation, but he was glad he'd booked the private room.

Even Franka's risqué jokes seemed subdued, and Lester spent the meal alternately frowning at his plate and fiddling with his cravat.

"Look, uh, Jonathan," he said. "Let me know if there's anything I can do to help. Seems I'm staying in the city for now, to help with training. And dealing with any unrest."

Jonathan gritted his teeth. The young man *wasn't* competition: he offered Susanna valuable support in her work. Jealousy about their relationship would be petty. "Could you keep an eye on Susanna? Left to her own devices, she'd work round the clock."

"Jonathan!" Susanna half-heartedly patted him on the arm.

Franka winked. "I'd offer to keep an eye on *Lester*, but I'm marching with the army. If either he or Susanna end up with us, I'll keep them in line."

"You'll get your chance." Susanna put down her fork.

"I'm splitting my time between Ascar and the army, depending on who needs help."

Jonathan met Lester's eye. "You see?"

Lester nodded. At last, something they could agree on.

On the day of the army's departure, Susanna had Keep commitments, so Jonathan attended a gathering in the city square by himself.

Eleanor stood on the platform, chin raised as she addressed the crowd. "I hereby transfer full control of the army to Commander-in-Chief Hastings."

Hastings saluted her while the technician adjusted the amplifier to his height. His face betrayed no triumph. But then again, Eleanor was still ultimately in command. Only if Eleanor declared their war status to be active would Hastings take charge of the entire realm, both military and civilian.

"We march to show the enemy we're a force to be reckoned with." Hastings' voice echoed around the square. "We do not wish to fight. But if those to the south are aggressive, we will match them in determination. If they initiate a fight, we will make them sorely regret it!"

Jonathan's neighbours in the crowd looked concerned but resolute. The man certainly had a way with words.

Hastings held out his hand. "I see Captain Shelley is here, a veteran of many missions. Captain Shelley, step forwards."

Me? Everyone turned to stare at Jonathan. Why hadn't he worn civilian clothes? Sweat beading on his neck, he paced up the steps and saluted Hastings. "Sir."

Hastings placed a heavy hand on his shoulder and turned him to face the crowd. "Good citizens of Ascar, Captain Shelley epitomises the best qualities of our people.

Loyal, hard-working and noble. He leads the reconnaissance mission which will dictate the army's strategy. Please keep our heroic blimp team in your thoughts when they leave tomorrow."

Damn the man. Praise from Hastings was even worse than having his enmity. Jonathan bowed stiffly, trying not to wince at the cheers.

Fortunately, Hastings moved on to other topics with his morale-boosting speech. After a brass band struck up a farewell tune and Hastings led the army out of the square, Jonathan slunk off.

When Susanna arrived home and he told her of the incident, she said, "About time he acknowledged your contribution. I wish I could have been there."

"No, you don't," muttered Jonathan.

And now the army was a day's march down the road, probably halfway to Holmbeath. The team had done their final checks and briefing that morning. It was time for the blimp to set off.

Jonathan stood on the roof of the Keep, Susanna's hand on his arm. Eleanor, Paton and a few blimp technicians were present.

They watched several porters load up the gondola under Artur's supervision with supplies, bedrolls, rope and other equipment. The gondola could hold six people: a compromise between capacity and the need for stealth. When fully inflated, the mottled sky-blue balloon would be some fifty feet in diameter. It was filled with a versium/levium mixture, and they took a spare canister of each plus several patches.

"If we use all those patches," Artur grumbled, "there

won't be a balloon left to repair."

Dressed in one of her silk captain's uniforms, Isabel ambled up and slugged Artur in the arm. "Got everything you need?"

Artur flinched. "Just about. I've already stashed spare parts and tools." He opened a folder. "And blueprints, in case I need to get creative with any repairs."

After Annetta arrived, Paton handed flechette guns to Jonathan and Isabel. He gave all four of them a steel bracelet engraved with their initials. "We hope Honeyman can track you with these. Plus the travel markers."

Jonathan fastened his bracelet with mixed feelings. The tracking system had been Silvers' idea, but this was a beneficial use.

Annetta handed him a belt pouch. "General medicinal preparations, antiseptics, painkillers... Yours and Isabel's contain stimulants and suppressants for your powers. Emergency use only."

"Thank you," said Jonathan. The suppressant might come in useful if blimp sickness got the better of him. No reason for the other two to have those preparations immediately to hand. Artur's power wouldn't be needed, of course, and Annetta had no power to stimulate or suppress.

"You're welcome." After wiping her fingers on her beige overalls, she fiddled with her bag. She frowned at a pair of rubber gloves and a sealed glass vial inside. Poison?

Eleanor cleared her throat. "Are you all ready?" At their assent, she continued. "We estimate the army will arrive at the border in three days, so you'll overtake them on the way. We'll allow your mission one week. If you don't return or send word within that time, we'll..." She swallowed. "We'll assume you have met with hostile forces."

"What will you do then?" Shoulders tense, Jonathan suppressed visions of blood-soaked fields.

"Of course it depends on the particulars. But I expect Commander-in-Chief Hastings would direct the army to march across the wastelands, fully prepared for battle. I hope it doesn't come to that." She met his eye. "We're depending on you."

"Don't worry, cuz." Isabel embraced Eleanor tightly, only releasing her on a muffled squeak. "We'll be safely laughing about our adventures before then. I'm sure Artur will race back as fast as he can."

Artur blushed. "We'd better get on our way. Eleanor..." Colour deepening, he took her hand and bowed over it. "I hope to see you again, soon."

Susanna stood on tiptoe and kissed Jonathan's ear. "Goodbye, Jonathan," she whispered, her eyes moist.

As they lifted off, Jonathan gripped his sabre hilt tightly in an attempt to keep his stomach under control. He didn't dare send Susanna a farewell glance. *Don't be such a wimp, Shelley.* At this point, he wasn't even needed. As Eleanor had said, he'd only be backup for the manual steering system, however that worked. The versium had been heated for takeoff by some gadget at the Keep. From now onwards, Isabel's fire power would heat the balloon's gas so they stayed in the air, and Artur would control their speed and direction. Jonathan and Annetta would be doing the mundane tasks. From convoy captain to tea boy. He'd accept the role gladly if it staved off a war.

He concentrated on regular breathing rather than the land they were traversing. His only previous blimp ride had passed over the Ascar Mountains. For this one they'd keep a lower elevation. Artur had said something about conserving energy as well as being less visible from a distance. For Jonathan, it was a disadvantage being able to see the terrain features in such detail as they whizzed by, far faster than he could run.

They headed south, across Ascar's southern fields. Workers looked up and waved.

"Woohoo!" Isabel leaned out and waved back. "Jonathan, you should wave too. Keeps their morale up."

Ugh. Screwing his eyes shut—hopefully they couldn't tell at this distance—he flapped a hand over the side.

"You too, Annetta," shouted Isabel.

"Like this?" called Annetta.

Jonathan cracked an eye open and groaned. Even the herbalist was coping better than him.

Fortunately, they were soon past Ascar's fields and over unpopulated woodland and hills, following one of the new roads. He slumped against the side.

"Jonathan?" Annetta held out a pill. "To settle your stomach. Sorry, if I'd known earlier—"

"Thank you, but I'll decline." He smiled weakly. "Need to get used to this."

"If you change your mind, let me know..."

His roiling innards gradually settled. As the sun progressed across the sky, he forced himself to watch the land pass beneath them. It wasn't *too* bad, really. Following Artur's instructions, Isabel occasionally put her hand on a metal rod attached to the balloon. It heated the versium inside. Or so he gathered. The engineer's mutters about heat capacity and insulation could probably be ignored.

Artur pointed down the road at a cloud of dust. "There they are."

Jonathan squinted. They'd reached the army already?

After some thirty years of walking around the entire realm, he might be forced to agree that flying had advantages.

As they passed over the army, he looked down at Hastings' thousand troops. The soldiers marched in squads of six, faces turned up at the blimp. Groups were separated by pedalcarts holding their supplies. "Runners"—now bicyclists—sped up and down the line, presumably carrying messages.

"Eleanor's idea about the handcarts was inspired," said Artur, a smile on his face.

"What was that?" Did she know about handcarts as well as blimps?

"Pumping versium into the frames to make them lighter. Not so much that they lift off, but they're easier to handle. The water barrels were treated similarly, including the ones we're carrying."

"Ah." Jonathan returned his attention to the troops.

The soldiers were dressed mainly in light green, although convoy and city guards were mixed in too. David's grey-clad muscular form stood out among the rest.

At the front marched Hastings, distinguished by his dark green uniform. As the blimp's shadow touched him, he halted, raised an arm and saluted.

A cheer rose, and the soldiers waved. Isabel jumped up and down, pumping her fists in the air. The floor rocked while Jonathan's stomach turned somersaults.

"Steady on, Isabel," said Artur. "Can you calm down, please?"

"Sorry." Her face still bore a grin. "But it's pretty spectacular. Eh, Jonathan?"

"Sure." He clamped his lips shut. It would *not* do to vomit over Hastings.

They left the army behind and were back to unpopulated territory. Occasional groups of travellers with pedal-carts—likely traders—stopped to stare. Jonathan lost track of time, and his nausea returned. *Why* had he agreed to this? Why had Eleanor thought *he* was a good choice? And, most importantly, when would this be over? The shadows grew longer, tempting him to wish for night. Surely they would land soon.

"Should be close to Holmbeath." Isabel squinted through a spyglass. "Let's see... Yep, there's chimney smoke. I wonder if they can see us too."

"I suppose if someone were looking this direction and also had an equally powerful spyglass..." said Artur.

"True. Though this is top of the range." She offered it to Jonathan. "Want a look?"

He swallowed. "No. I'm... fine as I am." His grip tightened on the handrail.

"Annetta?"

The herbalist accepted the instrument and raised it to her face. "How does it—" She turned the focus. "Oh! That's amazing! This would be a great way to spot patches of herbs. I must try this next time." Her face fell. "Well, if there is a next time."

Isabel snorted. "Pessimists!"

Artur shook his head. "This time of day, the air temperature is falling, so the versium isn't lifting us so well. We should land before it gets dark. I need to do final checks once it's light, before we cross into the wastelands. Does that sound alright?"

At last, some respite. "Very sensible." He tried not to sound too eager.

"Something else, while I remember," said Artur.

"Jonathan and Annetta, you should have a go at steering the blimp."

Jonathan froze. "Me?"

"Us?" squeaked Annetta.

"Sure. It's very straightforward—you'll pick it up in no time. We're unlikely to need it, but best to practise while we're still in friendly territory. Now we're past Holmbeath, there's no need to worry about landing on anyone."

This wasn't something he could refuse. "What do we do?" He managed to keep his voice steady.

"Right," said Artur. "I won't confuse you with how the *techne* works, since I'd be controlling the powered propellors myself. But if the weather gets rough, we might need to supplement the steering with passive, manual fins. If you put your hand just under the rim of the frame"—he pointed—"you'll find a handle on either side."

With Annetta holding one, Jonathan grasped the other, and they followed Artur's instructions. He tried to ignore Isabel's whoops of amusement as the two of them spun the blimp in lopsided circles.

With the air cooling, the ground grew closer. Clenching his jaw against an escaping whimper, he squeezed his eyes shut.

The floor tilted, and he flexed his knees, bracing against the impact. If he got tossed out, he'd have to roll—

"Jonathan?" Artur's voice sounded by his ear. "We've landed. You can let go now."

"Oh." He opened his eyes and cleared his throat. "I guess we'd better set up camp."

Once back on the ground, he tottered into a copse and spent a minute clutching an unmoving tree. Then he gathered dry wood for a campfire. Annetta explored and returned with a cooking pot holding foraged greens and water. As yet, they'd no need to breach their water barrels. The other two laid out the bedrolls.

After Isabel lit the fire, Artur emptied a sachet into the pot and set it to heat up. Jonathan's nose twitched. In his convoy days, each village or town they visited gave them local food sufficient for travel to the next settlement. These dried rations might be convenient and easy to reconstitute, but he doubted they'd taste pleasant. Still, he shouldn't complain: it was all food.

"Not bad." After scraping her bowl clean, Isabel patted her stomach. "Before I drop off, I'll go over what I found again..."

Fifty feet tall. It didn't sound any better this time round than it had at first. The reference photograph they'd brought still made Jonathan sweat.

Artur scrunched his face at his notepad and scribbled some calculations. "Going by our speed today, we should be be within sight of the sentinels tomorrow evening about this time. It was Eleanor's idea that we drop travel markers every hour." He eyed Jonathan. "That was the tub of numbered metal clips. They're too small to be easily visible, but Richard can locate them with his power."

Jonathan spread his hands. "I'm amazed at these bright ideas you young folk come up with. I hope I can contribute to the mission too."

"Hey, don't go all mopey on us." Isabel poked him then turned to Artur. "Any ideas about how to approach the sentinels?"

"Given their size and positioning, it seems they might be monitoring the skies. Not sure the blimp is the best way to pass them. But need to think about that nearer the time.

I brought a decoy balloon that might come in useful, especially with Jonathan's power."

"What if they attack us in the blimp?" Annetta's voice quavered.

Artur frowned. "This blimp isn't built for speed, but I'll do my best to steer us back. Isabel, if that happens, keep heating the balloon's core so we rise out of range. Don't worry, you can't burst the balloon. Jonathan and Annetta, you hold on to the passive fin controls and keep us moving in a straight line."

"And if that doesn't work?" asked Jonathan.

Artur's shoulders straightened. "Settlers help us."

Chapter 18

Susanna accepted David's arm while she clambered down from the blimp. Some day she'd manage this unaided, and without making a fool of herself. Pretending not to notice the soldiers' curious glances, she smoothed down her overalls. She left Samuel chattering at the blimp operators and walked with David towards the nearby camp. The army had stopped where the road forked towards Holmbeath.

"Any problems?" asked Susanna. She'd agreed with Hastings that David should coordinate the "special forces"—anyone with powers, no matter how practical or otherwise.

"Not with their powers, no." David smirked. "Richard's whining about not being able to sleep properly in a tent, but you know what a fusspot he is. He asked why we couldn't overnight in Holmbeath. These city-based captains have no idea."

She returned the smile. Trust Richard to be ignorant of rural populations. A thousand soldiers certainly couldn't fit into thirty dwellings. "I hope that's as bad as it gets. I'm working with him today, which might help take his mind off things."

"Commander Hastings is this way." David led Susanna past a row of part-dismantled pedalcarts. The old roads had only been cleared as far as here, so from now on the old-fashioned handcarts would be of more use.

The former Chief Councillor stood beside two soldiers

checking over a crate labelled "CAUTION: FLAMMABLE". A year ago, Susanna had viewed him as the archetypal politician, more comfortable at a podium than in the field. She hadn't expected his air of easy authority to sit so well on him as a military commander too. If war broke out... it was a relief they were on the same side.

After David saluted, Hastings told him, "We'll break camp an hour after dawn. It's an easy day's march tomorrow, and we'll station ourselves just back from the border. Once the survey blimps are in position, they'll see any approach in time for us to respond. Let the others know."

"Yes, sir." David walked off, shouting instructions to the guards.

Hastings nodded at Susanna. "Thank you for bringing Samuel. I hope this works."

"Me too. But remember how young he is." The decision to bring the boy here had been painful. With Jonathan on his exploratory mission, Samuel's drawings could be invaluable. Hastings had wondered if his power would be more effective while closer to the wastelands. She'd told Hastings that he might draw only Jonathan, but not the reason: the information was still too raw.

I will do all I can in my power to return to you. Samuel might be all she had left. She shook her head at her morbid thoughts and watched him climb a tree.

"Do you need any... equipment?" Hastings winced as Samuel clumsily descended, tearing his shirtsleeve on a protruding branch. "I can see why you want to keep him out of the way."

"We're fine, thanks. He has a sketchpad and pencils. Be aware it might not work this time. Once you're set up near the border, we'll both join you permanently. Just a case of seeing what he does. Best to leave him to his own devices while I deal with Captain Honeyman."

Richard, with his ability to sense item location, was travelling with the army in order to keep track of the exploratory blimp. Given the distances involved, and his difficulty in locating the blimp Isabel had stolen, Susanna was attempting to help. She would monitor his power while he tracked the identity bracelets and the marker clips: if his power went out of focus, she could nudge him.

"Captain Honeyman is over here." Hastings walked towards the tents. "Any news from Queen Eleanor?"

"She's still working in the library, tracing old references for anything useful. She was wondering if people on the other side of the wastelands might have powers. But if they have powers, why would they need advanced *techne* like those sentinels? She didn't give me any specific messages. Oh, she did mention she'd bring some papers when she joins you." Eleanor wouldn't remain in the safety of the city once the army reached the border, though she'd agreed there was little point in marching with them. Solidarity only went so far.

When Hastings accompanied her inside the tent and helped Richard set up his folding table, Susanna's eyebrows rose. "I didn't think you would be staying."

He spread his hands. "I'm keen to learn what you find. But if you'd rather I waited outside..."

"No, it's fine. People aren't usually keen to watch the pain boxes in action." If only the Council had been more interested in the bad old days when everyone used pain to trigger powers.

Richard sniffed. "I'm ready when you are, Susanna."

After they both switched on their pain boxes, she absorbed the pain and took his hand. "They should be dropping the clips sequentially, so try to find Number One first. It'll be the closest." That was assuming Jonathan hadn't got blimp sick and muddled.

"Right." Richard closed his eyes, his hand hovering over the map. "Yes, Number One is here." He tapped the paper.

Hastings marked a cross in pencil.

"And Number Two..." His finger prodded a spot further south. "Here?"

Susanna focussed on the weave of Richard's power, now slightly bent. "Doing well," she murmured. "Can you manage a little more? Your power is holding up."

After several long seconds, Richard jabbed the map with a wince. "Number Three." Taking a deep breath, he mopped his brow with a linen handkerchief. "Number Four is still moving..."

"Number Three is thirty miles in." Hastings marked the map again. "Halfway to the sentinels. They should be within sight of them by the end of the day."

"I'm done." Richard flicked off his pain box with a trembling hand.

Hastings frowned. "Using your powers is more arduous than I'd expected."

Susanna concealed a smile as his truth strands confirmed his sincerity. Perhaps this was a useful lesson.

"Sir?" David's voice came from outside the tent.

Leaving Richard to recover, Susanna followed Hastings outside.

Samuel tugged Hastings' sleeve. "I did a drawing, mister. Just like you wanted."

Hastings' lips twitched, but he accepted Samuel's drawing graciously enough. Susanna had a look too. It showed a blimp in the air, jagged rocks underneath. The gondola held four figures, but only one was detailed enough to recognise.

Leaning over the side, Jonathan was clearly not enjoying the journey.

"Oh, dear," said Hastings with some amusement.

Jonathan groaned again and wiped his mouth. He'd thought he might get used to this mode of travel, but his airsickness was getting worse. At least in the wastelands there were no people to witness his bouts of illness, other than his fellow travellers. Who cared about dignity when they were in this together? But he was being a burden rather than setting a good example.

After crossing the border that morning, it had been as Isabel said. Shrubs and grass dwindled behind them. The grey soil gradually took on a reddish tinge. Rare pools of water, seen in the light of the now-descending sun, resembled splashes of blood rather than a natural resource. The dry air made Jonathan cough and threatened to distract him from dropping the marker clips every hour.

Peering through his spyglass, Artur inhaled sharply. "I can make out the sentinels on the horizon, all lined up. Maybe half a mile between them? Jonathan, what should we do?"

That decision wasn't difficult. "We should land. Maybe there's a dip where we're not so visible? We'll reconnoitre in daylight, see if they react to us. Might delay us slightly if we then decide to pass them tomorrow night. But it'll be safer."

This time, Jonathan didn't feel better with his feet on the ground as he scouted around their landing site, his steps causing puffs of red dust. Pebbles skittered underfoot, and he tripped a couple of times in ruts of hard-baked mud. No water was to be found nearby, and they opened the first of the barrels they'd brought.

Being so close to the sentinels, he ordered a cold meal. The cooled, shrunken balloon might escape detection, but a fire would shout their presence. Jonathan declined Isabel's offer to heat their reconstituted rations. No point in her expending power unnecessarily. He choked down the resulting gloop without complaint, but his gut silently protested. They opted to sleep in the blimp rather than on the uneven ground, and Jonathan agreed with Annetta to share the watch. The following day, they'd need Isabel and Artur in good form.

The night-time ambient temperature was mild. Disconcerted by the absence of noise, Jonathan strained his ears to hear *anything* other than his companions' soft breathing. An hour before dawn, once he could no longer keep his eyes open, he awakened Annetta for her turn, then he curled himself around his aching belly to sleep.

He awoke from a bad dream to the sound of retching. The sun had risen. Isabel and Artur snored softly, but Annetta was throwing up a short distance away.

Jonathan averted his eyes and panted until his reflex nausea abated. Annetta returned, rummaging in her bag. She offered him a pill. He took it.

Isabel squirmed around and stretched luxuriously. "Wassup?" She prodded Artur, who jerked up and scowled.

Annetta swallowed her own pill. "I'm feeling a bit off."

"Me too," said Jonathan. "I don't do well in blimps, but I thought I'd have recovered by now."

"Maybe the longer journey?" suggested Annetta.

Isabel grinned at Jonathan then eyed Annetta. "Pregnant, are you?"

"What?" Annetta gaped then turned red. "I shouldn't be! Sundrop root is *extremely* effective, and we took great care... Um, I suppose in theory there might have been a failure. Anyway, it's no business—"

Isabel held up a hand. "Sorry, I'm only teasing. Feeling a bit squiffy myself, actually. Wasn't like this last time." She went uncharacteristically quiet.

Artur's brow wrinkled. "I guess it's no surprise people get airsick, but I've never seen such a delayed effect before." He reached for his mug of leftover gloop and a spoon. "So, are we heading out on foot or in the blimp?"

Jonathan tried not to watch Artur eating, even if he couldn't completely ignore the slurping noises. "Isabel, can you take the spyglass and have a quick look at the sentinels? See if they're moving? Then we can try the decoy balloon."

"Gotcha." She slid over the side of the blimp—he envied how she could do that without getting her sabre tangled—and held out a hand for the spyglass. "Back in a few." She strode up the gentle slope.

"How are we for, uh, fuel?" Jonathan asked. Was that the right word?

"Electrical power? We're good," mumbled Artur around a mouthful of slop. "Propellor units still have three-quarters charge, so we're nowhere near needing the spare power cells. My only concern is the gas." He waved a hand upwards. "Even while cool, the gas in the balloon has upward lift. Good, in that we don't need much heat to take off, but bad, in that it's pretty visible. We'll have to dump the gas if we seriously need to hide. Still, that's why we have spare canisters."

That sounded good, didn't it? Artur was knowledgeable and experienced, and he could probably build a blimp from scratch. Isabel was naturally competent—nobility and a lethal power were just additional seasonings. Even Annetta had a good head on her shoulders when she wasn't dithering. So what was he, Jonathan, doing here? Being stubborn, of course. He'd do everything in his power to look after his comrades and stave off danger to Susanna and Tabitha.

Crunching footsteps announced Isabel's return. Looking up at them, she leaned against the gondola's side. "You landed us perfectly last night, Artur. The sentinels are exactly as I remember them. Maybe they're really fixed in place? Though their weapons are still moving to and fro. Mainly pointing upwards. Seems we'd be better on foot, tiptoeing past—Jonathan, can you hang on to this a moment?" She held up the spyglass.

Jonathan reached out of the gondola and accepted it. Then Isabel pulled a handkerchief from her pocket, coughed and spat out a gobbet of blood.

"Look," said Lester breathlessly. "You can't just run off like this."

"Just watch me!" Tabitha didn't even pause in her stride.

They were walking rapidly past Ascar's southern fields, and it looked as if Tabitha wouldn't stop until she arrived at the border. It was sheer luck Lester had passed the Royal Compound that morning and noticed her departure: in the absence of specific orders, he'd defaulted to patrolling the streets.

Tabitha wore a bulging backpack over her beige overalls, a couple of poles strapped to the outside. He glimpsed travel rations in the bag she held.

He grabbed at the bag, but she swung it out of the way. He raised a placating hand. "But why? What happened?"

At that, she stopped and looked up at him. "Do you know why they asked me to help in the infirmary? Even though there aren't any patients now?"

"No?"

"Because *Jonathan* told them I was to be kept safely out of the way, away from the front line. *That's* why he agreed to go!"

Lester's brow wrinkled. "He wants to protect you. That's nothing new, is it?"

"If it weren't for me, he wouldn't have had to go!" Her face worked, and her eyes glistened with tears.

He reached out to her, then paused. Of course it wasn't her fault, though he could imagine why she might think that. Even if he could bodily carry her back to the city, he could hardly lock her up. Best to reason with her. "Look, it's nothing to do with you." *Probably.* "The war—"

"I can help! I've learnt stuff in the infirmary, and I can help with chirurgery. There will be injuries on the front line, and I should be there, not kicking around in the empty Keep. Not even if that's what Jonathan wants. Anyway, you told me to grow up."

Damn. He should have kept his big mouth shut. "Well, how about we return to Ascar"—*while we still can*—"and request a blimp? That would be quicker."

She eyed him sideways. "You know they'd never agree. And if you try to drag me back, physically, I'll make such a fuss you'll wish you'd never been born."

Well, he wasn't doing much good in Ascar. What could he do but travel with her and offer his protection? At least he had his sabre. "How about I carry your bag?"

She glanced at him and handed it over, mumbling, "... didn't pack my dress..."

"Sorry?" He must have misheard.

"Nothing."

They walked on in silence. At her pace, she'd be at the border within two days. He hoped he could keep up.

"Uh, Tabitha?"

"What!"

"I hope you have enough food for me too."

Chapter 19

After assisting Isabel back into the blimp, Jonathan rechecked his flechette gun's power level: since he hadn't used it, it was still full. Artur pulled a multi-tool from his pocket and muttered something about calibration before inspecting the console.

Annetta scowled at Isabel, now slumped against the gondola's side. "You shouldn't sit up so quickly. It'll make you dizzy."

"I'm fine." Isabel sipped from her canteen.

"Nobody coughs up blood for no reason." She grabbed Isabel's other wrist. "Why didn't you seek medical care when it first started? Or when you got breathless? Any tendency to bruising, or excessive bleeding when"—she glanced at Jonathan and Artur—"um, you know..."

"Really. I've never had this before. And the coughing's settled. You fuss too much."

Annetta's gaze flicked around their arid surroundings, then she sagged. "Well, I guess we can't do anything about it now."

"Do we need to turn back?" asked Jonathan.

"Did anyone ever tell you how cute you look when you're concerned?" Isabel patted his cheek with a clammy hand while he tried not to snarl. "Your nose kinda scrunches up. We have a job to do. I can still lift the blimp when needed, so we should carry on. At least, until we see how the sentinels react."

Artur returned his tool to an overall pocket. "It's not a case of lifting—"

"Yeah, whatever. Jonathan, what's your plan?"

Great, *now* she let him take charge again, after that crack about his nose. "Since those sentinels don't seem to have noticed us, and they're aiming upwards, I'd thought of splitting up and sneaking past on foot. Though it would be safer if Annetta and Artur stay here while Isabel and I go." He glanced at Isael's wan face. "Or... I'll go by myself. That's safest."

Isabel shook her head. "What if you need backup?"

"Or what if you get injured or sick?" Annetta frowned at him, then she regarded the others. "It's not impossible. We've all been ill, apart from Artur. Hmm, I wonder..."

"What are you thinking?" asked Jonathan.

"Although we landed last night, Jonathan and I got sick this morning, after we'd both been on watch." She ducked her head. "Jonathan more than me. Isabel didn't become ill until after scouting. Artur's been fine, but he's hardly left the blimp. I bet there's something in the soil that's making us ill. If that's the case, we can't afford to stay here. We have to leave. All of us. And in the blimp rather than on foot."

"Are you sure?" asked Isabel.

"Of course I could be wrong, and it's not as if I've come across this before... But with how we've been feeling so far, it fits."

Jonathan stared. "I'd never have thought of that. I'd just assumed it was my blimp sickness. So we need to get moving, and the sooner the better. A damn shame it's daylight now. Artur, I'd intended to send the decoy balloon past the sentinels from the ground, but it won't be healthy to do that on foot. Can we do it from the air?"

"Sure. In fact, it's easier since we can launch it from a good altitude. But since we'll already be moving, you'll need to decide quickly whether we should follow it or back off." Artur glanced up at the balloon. "Assuming we carry on, we should aim to pass through the line of sentinels equidistant between a pair."

"I see. Any other ideas to minimise our risk of being noticed?" Or at least not provoking them.

"Hmm." He patted the console then peered over the side. "Their advanced *techne* might detect the powered propellors. We should switch all the power off and steer the old-fashioned way. I'll direct the three of you, watching for movement via the spyglass. Isabel provides lift to the balloon, with Jonathan and Annetta steering." He smiled weakly. "It's a good thing you had some practice already."

Sure. Ten minutes of wiggling levers made them experts. Jonathan attempted to return the smile.

"If it comes to the worst and there's a hostile response—" Artur swallowed. "Captain Richard will know how far we got, since we're wearing those tags."

"With luck, Samuel will draw Jonathan," added Annetta. "That might help too."

Jonathan's brow wrinkled. "I don't think he's guaranteed to draw me, is he? He might draw someone else."

"Um, maybe." Annetta wouldn't meet his eye while she rummaged in her bag. "We need to get moving quickly. Isabel, here's a tonic to soothe your throat."

Why was Annetta so uncomfortable when talking about Samuel? Hmm, she shared a suite with him in the Keep. Had the boy said something embarrassing about Jonathan? Whatever the reason, it didn't matter. Better concentrate on their mission, not get distracted by irrelevancies.

Jonathan held the decoy balloon's tethering string while Artur attached it to the levium canister and released the valve. Once fully inflated, the red and white-striped balloon was twice Isabel's height. It bounced against their full-sized balloon. Jonathan winced at its appearance, but it needed to be conspicuous. The team's next move would depend on how the sentinels reacted to it.

"Time to go?" Isabel grabbed Jonathan's arm and hauled herself up. Closing her eyes in concentration, she gripped the heating rod.

The balloon expanded, and the gondola left the ground.

Artur spat over the side and muttered, "We're in luck. Wind's pushing us in a good direction." He tucked the spyglass into a pocket and held up his hands where Jonathan and Annetta could see them. They'd adjust the passive fins according to his signals.

The balloon drifted towards the sentinels, one on either side. Artur had ordered no speaking, and Jonathan suppressed a moan as he tried to keep his balance on the wobbling floor. He hadn't realised how steady the powered propellors kept them. With one hand clutching the decoy's string, the other on his steering lever, he concentrated on Artur's hands.

The sentinels grew closer. Glinting reflections caught his eye as the spears swung back and forth.

Artur held up a hand and pointed at the decoy.

Right. Jonathan uncurled cramped fingers and released the stripy balloon. It rose, bumped gently against the large balloon and floated ahead.

Too slow. The quicker it moved, the more time they'd have to react. Jonathan clenched his jaw and reached into his core to summon his power. It thrummed, seeking release. He extended his free hand and *let go* towards the decoy.

The striped balloon picked up speed.

The sentinels' spears broke their rhythmic movement and aimed towards it.

Jonathan's eyes smarted as he tried not to blink. Would their decoy be obliterated?

The spears tracked it while it passed, and then they resumed their regular movements.

The decoy continued sedately on its way.

So far so good. Now it was their turn, but they were a much larger target. Only one way to find out. He licked his lips and nodded at Artur. They continued on towards the sentinels.

The breeze cooled Jonathan's sweating face, and the only sound was creaking from the ropes and an occasional clunk from the steering mechanism. A glance to each side confirmed they were passing the sentinels. The giant legs remained planted firmly on the ground.

The sentinel's weapons swung towards the blimp.

His breath caught. Did the sentinels know there were people now, or would they do no more than they had last time?

As Jonathan tensed, his power surged again, more than before. *Move!* He *let go*, pushing against the huge balloon. Nothing happened. An idiotic attempt. Powers could only achieve so much.

No attack came. Not yet.

Isabel waggled her fingers at him. Now what? Then she drew her flechette gun.

Shit! Jonathan shook his head and waved a frantic hand in negation. The guns would be useless at this distance.

And he didn't want to risk provoking the sentinels.

To his relief, Isabel rolled her eyes and put her gun away.

After several long, painful breaths, he was sure the sentinels were shrinking. They'd passed them unscathed. Still, they'd better get further away before counting their hatchlings. They continued on in silence.

An hour later, Jonathan could see no sign of the sentinels behind him. He sniffed. The air carried the scent of damp grass. Annetta peered over the side and pointed. Steeling his stomach, he looked down. Ordinary-looking soil, not red earth. Even patches of greenery. A bird warbled.

Isabel whispered, "Artur, time to start up the propellors and get us landed somewhere safe."

"Sure." The engineer pressed a few buttons, then he frowned. He tapped the console, jabbed more buttons and leaned over the side. Clenching his jaw, he returned to the console and thumped it with a fist.

Jonathan swallowed. "A problem?"

"The engines are dead!" Artur's eyes were the widest he'd ever seen them.

His stomach dropped into his boots. Of all the misfortunes, he hadn't even considered the possibility of a *techne* failure. "Are we going to die?" He managed to keep his voice steady.

Artur hunched and muttered something to himself. Then he stood up straight. "No, we can manage. Isabel, keep us at this altitude. I'll pick a suitable landing spot, then we just need to steer there manually. Thank the Settlers the backup equipment is still standard, even if it adds extra weight..."

From the glimpses Jonathan caught while steering, the terrain was hilly. Even he could tell it wasn't ideal for landing.

Artur pointed to a flat spot of grass by a copse of trees. He directed Jonathan and Annetta to nudge the fins until the balloon's gas cooled enough for descent.

It was a relief when the gondola settled on to moist, grassy ground. Normal ground, not like the cursed or whatever terrain they'd spent the last two days passing over.

Jonathan climbed out. "I'll check it's safe before we tie up. Or whatever you call it."

"Hang on," said Artur. "Does your flechette gun still work?"

Jonathan flicked the switch on his gun. Nothing happened. He tapped the power display, which remained stubbornly blank. His shoulders tensed. "Isabel?"

After returning a bloodstained handkerchief to her pocket, Isabel drew her weapon and fiddled with it. "Nope."

They were stuck in hostile territory with no power. What was this land, that *techne* didn't work?

Susanna squinted down at the army encampment while the operators readied the blimp for landing. Cooking fires and handcarts separated neat rows of tents. Two tethered blimps hovered on either side of her. From this vantage point, she could see the border with the wastelands a mile away: a blurred demarcation where the terrain changed from grassy flatlands to a dull brown.

"This is fun!" Samuel beamed as he scooted from one side to the other, craning his neck to look around.

As the gondola wobbled, she resisted the temptation to clutch his blue overalls: an indicator of non-combatant status, similar to her own attire. The child wasn't addled enough to climb out before they landed, she hoped. He'd not inherited his father's serious attitude or sense.

"I believe the Armstrong coefficient doesn't apply at this altitude," said Eleanor. Dressed in purple overalls, she was in full flow speaking gibberish with the operators.

"Did you understand any of that?" muttered Paton in Susanna's ear. Still in his red uniform, he'd spent the journey from Ascar alternately gawping at the scenery and scowling at Eleanor's back.

The boot was on the other foot, for once, but Susanna resisted the temptation to tease him. "Not I, Paton. It's a completely different language. Worse than Noble Ascarite. Are you enjoying your first blimp trip?"

"I go where Her Majesty goes. I can hardly protect her by remaining on the ground." His voice took on a plaintive tone. "But I wish she wouldn't try to *explain* this stuff to me. It makes my head hurt."

Hastings waited at the landing site with six soldiers. He offered an arm to Susanna as she climbed down from the gondola, then he lifted a giggling Samuel out from Paton's grasp before setting the boy down. Eleanor finished her conversation with the operators and slid over the side as if born in the gondola. Paton clambered awkwardly down the rope ladder.

The soldiers unloaded Eleanor's belongings—mainly documents—and accompanied Paton to the royal tent.

Standing behind Hastings, Franka waved at Susanna. "Want me to take Samuel?"

Susanna pushed Samuel in her direction. "Go on. I'll catch up with both of you later."

"Hey, kiddo." Franka led Samuel away. "Sweets first,

or..."

Hastings bowed to Eleanor. "Your Majesty, welcome to our encampment."

Eleanor drew herself up. She didn't even reach Hastings' shoulder. "Thank you, Commander Hastings. I was pleased to see everything so well organised on my aerial survey. And I noticed you have squads clearing the old road towards the south."

"Indeed. Marching will be no challenge along that route."

"I commend your forward thinking and preparation, but remember—we must not initiate any hostile interaction."

He stiffened. "Might I ask why you agreed to my establishing a base here, if you don't intend us to fight? Our brave lads and lasses are fully prepared—"

"To keep our people safe. Not to attack without provocation."

A few soldiers paused to stare. Susanna's neck tightened. It wouldn't do for rumours of disagreement to start.

Eleanor swallowed. "Perhaps, Commander Hastings, we could continue this discussion later?"

He nodded sharply. "Agreed."

"The tethered blimps are an excellent idea." The queen's smile didn't touch her eyes. "I take it they're watching the border round the clock."

"They are. I'm grateful to Your Majesty for assigning all the blimps for army use. I hope this doesn't inconvenience the scientists' plans." Hastings nodded at Susanna. "Although I understand that road travel has rendered blimps unnecessary for your work."

Susanna waved a dismissive hand. "Not a problem.

Only Lester travelled by blimp, and he hasn't needed one for some time." The young captain was better off staying in Ascar for now.

Hastings gestured to the encampment, and Eleanor accepted his invitation to show her around.

"I hope you don't mind if I tag along and stretch my legs," said Susanna. If there were trouble brewing, better that she know about it.

Eleanor nodded politely to the soldiers who were seeing to weapon maintenance while others repaired uniforms. Susanna's fingers twitched. It had been a long time since she mended her own uniforms, and it would have been inappropriate to bring her embroidery.

As they approached the cooking fires and the soldiers preparing lunch, Franka approached and saluted Hastings. She held a paper. "Sir, Samuel's made another sketch."

"Good." Hastings accepted the paper and held it up so Eleanor and Susanna could see.

Susanna's shoulders relaxed when she scrutinised the drawing. Jonathan stood by a clump of green trees beside a blocky blue structure resembling a blimp if she squinted. Three vague figures in the background reassured her they'd all landed safely.

"Where is the boy?" asked Hastings.

Franka smirked. "Raiding the mess tent. Said he was too hungry to wait for lunch."

Chapter 20

After Jonathan checked that the immediate area was unpopulated—undulating grasslands with copses of deciduous trees—he returned to find his three companions filling the gondola with rocks to weigh it down. The balloon bobbed half-heartedly, its fabric sagging.

Artur squinted at the foliage and shook his head. "Still too visible. I was afraid of that. Jonathan, we need to dump the gas."

Jonathan's gut clenched. "But then we can't return." They couldn't hold back an army by themselves, could they?

"It's fine." Artur didn't look that convinced. "That's why we brought extra versium." He ran his hand along the balloon fabric and unscrewed a cap. Gas hissed out, and the balloon deflated while he climbed back into the gondola.

Annetta picked up a handful of soil and rubbed it between her fingers. "Feels normal." She sniffed it. "And smells normal." She peered at the ground. "And I can see lady's blossom leaves and... some kind of sage. I think we're safely away from the toxic area. But Isabel needs to recover."

"I'm fine." The sweat on Isabel's face belied her words.

Annetta scowled. "You've been coughing up blood again. Don't think I haven't noticed. And I can hear you wheezing from here. Unless it's a dire emergency, it's rest time for you, young woman!"

Isabel's eyebrows shot up. "That's me told, eh?"

Artur's laugh turned into a cough at Annetta's glower. "Here." He tossed a bedroll over the gondola's side, and she unrolled it.

Jonathan shook his head in bemusement. "If you pass me the hand spade, I'll fix up a smokeless fire. Or do you need help with the blimp?"

Artur handed over the tool and returned to flipping through his plans. "Not right now. I may be able to rig up better steering. Plenty of rope with us, fortunately, since it's standard-issue for tethering."

After Jonathan gathered kindling and dry wood, he constructed a fire. Then he sought something else to do. Artur and Annetta both declined his help—no surprise, since he had nothing to offer—so he paced around, scanning the horizon.

When he nearly tripped over Isabel, Annetta said, "Why not sit down for a rest? It's only a couple of hours till the sun sets, and we can hardly explore in the dark. Plus, we all need to recover, not just Isabel."

He couldn't explain why he felt restless, or his sense of disquiet at the contrast between those sentinels and this seemingly harmless terrain. Where was the unseen hazard? "I need to stretch my legs, so I might as well explore further. Might even find something edible."

Spyglass in hand, he set off southwards. He left his useless flechette gun behind but took his sabre.

As he walked, he took in lush grass, bushes dotted around, even clumps of yellow flowers pushing their way through the soil. The fresh scent of leaves relaxed him. He panted while ascending a slope, enjoying the burn in his leg muscles. Far preferable to being stuck in the air while sick.

Maybe he could find a stream where they could wash off the stench of illness.

At the top of the hill, he pulled out his spyglass. On looking east, his grip on the instrument tightened.

The slopes of the neighbouring hill bore fields of crops and a cluster of huts, smoke rising into the air. People moved between the houses. Even at this distance, he could make out vibrant clothing: shirts, skirts and tunics. Susanna would have been envious of the colours. Any weapons weren't obvious, and one woman carried an infant. Maybe a civilian village? Tomorrow he would approach more closely and glean further information—

The glint of another spyglass reflected back at him.

Shit. Of course he was silhouetted against the setting sun. How foolish.

He'd better warn the others. Poised to lope back to the camp, he hesitated. An image of Isabel, pale and sweaty, arose in his mind. The other two would be no help in a fight, and even Isabel would be vulnerable. What use would warning them be? He'd simply lead the enemy to the others and then they'd all be caught or worse. No, better that Jonathan lead the enemy away. If he didn't return, they'd know he'd run into trouble: trouble he couldn't overcome. Once Isabel recovered—of course she would—she'd be able to look after the others.

Pulling a pencil and paper from his pocket, he wrote:

Some friends to the east noticed me. I've gone to say hello.

His forehead wrinkled as he regarded his sabre. Approaching with it would signify hostile intent, and his companions might need the spyglass.

He left the two items on top of his note and walked eastwards, empty-handed.

Eleanor frowned at Hastings, who sat opposite her in his tent. Cooking pans rattled outside, and the smell of burnt onions drifted through the flap. Paton still hadn't returned from sorting her accommodation. Not that he could help her with politics, but his presence would have been a comfort. Especially now, when she was in Hastings' territory. "We agreed on a week, John. I see no reason for haste."

The folding table creaked under his elbows. "Your desire to avoid conflict is admirable, but I fear inappropriate in the current situation. I fully agree it was necessary to send a scouting team. But on further consideration, a week seems too generous. The blimp is moving much faster than we can march. If the blimp's approach forewarns the enemy, that gives them greater time to prepare. We should start moving tomorrow. The initial terrain looks easy to traverse—bare but flat—but it may become more difficult further in. The sooner we set off, the less overall strain on our troops."

She clenched her fists. "I agree that we should be prepared to move, not that we should initiate hostilities."

"My reading got me to wondering," murmured Hastings, "just when the monarch should hand over command in times of war. Rapid decisions may be needed, and uncertainty over leadership could lead to dangerous misunderstandings. At this time, it would be better for someone who has studied the craft to be in command."

"But I haven't declared us at war." Once she did, her absolute power would be suspended for the duration. She didn't believe they'd reached that point yet, but maybe she was causing harm by not allowing Hastings to take charge.

She couldn't fully disagree with him about her unsuitability.

"I'm as hopeful as you are that whatever they discover will be innocuous." He leaned forwards. "It's laudable that you are so concerned about the party. And completely natural that you worry about Captain Hanlon, as she's your only living relative." He lowered his voice. "It's such a pity there's no Queen's Discretion allowed in cases of regicide."

Now he chose to act on what he'd overheard. Eleanor struggled to keep a calm expression.

"I discovered in my reading," he continued, "that once we are at active war, all civilian laws—including those pertaining to regicide—are suspended. It seems a logical practice since it would be a time when desperate measures might be, ah, forgiven. I have a lot of admiration for Captain Hanlon. Should she survive, I'm sure her continuing contributions to the realm would be highly valued."

Thank the Settlers, Hastings wasn't the only one who did his research. Those days in the library had yielded information she could use here. "Would such forgiveness be retrospective?"

Hastings' smile faded. "I'm not clear on that. You have truly been under a lot of strain, and it would be quite understandable if you wished to step—"

"I also found something out." Nerves twanging, Eleanor gave Hastings a hard stare. It was as well she'd brought those papers. "If I dissolve the monarchy—and it's certainly a royal prerogative to do so—all specific crimes against royalty are rendered void from the moment of the declaration. Of course, that doesn't signify a general amnesty. A new head of state would be chosen by the populace. Who knows who might win an open election?"

Her heart hammered while she maintained eye contact with him. A muscle in his cheek twitched, and she fought the urge to blink.

At length, Hastings sighed. "It looks like an impasse. I have the good of the realm at heart."

"So do I." They just had different approaches towards it.

"I am not your enemy, Your—Eleanor." His expression was grave. "But for many years I worked with your father. He'd mentioned your innovative mind and gentle nature. I am concerned that the latter may prove a handicap when ruthlessness is called for. He wouldn't have hesitated—"

"Then maybe my father was wrong as well. I am not declaring us at war." Her shoulders sagged. "Not yet."

Eleanor left Hastings' tent feeling ill. She'd delayed his advance, but for how long? She couldn't think what to do. Isabel might have provided advice and a smile, but it was Isabel who was the problem now. Could she give up her realm to save Isabel's life? *Should* she? What might happen to her people under Hastings' governance? It would be easier if she knew Isabel wasn't coming back—No. She wouldn't think of that.

Chapter 21

Jonathan descended the hill and walked in the direction of the people he had spotted, making no particular attempt at stealth. They'd already noticed him, after all. If they attacked him, he'd defend himself as best he could. If they merely captured him, that might be a good thing: an opportunity to observe them more closely. And he wasn't a novice at escaping. Such an irony that his formerly reviled power was now a secret weapon.

His route took him past clumps of trees, and he splashed across a narrow stream. On the other side, he paused to wring water from his trouser legs. Laughter and the chatter of children's voices came from the direction of the village.

Strange. There were no sounds of alarm. He should use his time wisely.

If he offered no threat, might children be less wary than adults? Perhaps he could learn something from them. A pity he had no prior experience with children of his own. Well, in theory he might have—most convoy guards obtained companionship on their travels—but there was a tacit acknowledgement such arrangements were transitory. The guards weren't encouraged to make enquiries afterwards.

As he passed through a wooded area, a low grunt came from the clearing ahead, along with an odd, rank smell. His forehead creased. That didn't sound like children, or even adults. Knees creaking in a half-crouch, he crept behind some bushes and peeked.

Beasts! Jonathan's breath caught, and his hand slapped his empty scabbard. Three of them, facing away from him, one so close he could have reached out and placed his hand on its back. Two curved horns carved the air as it raised its head, muscles twitching under its shaggy grey pelt.

His leg quivered, and he eased back half a pace, trying not to shake the concealing foliage. Did they depend on sight or smell? Could he circle around? And why were they so close to the village?

Leaves swished to his left, and a small girl—maybe six years old—marched into the clearing. An equally small boy followed her. Each held a short stick.

While Jonathan gaped in horror, the two children giggled and waved their sticks in the air.

The beasts snorted and turned towards them.

No!

He launched himself out of the bushes and stumbled in front of the children, pushed them away and spun to face the beasts. "Run!"

Squeals and the patter of departing footsteps gave him some relief. The children would remain safe. He spread his arms to draw the beasts' attention, dropped his right hand and squeezed the old injury on his thigh.

Pain. His power surged, and he extended his arm towards the frontmost beast. It lifted a forefoot and snuffled. Would that one attack first? If he drove off the leader, would the others flee? How long could he hold them at bay? His power was still recover—

Jonathan opened his eyes and squinted. Outlined against the sky, a ring of faces looked down at him. Human faces, not beasts. Three belonged to fair-haired women, and one to a bearded man who leaned on a staff. Peeping out from behind a striped blue skirt were two chubby little faces: one with a blonde braid, and one with short dark hair. The children he'd rescued. He eased out a breath.

Why was he lying down? He didn't *feel* injured. He wriggled his toes in his boots, took a deep breath, flexed his fingers—

Someone was holding his hand.

He turned his head. A young woman with black, waist-length hair and a homespun tunic crouched next to him, her eyes closed. As his gaze reached her face, she smiled. Ears heating, he smiled back and tried to tug his hand out of hers without yanking.

She opened her eyes, patted his hand and released it, then waved at their audience who retreated a pace. Each of them lifted a staff in a firm grip. *Careful, Shelley.* They might not have attacked him yet, but he didn't want to provoke anyone.

After rolling on to his side, Jonathan slowly pushed himself up into a kneeling position. Spots danced in front of his eyes. Bracing himself, he took a few breaths and looked around again. He blinked.

Behind the bearded man stood the three beasts he'd seen earlier. One now had a rope round its neck, tethering it to a staff planted in the ground. As he watched, it lowered its head and tore up a chunk of grass. It regarded him with incurious eyes while it chewed.

He gaped. Of course there were vegetarian animals— beasts had to eat something—but he'd never come across anything that size. And these people domesticated them? Treated them like chickens and geese, maybe?

The tallest fair-haired woman stepped towards him and said, "Ooroowayrow?"

He shrugged. "Sorry."

She scowled and lifted her staff.

He didn't need to pretend fear and confusion as he raised his empty hands. The black-haired woman shook her head and muttered something. His interrogator pursed her lips but lowered her staff.

The black-haired woman grasped his hand again, and he tensed. Did she plan to restrain him so the others could beat him up? He narrowed his eyes at the tall woman. She'd be his first target. If he could snatch her staff with his power—

The grip on his hand tightened, and his scalp prickled. The woman placed her other hand on his shoulder, leaned forwards and murmured into his ear, "Who you name?"

Jonathan's jaw dropped. She was speaking Noble Ascarite rather than the modern language used by all citizens. Where had she learned that? Only officials, captains and the occasional historian learned the archaic tongue, and only in its written form. Damn. Of his companions, only Isabel would have a chance to understand it, and she was unwell. Even if Artur or Annetta found this place, they would have no idea.

Regarding his face, the woman cocked her head quizzically. His hand started to sweat in hers as he groped in the recesses of his memory. *I am. You are. He is. We are.*

"I is Jonathan," he managed.

"I be Mirra." She pointed at the others, giving each a name. The tall woman was Berna, the man Gregor. The two other women were Tasha and Yvette, although he could only differentiate them by their clothing. Tasha's blue skirt—to which the children Tonio and Astra clung—was more voluminous than Yvette's red skirt.

Jonathan's shoulders relaxed with the introductions, and he let his free hand drop. Mirra still held his other hand, now in both of hers.

He faced her. "What you do with me?"

She frowned briefly, and he tried not to squirm as her gaze tracked from his face to the ground where he knelt. Even during the medical checkups in the Keep, he'd never felt so closely evaluated.

At last, she said, "You captive."

That was no surprise. It was he who had intruded on them uninvited. Of course they'd see him as potentially hostile. Still, given the rural feel of the place and lack of *techne* so far, he couldn't see these people controlling the sentinels. Despite that, he'd better not let slip that he had companions. Once he'd learned what he could from these people, if they didn't release him he'd have to escape.

Mirra pointed at the horizon, where the sun was setting. "We feed you, watch you overnight." She had a brief exchange with the others, speaking too rapidly and fluidly for Jonathan to understand.

Shortly afterwards, Jonathan was marched to the village. They passed a few darkened huts on the way to the centre. In the village square a fire crackled underneath a cauldron of simmering stew. The villagers queued up with pottery bowls while the cook ladled out the evening meal. Hmm. Such a communal practice supported his initial impression the village was small.

Jonathan's captors rigged up an awning near the fire and set a quilted blanket on the ground.

"Warm, see?" Gregor grinned as he tied Jonathan's ankles together with a rope, allowing him enough slack to shuffle. He then fetched a bowl of food, which he handed to Jonathan with a wooden spoon.

The stew included chunks of succulent tender meat in a rich, thick sauce lightened by tart, crunchy vegetables. All in all, a favourable comparison to their blimp rations. He mopped up the last traces with a piece of soft bread. After he finished eating, Gregor tied his wrists together. On the other side of the dying fire, his allocated guard—Berna—sat on a wooden stool, a heap of knitting on her lap.

Carrying a toddler, a woman plodded past. She greeted Berna while the child stuck a thumb in its mouth and stared at Jonathan with wide eyes. He waggled his eyebrows and was rewarded with smiles from both mother and child.

The sun set, and Jonathan lay down, gazing into the embers. The click of knitting needles encouraged him to relax. Even though he was a prisoner in a village apparently lacking advanced luxuries, he was pretty comfortable. And initial encounter aside, they seemed peaceful.

Skirt swishing, a dark figure approached. It was Mirra.

"Tomorrow morning, you tell where from." She stroked his cheek. "You sleep now."

"Yes," mumbled Jonathan. His lids lowered. He was so very sleepy.

"Then we fetch your friends."

He forced his eyes open, but she was gone.

"Your Majesty?" Paton's worried voice came from outside the tent.

"Come in." Eleanor returned her maps to their folder and turned down the oil lamp. No point wasting fuel, and the sun was nearly up anyway. She flexed her neck from side to side. "You don't need to stand on ceremony here."

Paton coughed. "Commander Hastings and Chief Scientist Longleaf need to speak with you."

"Oh. One moment."

Outside, Hastings stood rigidly at attention beside Susanna, who was rubbing her temples. Even in the pre-dawn dimness, shadows gathered beneath her eyes.

Eleanor frowned. "What's the problem?"

Hastings proffered a paper. "Samuel's done another drawing. It's of concern."

The boy had again drawn Jonathan, tied up beside a bonfire. Beside him, an indistinct figure wielded a spike in each hand.

Eleanor's blood chilled. Captured, and under threat of torture. She took a deep breath. First things first. "I don't suppose he's drawn the others?"

"He only draws what's around Jonathan." Susanna's cheeks darkened, and her voice wobbled. "We're not sure why. Richard checked their locations. They're all past the border. The other three are clustered together, and they haven't moved from the campsite Samuel drew earlier."

Chest tight, she bowed her head. Given Isabel's fragility even before the team left, it seemed likeliest she and the others had met their end, with only Jonathan surviving.

Hastings patted his sheathed sabre. "Captain Shelley has been captured. The others may be"—he glanced at Eleanor—"ah, unavailable. Is that a good enough reason to get moving?"

Grief clogged her throat. She'd sent them to their deaths. Her naïve wish for a peaceful outcome had killed them. After such a misjudgement, how could *she* decide what to do next? Hastings had been right all along. "Yes.

You've got what you've been pushing for."

Paton gave her a sympathetic glance and extended his arm.

"Pay heed to Her Majesty!" Hastings' voice boomed across the encampment.

Nearby soldiers paused in their breakfast duties while sleepy faces appeared at tent flaps.

Clutching the solidity of Paton's arm, Eleanor raised her voice to a shout. "I, Queen Eleanor, declare that our war status is active. Commander-in-Chief Hastings is now in charge."

Before the echo of her words died away, Hastings saluted her and called, "Troops, we march at midday. Pack up and prepare."

Excited chatter met Eleanor's ears. She pinched the bridge of her nose, wishing for nothing more than a quiet spot to mourn. But she still had duties to—

"You're *not* sending me back!" came a girlish shriek from the edge of the camp.

Susanna's head jerked up. "That's Tabitha!"

"Paton, can you fetch her?" Eleanor frowned. She'd promised Jonathan she'd keep Tabitha in safety. She should respect his last wishes.

"Who's that?" asked Hastings.

Susanna sighed. "A fifteen-year-old girl who's been training her telekinetic power in the infirmary. Jonathan was—*is*—very fond of her." Her voice cracked. "The daughter he never had."

Paton returned with Tabitha, who stomped up to the group with a scowl.

Lester limped after them while brushing dried mud off his uniform. "I tried to stop her," he muttered.

Susanna jabbed a finger at him. "You idiot! Why did you leave Ascar?" Her head swivelled round at the others, and she let her hand fall. "I'll talk to you later."

Lester flinched and backed away, his mouth dropping open at the sketch in Hastings' hand. "That's Jonathan!"

"Show me!" Tabitha extended a hand.

Hastings' eyebrows rose, but he handed it over. "You certainly have gumption, Miss Tabitha."

"Paton," said Eleanor, "arrange a blimp to take Tabitha back to Ascar. And maybe Lester."

"As you command, your Maj—"

"Wait." Hastings held up a hand. "Since she's medically trained, she'll be invaluable in the treatment tents. She should stay."

Eleanor tensed. Now she'd handed over power, she couldn't order him around anymore. Her status was reduced to a precious token, but she could still argue. "A battleground is no place for a child—"

"I quite understand, Your Majesty, and I shall do all I can to protect her. Tabitha, you want to stay, don't you?"

"Yes." She thrust the paper back at him. "I want to help you get whoever did this to him!"

"That's settled, then." Hastings nodded at Eleanor. "It will take us five days to march across the wastelands at a moderate pace. You have expressed an intention to travel with the army, and I'm sure morale will benefit. But if physical danger approaches, you must flee. A blimp will be kept on standby for you at all times. Take Paton with you, of course..." His eye fell on Tabitha. "And Tabitha too. Satisfied?"

What could Eleanor say? "Yes, Commander-in-Chief Hastings."

Chapter 22

Jonathan awoke to a rooster's crow. The air was pleasantly cool, with a hint of damp. He massaged his jaw where the wrist bindings had left a crease, then levered himself upright with a groan.

Gregor tended a pot of porridge bubbling on the fire before him. The guard from last night had disappeared.

After giving the porridge a final stir, Gregor untied Jonathan's ropes. "Morning good."

"Morning." He accepted a bowl containing a dollop of porridge. When Gregor picked up a jug and poured a white liquid on top, his brow wrinkled. "What this?"

"Milk." At Jonathan's uncomprehending look, Gregor screwed up his face, then extended his arms and made squeezing motions with his fingers. "Unnerstan?"

"Huh?"

"Good for healthy bones." Gregor laughed. "See later."

How strange. Still, it tasted fine, a rich coating on his tongue as he swallowed, and there was no reason to suspect poison.

Hunger satisfied, Jonathan cautiously stood and took a few experimental steps away from the fire. A pair of villagers nodded as they passed him, each carrying a bucket of water. On the other side of the square, a few children played hopscotch in the dirt.

Under guise of stretching exercises, Jonathan glanced around. Several wooden huts surrounded the square. For rural buildings, they were of remarkably uniform size and shape with thatched roofs and shutters covering unglazed windows. Maybe a couple of dozen dwellings, from his spyglass survey yesterday. That would make the village population somewhere between fifty and a hundred? About the size of Keighley, that village Annetta and Samuel hailed from. Would the villagers pursue Jonathan if he fled, or be glad he was gone?

Or maybe they communicated with some larger, more advanced settlement. But in that case, why untie him rather than waiting for orders? No. They must be what they seemed: a small, peaceful village. No signs of wanting to invade anyone. Might they even face the same danger of invasion as Numoeath did? It would be wise to stay for a while and find out what he could. Susanna had chided him for impulsive behaviour in the past. He'd take her advice to heart and be patient.

Mirra approached, and he gave her a tentative wave. Today she wore a dappled green tunic and leggings. On her feet were sturdy rope sandals of the type ruralites wore for travel, and she carried a staff.

She took his hand and squeezed his fingers. "Morning good."

"Uh, morning." Under other circumstances, Jonathan would have disengaged, but he didn't want to appear unfriendly.

She sank gracefully into a cross-legged position, and his knees creaked when he attempted to do the same. Maybe he should have worked harder on those stretching exercises.

She gazed into his eyes. "What is the place you come from?"

He blinked. "How come I understand you so well now?"

"Ahh..." She tapped her temple. "I can tell what you mean, yes? Help to learn."

Oh. She was a mind reader? Like Susanna? Last night's words about his friends fell into place, and his hand trembled in her grasp. Had he inadvertently put them in danger?

"Shh." Mirra stroked his hand. "Your friends are in no danger from us. Why would they be?"

He tried to concentrate. "You want to invade—"

Her laugh showed even, white teeth. "We're happy here. The land provides for our needs. What more could *your* country give us?"

Weapons? Blimps? Mass production? Why would such a small settlement need such things? He relaxed. Certainly, from what he'd seen, the area was fertile. There was plenty of space to expand, just like with the rural towns in Numoeath. And those places like Maldon and Keighley would have been flabbergasted at the idea of attacking someone else's territory. "Why did you capture me?"

She raised an eyebrow. "You appeared from nowhere, frightened our children, threatened our livestock."

"Uh, sorry." The back of his neck warmed. She was right.

"I had to make you sleep. And then checked you weren't dangerous."

"Right." Those poor children. What must they have thought? And he'd believed he was helping them. It just went to show how different—

"Now we know you're not, we can go and fetch your friends. They must be worried about you."

Jonathan's brow creased. Was that a bad idea or not? Mirra placed a cool hand on his forehead. Well, she knew about the others already, and the villagers certainly hadn't mistreated him. It wouldn't do any harm. Besides, he was worried about Isabel. She might need more medical help than Annetta could provide.

He cleared his throat. "Good idea."

Avoiding the spot where he'd left his sabre, Jonathan retraced his steps towards the campsite. Mirra walked beside him while Tasha and Yvette followed. Each held a staff. Yvette also carried a canvas sheet, which Mirra explained could be used as a stretcher.

Annetta met him with a worried expression, wiping her hands on a cloth. "I'm so glad you're back, and that you've brought help! We had no idea where you'd gone. Isabel's fevered, and I gave her a sleeping infusion…"

Isabel was snoring, cocooned in a singed, damp bedroll.

Fever and a pyrokinetic certainly wasn't a good combination. Tasha and Yvette pointed at the collapsed blimp and whispered to each other. He tried to ignore their giggles as he briefly explained to Annetta and Artur about the village and the odd language.

"Mirra's been very helpful." Her fingers twitched in his. "She understands what I mean, even if I can't say it too well."

Annetta nodded awkwardly at the three villagers.

"They certainly look friendly enough." Artur rubbed the back of his neck. "We'll follow your lead."

Under Annetta's instructions, they transferred Isabel to the stretcher carried by Tasha and Yvette.

Jonathan frowned at the blimp, its balloon weighted flat with rocks. "Artur, should we do something with this?"

Artur shook his head. "I think our gear is as safe here as anywhere. Best not to move it. I know the balloon looks pathetic, but it's the best configuration for reinflation. Once the canister's attached and the valve released, the pressure will—"

Jonathan raised a hand. "I believe you."

When they returned to the village, Mirra allocated an empty hut by the square for Isabel and Annetta's use. One of the twins—he'd already lost track of which—fetched the village healer. He was a plump bald man in a homespun robe.

Jonathan and Artur hovered in the doorway of the hut until Annetta stepped forwards.

"Artur, you're no use here," she said. "Go and rest or something. Jonathan, I can't understand Healer Markov, so you need to stay and translate. I believe he might be able to help with Isabel's chest." She glared at him. "But no ogling when we undress her."

"Of course not." What did she take him for?

Aided by Jonathan's dubious translation attempts, Annetta obtained a bowl of hot water. Meanwhile, Markov placed his hands on Isabel's chest and frowned at the ceiling.

With Annetta's herbs added to the bowl, the hut filled with a bracing vapour.

Markov lifted his hands, shaking them lightly. "Not too late for her. Good. Now we eat." He led Jonathan to the cooking fire where the villagers had gathered for the midday meal and pointed at a space beside Artur. "You stay here. I take food back to your friends."

After the healer had left, Artur nudged Jonathan's arm. "Did you see how they lit the fire? That bearded chap"—he pointed at Gregor—"placed his hand on top of the kindling and set it alight. With his bare hand!"

"Like Isabel?"

"Yes! And nobody even stopped to watch. Well, apart from the woman with the cooking pot. What's the food like?"

Jonathan shook his head. From a land where powers were a governmental secret, to a society in which they seemed unexceptional. "Food's good. Though I'm not sure I want to know what's in the stew."

Artur rubbed his belly. "I was getting a bit tired of those travel rations."

After relaxing under a leafy tree for a post-lunchtime nap—when did he ever get the opportunity for those?—Jonathan checked on Isabel and Annetta. They weren't alone. The two children he'd "rescued" were giggling as they rolled polished stones around the wooden floor.

Annetta removed her hand from Isabel's wrist. "Pulse is good. She's breathing more easily, and she woke up for a few minutes. But we shouldn't disturb her while she's recovering."

"Uh, and..." He waved a hand at the children.

"I'm keeping an eye on them for Tasha, and Tasha can watch Isabel over dinner." Her nose wrinkled. "I did feel a bit trapped in this hut while you and Artur were strolling around."

Jonathan winced. He'd thought Annetta would want to avoid all these strangers, but he shouldn't be assuming things on her behalf. No. He wasn't being honest with himself. He hadn't really thought about her that afternoon. "Sorry."

"Never mind." She pursed her lips.

Annetta joined Jonathan and Artur for dinner, but Jonathan was the only one who could communicate unaided. With some amusement, Mirra helped with introductions. Jonathan provided the background to their blimp mission and what he understood of the reasoning behind it. Although emphasising Eleanor's desire to avoid hostilities, he tried to make Numoeath's defensive army sound impressive.

Sweat trickled down his neck as he regarded the silent villagers. "We thought those sentinels were an advance force. We readied an army. And our ruler sent the four of us here to investigate."

Trying to ignore Mirra's lifted eyebrow, he sipped water from a pottery cup. The villagers murmured to each other, some shaking their heads and chuckling. Yvette giggled and patted Artur's arm. Mirra stood and walked away.

Jonathan frowned at her retreating back, and his breath hitched. Diplomacy wasn't his forte. His clumsy words might have endangered the realm. Had he made a mistake, lulling himself into believing there was no enemy here? Still, he could hardly have said anything else, not if they could mind-read and detect lies.

But there were no shouts of outrage. Annetta stared into the fire while the villagers cleared up after dinner. They dispersed, leaving Jonathan, Artur and Annetta sitting by the fire with Yvette. She seemed to have taken a liking to Artur. On the other side of the fire, a few men played dice, occasionally glancing over.

Mirra returned. She supported an old woman who walked with a cane. "Our eldest. Sofia."

The woman certainly looked ancient. Hazy eyes regarded Jonathan, then she reached out and patted his cheek. "You a mover. Using skill cleverly."

Right. That would be his power.

She shook her head at Artur. "Ouch, death reader. Nasty. Stay away from those facing death. Dangerous."

Artur's brow furrowed, and Jonathan murmured a translation.

Finally, she turned to Annetta and sniffed. "And a defective."

Annetta looked enquiringly at Jonathan.

What could he say? He owed her honesty. "She says you're a defective. Sorry."

Annetta went pinker than the cooking fire merited. "What?"

Yvette took Artur's hand. Mirra took Jonathan's and Annetta's. An initial tickle in Jonathan's head faded as Mirra spoke. It transpired that nearly all adults developed powers naturally, a gift from the land.

"In fact," said Sofia, "in ancient times, they would drive away defectives in times of famine and scarcity."

"When was the last time?" asked Jonathan.

"Hundreds of years ago." She waved a hand. "No need now. Plenty of resources, and there are always menial jobs for the defectives."

Annetta's lips twisted, and she withdrew her hand from Mirra's to pat her herbalist's belt pouch. "I wonder if those 'defectives' were the original Settlers."

Jonathan pondered. It was odd how he'd spent all his life thinking of curses and powers as detrimental. Isabel had mentioned royals maybe being immune to the curse. And here people *without* powers were regarded as inferior. "But if our ancestors were defective, where did *our* powers come from?"

"I'd view the curse as a type of transmissible condition." Annetta's voice had a bit of bite to it. "So if the Settlers took items from here, maybe they took the agent too. Something in the soil, or any other resource—"

"Exactly!" Artur wagged a finger at her. "Think of where cursed mounds are, several beside the old roads. Assuming the Settlers built those, they might also have created the mounds. Jonathan, didn't you describe one of the cursed mounds as a heap of junk?"

His ears warmed. "I didn't intend that to go into my official report—"

"But that's what it was! Rubbish dumps the Settlers left behind. Or at least stuff they no longer found useful. When we get back, I'll want to check..." His voice trailed off when Yvette whispered in his ear.

Annetta nodded at Artur. "Scavenger animals would have settled in there and become infected. And beasts too."

It certainly seemed a plausible explanation. But cleverer people than Jonathan could decide if it was right.

Artur leaned towards Sofia. "Do you not have *techne*?"

Sofia glanced at Yvette, who murmured something. "*Tech-ne*. Like, machines?"

"Yes?" He sat back, bumping into Yvette. "Oh, sorry." He blushed and returned her smile.

"Bad business." Sofia frowned. "Don't get involved."

"Why not?" asked Artur.

"Big war in the old times, further south. One group said *techne* was better than powers. To say such a thing! Only defectives need *techne*. It killed the land, like further north."

Jonathan's brow wrinkled. Was that what they'd passed over? Land killed by *techne*?

"That was the last time defectives were banished. When they left, they stole all the gear they could find."

"What kind of gear?" asked Artur.

Sofia shrugged. "Powered wagons, equipment, books and plans, even."

"Hmm," said Artur. "I wonder if some of those books are in El—the royal library. Or maybe with the historians."

"If the land was killed," murmured Annetta, "that might be why we got sick too."

"Makes sense," said Jonathan.

Mirra squeezed his hand. "You're very clever to think that."

Straightening up at her praise, Jonathan ignored Annetta's scowl. "But what about those sentinels? They weren't left behind by the Settlers, were they?"

Sofia screwed up her face. "After the banishment, our fathers installed those devices. They destroy *techne* that passes in either direction. Means your 'Settlers' can't attack."

"I bet those devices are what poisoned the land." Annetta poked around in her bag. "We felt worse the closer we got to them."

"Yes, poisoned the soil. No good for crops or grazing. Bad to walk on, even. But useful as barrier."

"But you still had *techne* here, didn't you?" asked Artur. "Why not use it to complement your powers?"

Mirra shook her head. "The war destroyed most *techne*. *Techne* machines against each other, killed many people and towns."

"Who won?" asked Jonathan. Perhaps that's why these people had such a small settlement, trying not to attract attention from superior forces.

"Nobody," said Sofia. "Both sides lost. That's what happens in war. Enough. I go sleep now." She called to one of the men who abandoned his game and escorted her away.

Making a sour face, Annetta drained her cup. Yvette curled an arm around Artur's.

"That's a shame," said Jonathan. It seemed like such a waste of life, for no good reason. Just because of an argument over which was better. "But it explains why your village is so small."

Leaning closer, Mirra lowered her voice. "All villages are small. This is the smallest. We rejoice when friendly visitors arrive. Keeps the bloodlines from getting too close. I'm sure you understand."

He blinked. It had been over a decade since he'd received such an invitation. In those days, free from cares, he'd enjoyed visiting the settlements. It hadn't been entirely a duty. But... "I'm flattered. But I'm an old man, uh, Mirra." Now she'd assure him he wasn't old, and they'd both know she was being kind.

Her breath tickled his ear, sending tingles into his brain. "All the more reason. A chance for part of you to live on."

When she put it like that, it made perfect sense. And hadn't he been regretting his lack of progeny not so long ago? Why not do this pleasant young woman a service in appreciation of her help?

Standing up, Annetta shot him a glare and stomped off, muttering something about seeing to Isabel. One of the men nearby caught her arm. She glowered and patted her belly. "I'm pregnant, understand?"

Mirra called something, and the man laughed, waving Annetta away.

"Never mind her," whispered Mirra.

Indeed, why mind Annetta? Jonathan gained his feet and followed Mirra to her hut.

Chapter 23

Stifling a yawn, Susanna regarded Samuel and Franka with bleary eyes. "I thought you'd be asleep."

The boy's gaze flickered between her trunk of notes and the standard-issue camp furniture. "I was, but I woke up with a gurgly tummy. Then I wanted to draw. Here." He handed her a sketch.

"Thank you." The first day's march obviously hadn't worn him out. But it had been an easy one, not even reaching the first marker clip ten miles in.

"Sorry to disturb you." Franka's stance was a touch less robust than usual, and her cheery grin was missing. "But I thought you'd want to know straight away. Though maybe *want* isn't quite the right word..."

Susanna squinted at the sketch under the lamplight. Cold gripped her chest, and her breathing shortened. With that scar on his leg, there was no mistaking Jonathan, but how she wished the boy hadn't drawn it. Admittedly, she'd had sleepless nights about Jonathan's previous bedmates—but that had been in the past! This was *now*. From prisoner to...

Jonathan, lying on his back in a bed. Beside him lay a woman, her arm flung across his chest, strands of dark hair obscuring her face. Both naked. As usual, only Jonathan was sharply defined, even down to the identity bracelet on his wrist. Driven by a need to explore her pain, Susanna examined the woman's blurred features. Her hair wasn't streaked with grey as Annetta's was, and the length ruled out Isabel's boyish crop. The tangle of sheets and clothing on the floor hinted at grey—that would be Jonathan's uniform—and something green. No sign of other people.

"He looks like he's having a nice sleep," offered Samuel.

"Very nice." She resisted the temptation to stalk outside and toss the paper into a campfire. Instead, she forced a smile for Samuel's benefit. "You've done very well. Franka, could you please take him back to his tent? No more sweets, given his bad tummy. And send Richard in."

Franka gave her a sympathetic look and departed with the boy.

How dare he! The moment he encountered a younger woman—Susanna bit back a cry. Declaring her outrage to the entire camp wouldn't help. *Breathe in...*

Richard arrived, rubbing his eyes. "The air here isn't exactly conducive to easy sleep, especially with the food challenging my digestion. I take it you're the reason Franka barged into my tent and yanked me out of bed."

"Tell me where everyone is." At his offended expression, she exhaled. "Sorry, bit stressed. I would appreciate your help."

With a sniff, he sat at her folding table with its pain box. "I suppose I start with Jonathan."

"Actually, could you check Isabel first?" If the other three had moved—or their identity tags had—that would offer her some hope for their survival. If not, maybe Jonathan had given up. If he felt trapped, with no way to return across the wastelands on foot, he might have decided to make the most of whatever lifespan he had left. She thought she'd found someone with whom to face life's challenges, someone who wouldn't desert her, but perhaps she shouldn't blame him, ignorant as she was of his situation.

I will do all I can in my power to return to you. That's what he'd said. She squeezed her eyes shut, then wiped her wet cheeks with a handkerchief. She should know better than to believe in romance. That was for young innocents.

Richard raised an eyebrow but went through his usual process in silence, scribbling a few notes between attempts. At length he sat back. "Good news, I think. They've all moved, which I take to mean they're alive. They're not far from each other, say within a couple of dozen yards? All separate."

Susanna closed her eyes and considered. Had Jonathan been singled out for special attention? Were they all being held hostage for the others' cooperation? That might make more sense. After all, even though she tried to stay out of his head, she *knew* him. He wasn't fickle or hasty in his affections. There was no logical reason he'd just abandon his duties. Right, and what duty would land him in bed with a woman? Surely not trying to seduce her for information, or giving comfort—ha!—to a fellow prisoner. The situation made no sense.

Massaging her temples, she opened her eyes.

Half-rising from his chair, Richard was staring at her in concern.

Her face warmed. "Another question. You can sense the metal of those identity tags. Is there much other metal close by? Like might be used in *techne* tools or weapons?"

He bent to his work again. Although he still needed the pain box, his powers had expanded since she'd worked with him. "Very little metal. A few knives, cutlery and suchlike. Various cooking pots, including a huge one. Assuming people cook their food, there can't be that many of them. Nothing like our flechette guns."

"Thank you, Richard. I think that's all. Could you send Lester in, please?" The relative lack of *techne* was reassuring, but she didn't want to speak to Hastings while feeling this frazzled. Poor Lester would have to bear the brunt of her worries. Served him right for bringing Tabitha here.

Richard's lips twitched. "With pleasure. Seems you're determined to disturb everyone's sleep."

She'd probably asked for that. Susanna spent the minutes before Lester's arrival brewing two mugs of tea over her oil lamp. It was unlikely she'd get back to bed.

When he arrived, she told him about the drawing and Richard's findings, as well as her suspicions Jonathan had given up.

Standing by the table, Lester gaped and set his mug down. "But he's so loyal to you! I can't imagine what would lure him—" He raised a finger. "But didn't you say our opponents might have powers?"

"Yes, I warned Hastings about that. He didn't seem worried." Or maybe he'd been putting on a confident front for his soldiers.

Lester took a few paces and turned, nearly knocking his mug off the table. "What if they have mind control? Might she have"—he wiggled his fingers—"*persuaded* him into bed?"

Much as she wanted to believe him, she couldn't help picking at the matter like a sore tooth. "I thought you couldn't compel someone to act against their natural inclinations." Jonathan's responsible nature simply wasn't consistent with casual bedding.

"*I* can't. But I'm not powerful. Someone like Denton, on the other hand..."

Could she afford to be hopeful, or was Lester just trying

to comfort her? "Even so, there are four of them. Richard's optimistic they're all alive. They know to be wary about powers, and Annetta has her herbs. Why wouldn't they do something?" Her voice cracked.

"Shh... We'll work our way through this." He gave her a brief hug.

She tried to smile. "Here's me, old enough to be your mother—"

He jerked backwards and collided with the table. The mug clanged on the ground with a splash. "What about mind control on top of an appeal for help?"

"What help? And why him? Why would she want him?" That sounded wrong. "I mean, he's a stranger to her. Jonathan and I have a long—"

"It seemed like he was in a small settlement, yes?" Lester waited until she nodded. "When I was out with Annetta, she had to explain to me that people don't migrate much. So they kinda... welcome visitors? Like, a lot of the convoy guards screw the local ladies?" His shoulders hunched. "That is, fit and fertile males are welcomed with open arms. So to say. Sorry."

"I see. Thank you for your insights, Lester." Of course she'd known about such customs. She just hadn't thought to apply it to Jonathan's current situation. "I suppose if that's really the case, I should be grateful he's not being tortured or worse." Not that she really *felt* grateful after such a blunt suggestion. She frowned at his anxious face. "Anything *else* you feel appropriate to tell me?"

Lester rubbed his unshaven chin then cleared his throat. "Just wondering. You know how protective he is of Tabitha, and he's not even her father."

"Isn't he?" Susanna regarded him gloomily. "Maybe he

is."

"Definitely not. I met her parents in one of the settlements. Anyway, I know the arrangement's not supposed to be permanent. But knowing Jonathan, if he has any children with someone over there..." He waved a vague hand.

"Damn!" If he'd agreed to fathering children, he might feel obliged to stay and care for them. He might prioritise such a duty over any personal preferences. Maybe even over loyalty to his realm. Why hadn't she mentioned Samuel when she had the opportunity?

"Uh, anything else?" He gazed longingly at the tent flap.

She straightened. "I don't need you right now, thank you."

"Sleep well," said Lester as he left.

Not likely. *Breathe in...* Susanna slumped back in her chair, temples throbbing. The headache she'd developed after marching into the wastelands still hadn't worn off. She retrieved a painkiller from her trunk and washed it down with the bitter tea before heading out.

In shirtsleeves, Hastings ushered her into his tent and unfolded a seat for her. He sat down on the other side of a table which held a hand-drawn map. "A problem, Chief Scientist Longleaf?"

"Quite possibly. Samuel made another drawing, and I—" She swallowed. "I was quite shocked..."

She told him of her suspicions, that Jonathan's captors were mind controlling him. After steeling herself to show him that drawing, it was a relief when he declined her offer.

"Perhaps we could view this as their initial strategy?" Hastings drummed his fingers on the table. "An attempt to, ah, soften him up? After all, we don't know if they'll treat him differently tomorrow." He shook his head. "It pains me to distress you, but I've read of some old cultures treating prisoners in a dreadful manner."

"On the plus side, Richard believes all four to still be alive." But for how long? Would that be a reason to hold off? "Might this affect your plans?"

"Not at all. All the more reason to march. I hope we'll be in time to rescue them. The odds are on our side..." From what Richard sensed, the small size of the settlement would be no match for the army's superior numbers, never mind their training and weapons. Their opponents couldn't mind-control them all. "We're committed now. If we don't need to fight, that's good. But if needed, we'll teach them a lesson they won't forget."

Susanna's breathing eased. Maybe it was selfish, but she was relieved he had opted to continue. "What about the sentinels?"

"If they didn't stop a blimp, they're not likely to stop a whole army." His expression was sympathetic. "Look, I can see you're perturbed, and no wonder. I suggest you get some sleep, and maybe things will look better in the morning."

Jonathan spent the next morning accompanying Mirra around the village and its environs. He watched the flock of long-pelted herbivores while she told him how animals provided food and clothing.

"And this is how we herd them." She pointed across the field. "See?"

A black and white beast wove its way among the larger animals. At Mirra's whistle, it yipped and bounded towards her. Jonathan flinched as it neared, his power stirring. But the beast halted and sat on its haunches.

Mirra raised an eyebrow. "She's friendly. I'll show you."

When she scratched the back of its neck, he gaped. "Careful—"

"It's fine." She smiled as it licked her hand. "You want to stroke her?"

His shoulders tightened. But Mirra was unafraid, and the beast he'd met on his previous travels hadn't been threatening. He should learn what he could here. It would be useful when—something niggled at the back of his mind—sometime in future. Slowly extending a hand, he touched the rough fur. "Like this?"

"Nearly." She grasped his hand and drew it firmly along the beast's back.

The beast's tail thumped the ground, and it grinned at him. He returned the grin, not even minding its sharp teeth. The vibration of its fur-covered chest beneath his hand was oddly appealing.

"This is amazing," he said. "Back home, everyone dreads beasts."

She laughed. "I bet your beasts are pets that the defectives—Settlers—took with them. No need to fear these. We understand each other."

Some Ascar nobles kept songbirds, but he had a hard time wrapping his head round the concept of "pets". "Do you have other helpful, uh, pets?"

She scrunched her nose then pointed at a tree where a multicoloured bird stretched its wings. "Not pets, but birds? I want to tell something to my friend in the next village, a day's walk away. Birds take messages."

"Like, messenger birds? We have those too." Hmm. Hadn't he once known a girl who enjoyed feeding them? Did that make them pets? "Is that village much bigger than this one?"

"A little bigger. Maybe one hundred people? They're south of here. If the dead lands expand in this direction, we might leave here and join with them."

"Have you moved before?" He'd wondered why the buildings looked so similar, but perhaps they'd all been constructed at the same time.

"When I was a child." She patted the beast's head, and it loped off. "The crops were doing badly, and Sofia said moving was safer."

"That's a shame." Jonathan's gaze skipped over the grazing herbivores to the clustered huts. What would it be like to abandon his home? At least the livestock could move with them.

"We hope that the land will heal itself. Even if we did think of invading you, the land is telling us not to."

There was no good reason she would lie to him, but it would be wise to learn more about the next village—

"Astra! Tonio!" Mirra waved the children over. "Fetch the spyglass, and climb the big hill with Jonathan. Take him to the viewing point. Show him where our neighbours live."

As he allowed the giggling children to usher him away, a smile tugged at his lips.

While they walked, Jonathan held the spyglass in one hand, Astra clutching the other. Tonio skipped ahead up a well-worn trail towards the hill's summit. Grass and wildflowers coated the ground, and a solitary herbivore paused in its chewing to watch them.

Astra's grin revealed a missing front tooth. "They don't let us borrow the spyglass. You can show us!"

Even with the spyglass, Jonathan could barely make out the other village, just a vague impression of regular fields and maybe some wisps of smoke. But a closer structure caught his eye: a derelict building, surrounded by jagged debris.

"Children?" He pointed. "What's over there?"

Tonio peered through the spyglass. "Old town. Long gone."

Jonathan shivered. Wooden buildings might fall into disrepair over time, but those fragments had been stone. What forces had caused such destruction?

When Mirra rejoined him at the communal lunch, she confirmed the ruins had been caused by the war. "Everyone tried to destroy everything else. We left things as they were. Reminds us to stay peaceful."

Artur scribbled in his notepad between mouthfuls of stew. "I've had an amazing morning. With coordination of heat and manipulation powers, the metalworker can make precision fittings. It's not easy, and for most jobs they use regular tools, but they've achieved so much without electricity or powered *techne*."

Steam rising from her bowl, Yvette sat beside him. Her shoulder rubbed against his. "The land provides."

"They don't even use—or need—calculating machines." Artur waved his spoon towards Berna. "When I showed her the blimp plans, she suggested an alternative configuration that could improve speed. I told her of the Armstrong coefficient first, of course. They have no reason to fly, so that was a new concept."

Jonathan scratched his head. "For once, I think I understood that."

Mirra smiled at him. "I helped."

He returned her smile. He was certainly benefiting from her company.

In the afternoon, Mirra left Jonathan at Isabel's hut

while she went to visit the midwife. Annetta and the healer were gesticulating at each other with confused expressions.

Isabel gave him a weak smile. "This translation business is a bit wearing. Give us a hand?" Her lids drooped.

"Of course." A pang of guilt struck him. His responsibility for the team had slipped his mind. Luckily, there had been no immediate danger. Maybe it was his age, plus the distraction of learning so many new things—

"Jonathan?" Annetta's voice was impatient. "Can you ask Healer Markov..." She rattled off a list of questions which he translated.

Markov nodded and flexed his chubby fingers. "I've healed Isabel's lungs, patched up the sick areas so she can breathe more easily, but she's still weak. Your friend has a good knowledge of herbs..."

Annetta beamed at his translated praise.

"... but we don't prepare them by cooking. Use powers instead. Still, she's quite competent for a defective."

Jonathan opted not to share that last part, but Annetta insisted on quizzing Markov about preparation methods.

"We use gas burners for distillation in the Keep," she said. "I wonder if there would be an equivalent here?"

Markov screwed up his face. "No gas. But we have oil lamps and heaters. Similar, maybe?" He headed towards the door. "Wait here for a while. I go to speak with Mirra and the midwife."

As soon as Markov left, Annetta said, "When are we heading back?"

Jonathan blinked. "Back?"

"Yes, *back*. To Numoeath."

"There's no rush, is there? We're not having a war."

"No, but we need to warn them about the poison in the

wastelands. If they try walking over it, they'll become sick. It'll be worse the further in they get."

"Oh, sure. But our speculations last night were interesting, and I'm sure it would be good to confirm things further for the scientists. Might as well benefit from the villagers' willingness to share information. Besides, it will be days before the army leaves, and Isabel needs to rest—"

Isabel cracked open an eye. "I'm getting better by the minute. Annetta, you were—"

The doorway darkened. It was Mirra, who held out a hand. "I'll show you the irrigation systems before it gets too dark. And Markov said you were interested in the oil press. Burns well for heat and light."

"Right." Jonathan stood and nodded at Annetta. Now she'd condemned him to a tour of heating facilities or something. "I'll, uh, speak to you later."

Annetta looked down. "That's fine. I'm helping prepare dinner, so I'll probably see you then."

Tonight's dinner was recognisably chicken. Scowling, Annetta served him a smaller portion of stew than everyone else got. He sighed but didn't complain. When had she become so temperamental? Well, being labelled a "defective" would be annoying, especially given her undoubted knowledge of herbalism. A pity her skills weren't valued as much this side of the wastelands. He'd better think up something nice to do for her tomorrow.

At a touch on his arm, he pushed Annetta from his mind and smiled at Mirra.

A sharp pain in Jonathan's ear yanked him awake. He blinked at the dim figure bending over him. "Annetta?"

"Put some clothes on," she hissed, releasing his earlobe.

"Isabel and Artur are waiting."

His brow creased. "But what are you doing here?"

"Rescuing you, you idiot!"

"From what?" He glanced at his sleeping companion. He'd returned to her bed tonight, because... because... *why?*

"She was mind-controlling you. Downplaying the importance of your mission." Annetta's voice rose. *"Our* mission. We need to warn Eleanor. You remember who she is, maybe? Loyalty to the queen and all that?"

Jonathan winced. "Shh!"

Annetta flapped a hand at Mirra. "That one won't wake for a good half hour. Lucky I brought my knockout powder, but we don't have time. Get moving!"

He eased himself upright, tugging the sheet over his midriff in an attempt to maintain some decency. *A bit late for that now, Shelley.* Talking of which... "But the midwife said she's pregnant."

"So? Then she's got what she wanted from you. This is a convenience, not a romance! And what about Susanna?"

Susanna! Jonathan's breath hitched as he imagined the pain on her face. She had welcomed him into her life, he'd promised to return, and *this* was how he rewarded her. He didn't deserve her. His heart ached at the thought of losing her forever. However, he now had responsibilities. "I should stay here." He pulled the shirt on over his head. "I can't just abandon Mirra and her—*our*—child."

She grabbed his collar and shook him. "And how do you know you didn't before? When you were a convoy guard? Can you swear you've never had a convoy tryst?"

With Annetta shoving him around so his teeth clattered, he could barely think straight. "No, but—"

"Why do you think Samuel keeps drawing you? Didn't

you consider he might be your son?"

"Samuel? *Mine?*" His head swam while the walls closed in on him.

"There are records and everything! Susanna was going to tell you, but..." Annetta deflated and released him. "That was the day the queen gave us this mission."

 Shit! The boy's age fitted with the time Jonathan had been cursed, although his memories of that time were hazy. "But what will I say to her?"

"Never mind that! Let's get back in one piece first." Her voice trembled. "We can't fly the blimp without you, so get a move on."

What a fool he was. Whatever problems he'd inflicted on himself, he had a duty to his companions as well. He snatched up the rest of his clothing, trying not to look at Mirra. Annetta's pursed lips were enough of a reproach. Once he was dressed, he followed the herbalist out of the village to a clearing, where the other two waited by a flickering oil lamp. Artur was yawning and rubbing his eyes.

Isabel's face was pale in the moonlight, and she leaned on a pilfered staff. She grinned at Jonathan. "Your buttons are squint. Looks like I missed all the fun."

Annetta grabbed the lamp and chivvied them along. "We need to get to the blimp before they notice we've gone."

As he walked, the night air cleared Jonathan's head, and he cringed as his memories came into focus. "Annetta, what did you do? How did you get us out?"

She sniffed disapprovingly. "Obviously I wasn't going to get through to you two *men*, what with you adapting so readily to your role as breeding stock. They were mind-controlling you to forget why we're here—it was obvious from your behaviour, plus I'd seen Lester's power in use. They were also mind-reading you in case you were thinking of leaving."

"Artur too?"

Head bowed, Artur flinched. "Yeah. Sorry."

"How did *you* get out of it?" When would he learn not to underestimate her?

Annetta snorted. "Clearly, as a *defective*, and supposedly pregnant already, I wasn't worth much. And fortunately Isabel seemed too ill to be a threat. So they didn't pay much attention to us, and I spent most of my time fussing around Isabel and helping with the kind of menial tasks assigned to defectives." She paused. "Including cooking."

"And?"

"I added bitter pinkweed to last night's communal stew. That's the herb that temporarily disables powers, remember? So the influence on you wore off. And it protects against being mind-read, which is why I ate some myself yesterday after realising there was a problem. I had to get you out quickly before anyone noticed their powers had failed."

Jonathan gaped. She'd disabled *an entire village?* "So I can't use my power?"

"Not yet. Not sure how long it'll last. I put my entire stock into the cauldron, though it's a pretty dilute dose for the numbers."

"So that's why you gave me a small portion. I thought you were annoyed with me."

"That too."

Oh. He could hardly blame her. "How will we leave?"

"Me," said Isabel. "Annetta told them I was still too delicate to eat anything, so my power works fine." She made a face. "Though I'm still not feeling great."

"And the steering?" asked Jonathan.

"The old-fashioned way," said Artur. "Picking an altitude where the wind's in the right direction. The manual fins give us further options."

Jonathan increased his pace. "We'd better get to it." On top of their travel time, he'd wasted two whole days! He'd never forgive himself if there were casualties because of his tardy return. "And thank you, Annetta."

"Um, you're welcome."

The team arrived back at the blimp while it was still dark. Concerned about pursuit, Jonathan retrieved Isabel's sabre from the gondola: the sabre and spyglass he'd abandoned before his capture were lost. Another misjudgement on his part.

"Before you came back with those villagers," said Artur, "I reinforced the steering fins with our extra rope. Now we just need to inflate the balloon, and then Isabel can power our ascent." He attached the canister of spare gas to the balloon with some tubing before inspecting the console. "At least we can leave the empty canister behind. It's excess weight."

"Need me to help?" asked Jonathan.

"You and Annetta, stand by the balloon. When I tell you, remove the rocks holding it down. Otherwise, we should be good."

"I hope they're not coming after us," muttered Jonathan. "I can't fight them all off, especially without my power."

"You still have me," said Isabel.

Annetta frowned. "Best to conserve your energy. This is the first you've been out of bed, and you've already walked—"

Isabel waved a hand. "Yeah, yeah."

Jonathan gripped the sabre tighter. He didn't *want* to fight the villagers. "Uh, Annetta? I don't suppose you drugged them to stay asleep, did you?"

She shook her head. "Couldn't. Not without drugging you and Artur too."

"Still," said Isabel, "they're not *that* likely to race after us in the dark, especially if they notice their powers don't work." She nudged Jonathan. "And you've already provided Mirra with what she wanted, eh?"

Jonathan winced. "Don't remind me." What was he going to say to Susanna? He wasn't sure he could face her again—No. He *had* to ensure they returned. They needed to warn the army about the toxic soil. If she sent him packing, that was his problem, and he'd deal with it later.

"You're not the only one." Isabel waved at Artur. "I'm sure Eleanor will also appreciate what he's learned—"

"Ready to inflate!" Artur's bellow nearly drowned out Isabel's laugh.

They removed the stones holding down the balloon and climbed into the gondola. With a flap of cloth, the balloon gradually expanded. After they tossed out the gondola's weighting rocks, Isabel grasped the heating rod and applied her power.

The blimp lifted.

"We're flying more or less blind," said Artur, "but I can aim us northwards from the stars. Even without a spyglass, I'm sure we'd see the army on the ground. It'll be easier once it gets light, but I don't want to wait until then."

Jonathan clutched his steering lever. It was going to be a long night.

Chapter 24

Eleanor coughed and rubbed dust out of her gritty eyes, squinting at the soldiers ahead of her. Those fitness lessons and walks with Isabel had improved her stamina, and she could maintain her position in the protected middle of the group. However, her footsteps dragged while weariness seeped into her bones.

She wasn't the only one feeling the effort. The troops had marched up to the border yesterday morning in tight, six-person squads. Now they meandered in ragged lines past stunted bushes interrupting the dried-out ground. Each time they stopped to rest, the queues at the medic stations grew longer. Even Paton didn't seem his usual overbearing self, though still he insisted on walking beside her. His royal red uniform bore dust smears and contrasted oddly with her own distinctive purple overall.

With the increasing dryness of the wastelands—brown merging into grey—the dust cloud nearly obscured her view. The two survey blimps floated above them, carrying operators and sharp-eyed soldiers with spyglasses. At that height, they wouldn't be hampered by the dust.

They would know they were nearing the sentinels when the soil turned red. After that, the survey blimps would become even more important. Eleanor wished she could be up there as part of the crew. She had more flying experience than many operators, and it was a useful contribution she could make. But Hastings had decreed it too risky for the queen to expose herself to possible attack from the giant guards.

No, the only chance she'd get to travel in a blimp would be in an emergency where she, as titular head of state, withdrew from the field. She glanced back at the royal blimp jouncing along close to ground level, tethered to a trolley bearing the gondola. With the balloon's lift, it wasn't difficult to push. The propellors were fully charged, and the rapid-heat system ready to go at a moment's notice. She had no desire to use it, not given the implications.

Hastings approached her. Sweat beaded his ruddy face.

"John, are you well?" she asked.

His smile flickered. "I've felt better. Days like this, I wish I was younger."

"I noticed we're moving more slowly than yesterday."

Hastings nodded. "Yes, and slower than when they were training with heavier loads. I can't explain it, but I ordered them to ease up on the pace. We're nearly at the second blimp marker, so not quite a third of the way to the sentinels."

Paton stuck his chest out for a few steps, then his shoulders slumped again.

Eleanor regarded both men with concern. "Something about this place isn't healthy."

Hastings mopped his brow. "Maybe. At first I thought we had malingerers, but Louis says the complaints are genuine. His medical supplies are running low. He's been treating stomach cramps, breathlessness and headaches. Maybe they're not used to the foreign air?"

Louis the infirmier wasn't prone to exaggeration. Eleanor chewed her lip. Much as she burned to rescue the team, she couldn't prioritise their welfare over that of a whole army. "If the march is making people ill—"

"I'm sure they'll get used to it within a day or two." Hastings nodded at the nearest squad. "Isn't that right, lads?"

"Yes, sir!" Backs straightening, the soldiers saluted and picked up their pace.

Hastings lowered his voice. "It's vital to keep morale up. We know the team is still alive, but we don't know for how long. We're committed now, and we can't afford a loss of confidence. That could lead to chaos, and with all the weapons they're carrying..."

"I see your point." Unable to find a counterargument, she sighed. Panicking troops were a more immediate threat than unwelcoming terrain.

A bell rang behind them, and a guard rode up on a bicycle. "Commander Hastings, Your Majesty. Urgent message from Chief Scientist Longleaf."

"Go ahead," said Hastings.

"The four identity tags from the exploration team are approaching from the south. Estimate they'll be within spyglass distance within thirty minutes. Captain Honeyman following with more details."

Her heart lifted. They were returning! "Well, John, it seems we were maybe too keen to start this rescue attempt."

Richard wobbled up on a second bicycle. Paton grabbed the seat and held it steady while he clambered off.

Hastings was frowning. "Is there any way of knowing whether they are pursued?"

"No metal chasing them." Richard wheezed. "But remember, they may not have conventional weapons. If they have powers like Isabel's—"

"Attack may yet be imminent." Hastings hopped on top

of the nearest handcart. At his shout of "Defensive!" the guards dropped their burdens and drew their flechette guns. The teams responsible for explosives ran to the handcarts.

David's tall form pushed through the mass. "Visualisers, to me! Report images from the blimps."

"Marksmen to the front!" shouted Hastings.

"Make way!" bawled a soldier, heaving a handcart forwards.

A hand fell on Eleanor's shoulder, and she flinched. It was Paton. "We need to move, Your Majesty."

Her gut churned. She was causing an obstruction. "You're right. Let's go."

Her blimp was only a few dozen paces to the rear. On her way, she dodged as running soldiers nearly bowled her over. Paton's bulk shielded her from the worst of it. By the time she arrived, the balloon was straining at the tether while the flight operator studied the control panel.

The ground operator said, "Nearly ready for launch, Your Majesty."

She rubbed a bruise on her leg. "Take your time."

Dragging Tabitha by the arm, Franka strode up. She winked at Paton. "Hey, big guy, wanna take care of the kid?"

Tabitha jerked her arm away. "I can look after myself!"

The girl's spirit engendered sympathy, but this wasn't the time to indulge her. Eleanor looked her in the eye. "I'm under Commander Hastings' orders too. We mustn't distract the troops."

Tabitha's gaze fell. "I don't like it."

"Me neither. I hope this comes to nothing, but we need to be prepared."

The gondola lifted slightly, and the flight operator called, "We're a bit on the light side. Shall I dump some gas?"

"No." No point wasting gas. "Tabitha and Paton, you climb in."

Paton helped Tabitha into the gondola, then heaved himself over the side after her. "And you, Your Majesty?"

"It'll take me only moments to embark." She folded her arms and watched Hastings as he gesticulated. "I'm staying on the ground unless there's dire need for me to leave."

Ignoring the parched grey earth passing beneath them, Jonathan frowned at Isabel's haggard face. She'd kept the blimp at the altitude Artur specified, but her hands trembled, and her eyes were bloodshot. Jonathan, Annetta and Artur weren't suffering ill effects: it must be Isabel's power taking a toll. If it failed, they'd be stranded.

At least the villagers wouldn't pursue them across the wastelands, and the sentinels hadn't done further damage when they passed by again. But that was no comfort if Jonathan's warning went undelivered. How much longer would their journey take?

With luck, the army wouldn't have left Numoeath yet. But what if they'd already stepped on to the toxic soil? His temples throbbed. His stupidity would lead to further deaths. Annetta had pointed out that they'd not become sick until they were close to the sentinels. But they hadn't been travelling on the ground. Maybe the soldiers would run into problems sooner, but too late to retreat without harm.

And what of Susanna? She'd be travelling with the army too. Even if he'd thrown her affection away, he would save her life. It was a mercy Tabitha was tucked away in the Keep.

Annetta rummaged through her bag and squinted at a sachet in dissatisfaction.

"Can't find any?" asked Isabel.

"All I have is the emergency stimulant. But you're so unwell that—"

"Give it to me."

Reluctantly, Annetta handed over the sachet. "Place a pinch on your tongue and let it dissolve."

Isabel tore the packet open, tipped her head back and poured the powder into her mouth. Annetta snatched the remains of the packet and scowled.

"I promised Eleanor I'd get you home safely or die trying." Isabel's smile revealed bloodstained teeth. "I might even manage both." She placed a hand on the heat transfer rod, and the blimp rose. "How's that, Artur?"

"Good, good. Even without *techne*, there won't be a problem. We've just about—" Clutching his chest, he pitched forwards. His face smacked the panel, then he slid to the floor.

"Artur!" screamed Annetta, kneeling down to feel his neck.

Why did the boy have to faint right now? The blimp lurched, and Jonathan's stomach spasmed. He staggered to the controls, staring at them in incomprehension. There were knobs and dials and some kind of lever, but what did they all mean? The blimp was coasting rather than plummeting, so he looked to Isabel for help. She had paled, her eyes like glowing coals in a snowbank. Wrapping a supporting arm around her, he sank with her to the floor.

He chafed her hands while her eyes closed and her breathing became laboured.

"Um, Jonathan."

"Not now, Annetta," he mumbled. "Isabel's dying."

"Jonathan!" She shook his arm. "I think Artur's dying too!"

That got his attention. "Huh?"

"One moment he was fine." She scrabbled through her bag, tossing sachets and vials aside. "When Isabel got worse, he collapsed. Death reading, remember? His power. That woman warned him about people facing death. This must be what she meant. If Isabel dies, Artur will too. I don't have any bitter pinkweed left." She gulped.

Shit.

Isabel's lips moved, and he bent closer to hear her words.

"Never mind me, idiot. Steer the damn blimp. Tell Eleanor I kept my promise."

Right. Isabel was sacrificing her life so they could warn the army. He swallowed the lump in his throat and gazed up at the balloon, hoping for inspiration. The two essential crew members gone, and him with a useless power—but wait! If Artur's power had recovered, so had Jonathan's. He certainly couldn't push the blimp around with his power, but they knew how to use the fins, sort of. Artur had said the blimp should go up and down to catch winds in the right direction.

Jonathan's glance fell on the lamp Annetta had brought, and he fumbled in a pocket for his tinderbox. Isabel had heated the balloon via a metal rod made for her. The fins needed two people to steer, and it wasn't possible to reach both the heat rod and fin controls. Although they had rope, they couldn't tie a burning lamp to the rod. But if he could use his power to hold the lamp up—

"Jonathan!"

"Now what?" The woman had the worst timing.

"If Isabel stays in the blimp, we lose Artur too. If, um, she doesn't, Artur might survive. Maybe even wake up and help us."

He gaped at Annetta. "You're suggesting we throw Isabel out?" When had she become so bloodthirsty?

She glowered. "I wasn't suggesting we toss her out like so much rubbish. I have an idea..."

Chapter 25

Nerves jangling, Eleanor paced around the evacuation blimp under Paton's vigilant glare. Straying too far would vex him, but she couldn't remain still. Her weariness had vanished, and her mood flipped between elation and dread.

A shout came from above. "They're coming! Empty skies otherwise. No pursuit seen."

Ha, Hastings had overreacted, both with his strategic advance and his battle fervour. Soon he'd hand control back to her, and together they could take the troops back to safety. Her excitement grew at the thought of welcoming the team home and hearing how their adventure had gone.

The army's dust was starting to settle, but the approaching blimp was only a vague outline. Something dangled from it: bartered goods, perhaps, from the new society they'd visited? She pulled out her spyglass for a closer look. Peaceful trade would be a disappointment to Hastings, but a huge benefit to the realm.

With a smile, Eleanor put the spyglass to her eye. The patchiness of the dust cloud made her inspection challenging, not helped by the blimp's erratic movements. Maybe the propeller *techne* had glitched, forcing Artur to use the winds at different altitudes. At least she could see no obvious patches. Might he return this time with his overalls intact? Her gaze slid down the balloon's main rope to the gondola, and she wondered if she would first glimpse Isabel's smirk or Artur's bashful expression.

She blinked.

Jonathan's grim face scowled towards her. He waved an arm, encompassing the entire area. "Poisoned ground!" he roared. "Flee!"

Poison? She froze. *That* explained the army's illnesses and the bare terrain as they moved southwards.

A skinny soldier with a pockmarked face flung his sabre down. "Better run! Captain Shelley's orders!" He shrugged off his backpack and broke into a homewards jog.

More soldiers abandoned their squads and followed him while others exclaimed and pointed. Trying to stifle hysterical laughter, Eleanor gnawed a gloved knuckle. If this was how they behaved under pressure, she was glad Hastings was in charge rather than her. Once he'd re-established order, she'd help him move everyone away from the dangerous area.

"Come back, you idiots!" Still atop his handcart, Hastings shook a fist. "Everyone, stay where you—"

"Catch her!" The shrill scream rose above Hastings' bellow. Beside Jonathan, pale-faced Annetta clutched the blimp rail and pointed downwards. "*Techne* failure! Help!"

A hasty scan of the gondola revealed no further occupants. The weight on the tethering rope came into view within the dust cloud. Eleanor gasped. Isabel, trussed up like a celebration turkey. Eyes closed, she dangled limply.

The clamour from the panicking soldiers made it difficult to think. Where was Artur? Even if he were at the controls, Isabel would be injured on hitting the ground. In his absence, the impact of an uncontrolled landing would kill her.

Eleanor sprang into her waiting blimp. "Lift off!" she shouted. "Meet the approaching blimp."

The flight operator seized the controls. The ground operator slashed the tether free. The gondola lifted off its trolley, propellors whining in protest under Paton's weight.

"Queen's fleeing!" shouted a soldier. "She's leaving us behind."

The poor ground operator disappeared under a mass of soldiers as they rushed the rising blimp. One grabbed the foreshortened rope and hung on. The gondola shuddered.

Paton growled and leaned over the side, shaking the rope until the soldier's grip loosened. The man dropped to the ground. The blimp leapt upwards.

Eleanor's heart pounded. "Thanks, Paton. I may need your strength again."

As they drew closer, she focussed her spyglass on their target, mind working furiously over the possibilities. Artur *had* to be inside the gondola, maybe incapacitated. If they could detach Isabel—No. Artur's blimp would drift away, landing who knew where?

She took a deep breath. Annetta had warned of a *techne* failure. For a safe landing, someone knowledgeable would have to operate the old-fashioned manual controls. Eleanor couldn't ask the operator to do it, so she'd have to get herself aboard. And without Paton suspecting her plans. He'd never allow her to endanger herself.

Such luck there was a telekinetic prodigy on board. "Tabitha. Your power—can you lift a person?"

Tabitha's jaw dropped. "No, of course not!"

Damn. She chewed her lip. Using both hands to steady the spyglass, she inspected Isabel again. "There's excess rope dangling from Isabel's tether. If we get close enough, can you pull it into Paton's hand?"

"Maybe." The girl's voice quavered.

Maybe. That's what Eleanor had to trust. She squinted at the distances. They were now some hundred feet in the air and nearly level with Isabel, who dangled two dozen feet below the gondola. Isabel weighed... say, half as much again as Eleanor. Maybe a bit more? Certainly impossible to budge when they were grappling. Not as much as Paton, obviously.

She flexed her fingers in her gloves and told the operator, "Stand by for extra weight. You'll need to lift quickly on my signal."

This blimp had several small emergency levium canisters. Just as well: Eleanor couldn't have handled a large one. She unstrapped one and hooked it to her belt. "I'll ready backup levium in case we need it. Paton, I want you at the side rail, ready to grab Isabel's rope."

"Ready, Your Majesty."

"Tabitha." Eleanor drew a jerky breath. "Can you see the rope? Are you ready to pull?"

"Yes? Yes!" Tabitha waved at Jonathan. "Don't worry, we'll save you!"

Jonathan's face paled. "You shouldn't be here. Stay away, child!"

"You should be glad I came! And I can hardly jump out now!"

"Right," said Eleanor. "I'll wait behind Paton, out of the way."

Paton grunted in approval.

Eleanor peered round his bulk. *Closer... closer...* "Now, Tabitha!"

Tabitha stretched her arm forwards, drew in a great breath and screamed. The dangling end of the rope twisted and then slapped into Paton's extended hand. Muscles bunching, he leaned backwards, pulling the rope and Isabel towards him.

"Operator, gain altitude!" shouted Eleanor. As they rose and the rope slackened, she slid round Paton and grabbed Isabel's jacket, easing her over the gondola's side. Isabel flopped on to the floor. She lacked the stiffness of a corpse, but there was no time to check her.

"Paton," said Eleanor. "Use your sabre. Cut the rope just above Isabel, to let the other blimp float free." She grasped a knot higher up the rope. "I'll hold it steady while you cut. Quickly, now! The longer we stay like this, the greater the risk."

"I'll help!" Stretching upwards, Tabitha grabbed the rope near Eleanor's hand.

"No, let go!" exclaimed Eleanor. "You need to... check Isabel. Like they taught you in the infirmary. Paton, ready?" She pointed at the rope close to Isabel. "Cut it there."

Tabitha's brow wrinkled as she loosed her grasp. "Hang on, if he cuts the rope and you're holding it higher—"

Shutupshutup. "Quickly, man!" She clamped her lips shut on a shriek. For the first time ever, she valued his lack of education.

Raising his weapon, he hacked through the rope.

Freed of Isabel's weight, Artur's blimp shot further up in the air, Eleanor hanging on to the tethering rope. Her foot landed on Paton's shoulder and she jumped, tucking her legs under her to avoid his instinctive grab.

"... of all the lousy friggin' tricks to play on me..." Paton and Isabel's blimp descended, his curses growing fainter.

Eleanor's arm muscles screamed as she eyed the rope below her. Dammit, there wasn't enough to use her legs.

With gritted teeth and shaking arms, she pulled herself up a few feet. She swung a leg, winding the rope around it. The strain on her arms eased slightly. She gasped for breath and whimpered.

A downwards glance showed the entire army pointing up at her, mouths agape. Hastings shook his fists at the sky while she swung in dizzy circles. No, it certainly wouldn't do for her to fall. She'd allow herself a few moments, and then she'd have to climb again. A groan escaped her. This was nothing like the gymnasium.

"We're pulling you up," called Jonathan.

"Excellent idea," muttered Eleanor. Why hadn't that occurred to her? All she had to do was hang on and let them do the work. She glanced to either side where the survey blimps hovered uncertainly. One soldier held a camera to his eye. *Blast.*

Once she was close enough, Jonathan grabbed her belt and hauled her in. She landed upside down on top of the levium canister. The camera man would get a nice shot of her flailing feet.

"You're a damn idiot," Jonathan growled as she righted herself, landing face to face with a snoring Artur.

She leaned over to touch Artur's face—

"But we're glad to see you," added Annetta.

Eleanor stood up and took a few wobbly paces, stepping over a warm, extinguished lamp. She inspected the controls. "Right. Let's get to work. Versium temperature falling smoothly... no hazardous loss of inflation..." It was nowhere as bad as she'd dreaded, and landing would be straightforward. For a moment, jubilation filled her, but it couldn't displace her growing queasiness.

Leaning over the side, she regarded the cheering soldiers. *Settlers' bowels.* This wasn't going to improve her reputation any, but she'd need to—

Her stomach heaved, and she threw up.

In Susanna's tent that evening, Jonathan bowed his head and focussed on the ground. Although they'd now retreated to less dangerous terrain, he felt worse than he had on the outward journey. It was a minor comfort she'd allowed him in her presence. "I'm so sorry. My behaviour in the village was reprehensible. When we get back to Ascar, I'll find somewhere else to live."

"Oh, Jonathan." Seated on her camp bed, Susanna sighed. There were bags beneath her eyes, and her shoulders drooped. "Lester suspected you were being mind-controlled. I'm relieved you survived unharmed, truly, but everything's been a bit of a shock."

"*Lester?* Oh. I must thank him. Uh, Annetta said something about Samuel?" Perhaps the herbalist had misled him for his own good? No, he was just being a coward and trying to avoid the truth.

"We believe he's your son. So you really have a family now." Susanna rubbed her forehead. "You said you'd do all in your power to come back. You kept your promise."

He started to kneel, but she patted the space beside her. "Let's work something out. We always have, before."

Tears rolled down Eleanor's cheeks while Louis rubbed a salve on her arms. It was only pulled muscles, but by the Settlers, it hurt! "I'm sure others need medical help more than I do."

It had been so embarrassing, being stretchered away from the danger zone. She'd been perfectly capable of using her legs. And to make things worse, Jonathan and Annetta had walked beside her to report back on their mission.

Louis pursed his lips. "Don't worry. Everyone's feeling better now we've moved away from the toxic area. Commander Hastings ordered me to attend you, but I'm keeping an eye on those dealing with Captain Shelley's team."

She turned her head towards the other bed in the tent. The carers crowding around Isabel obstructed her view, but the snippets of speech she caught were reassuring.

Louis followed her gaze. "There are plenty of volunteers to carry her stretcher tomorrow. Everyone wants some reflected glory. And young Artur is equally popular, though we'll make sure to keep him a prudent distance from anyone who's ill."

"Only stretchers? But a blimp—"

"Sorry. Blimp travel would be too much strain on them after that journey. Maybe in a couple of days..."

After Louis and his assistants left, Eleanor lay on her camp bed, gazing up at the tent canvas. What kind of queen was she? It wasn't for her to decide, not after what she'd done. All that disruption, alarm, soul-searching and mental anguish. And for nothing. No, not quite nothing. They were no longer completely alone, and the team had brought back new ideas. Maybe in time they'd communicate again with their not-quite-neighbours. Shared knowledge could be of mutual benefit.

Eleanor's reforms had integrated society better than ever before. Hopefully such progress would continue, no matter the outcome of this endeavour. Her brow creased. She'd manipulated people's fears to achieve her aims, and harmed the blimp team and soldiers. She glanced towards Isabel's sleeping form. Was the result worth the cost? *I feel*

like we've lost a war, somewhere. And we didn't even fight anyone.
Though surely that was better than the alternative. Maybe
future historians would curse her name and hold her up as
an example of egregious misrule.

"Your Majesty?" came a gruff voice from outside.

"Come in, Paton."

He entered and bowed, then remained hunched so his
head didn't hit the canvas.

The familiarity of his glower made her smile. "*Now* will
you sit down in my presence?"

The chair creaked as he sat.

Eleanor broke the ensuing silence. "I suppose you're going to shout at me."

He snorted. "I planned to, but the soldiers are all talking about your heroics."

"Really? It was an act of desperation."

"Of course it was, Your Majesty."

She tried not to laugh. He really had no idea how much
she'd improvised. Probably better she didn't enlighten him.
"Are the soldiers all talking about the mad queen?"

"No. They're talking about the queen who took enormous personal risk to save our intrepid explorers. Now they
don't see your previous caution as cowardice, but as a desire
to keep them safe. That matters a lot to them."

She sighed. "That's nice, I suppose. How's Hastings taking it?"

"With good grace. At least in public. He's praising your
grit."

"I see."

With the threat of war averted, she'd disband the army,
and Hastings would return to politics. And they'd be back
fencing with each other verbally and politically. He knew

about Isabel's crimes, but Isabel was now a heroine.

That didn't matter. No Queen's Discretion in cases of regicide. What concessions might he "invite", in order to keep his knowledge unshared? Would he demand more, year on year, until he ended up reigning in all but name? In his position, she might be tempted to do the same.

"A problem, Your Majesty?"

"It's fine. Go and get some sleep."

Chapter 26

A month later, Eleanor stood in Ascar's city square, Paton and Hastings beside her. In addition to the amplification system, trained televisualisers and telesonographers relayed her words to the settlements. The square was packed. Eleanor wasn't sure if the crowd had been drawn by her announcement. More likely it was the free food and drink, never mind the entertainers waiting to perform.

On one side of the dais stood Susanna, Artur and Tabitha. Jonathan had declined the invitation. If a hooded figure in the crowd had his profile, she'd pretend not to notice. Annetta had requested permission to return to Maldon and already departed. On the other side of the dais lounged Isabel in a wheelchair, Lester behind her. She could walk for short periods, and the infirmiers encouraged it, but two trips across the wastelands had softened her bones. Or so they suspected. She gave Eleanor a thumbs-up. Hastings tugged at the cuffs of his smart civilian suit, which hung loosely on him.

Eleanor cleared her throat. "Citizens of Numoeath, we have all been through trying times. It is an immeasurable relief that we are not, after all, at war. We have learned many things about our history, thanks to the massive efforts and considerable personal sacrifices of Captains Jonathan Shelley and Isabel Hanlon, and Annetta Benedict and Artur Granville."

In the silence while she licked her lips, Lester muttered,

"Right, Senior Research Blimp Engineer blah blah..." She tried to keep her face straight. This was serious business, but she looked forward to its completion.

"It seems that the development of our society has been based on a number of..." She couldn't call them lies. "... misunderstandings. Powers should have been viewed as beneficial from the start, and we need not fear beasts."

There were a few wry smiles in the audience. Some people had learned that already.

She swallowed. "Given the unstable values our society is based on, I am forced to conclude our form of government is not ideal."

Hastings stiffened to attention. He didn't know the contents of her speech, but he'd want to take advantage of her words. That was what politicians did, after all.

She raised her voice. "I therefore declare that in one month's time, the monarchy will be dissolved. Democratic elections will be held for the post of Prime Minister, a time-limited position. Information about the application process will be posted in the public library and distributed to the settlements. May the best candidate win."

Hastings blinked. Under cover of the crowd's exclamations, he murmured, "You would seriously step down from reigning? Give up the throne and absolute power?"

"I never wanted power," she said. "I wanted what was best for the people."

After the hubbub died down, Hastings stepped up to the amplifier and asked, "Who is allowed to compete?"

"Anyone may stand. And every adult citizen is allowed one vote. Whoever attracts the majority wins and sets up his—or her—own constitution, which must hold to his or her election manifesto."

"I see. And if I may ask another question, Your Majesty, or should I call you—"

"I am still My Majesty for another month. Ask away, Councillor Hastings."

"Will you yourself compete for this position of Prime Minister?"

She laughed. "Not at all. I'll dedicate myself to applying blimp technology to improve living standards for everyone. To be honest, I'll welcome the freedom." She met Artur's gaze and held it, then stretched a hand out towards the crowd. "Let the queen's retiral festival begin!"

After the crowd cheered and dispersed to seek their entertainments, Hastings rubbed his chin. "I wonder if there will be many other candidates." He left the question hanging in the air.

"In addition to yourself? At least one, I would imagine."

Hastings glanced at Susanna, who blandly returned his gaze, her cheek dimpling.

"Of course Chief Scientist Longleaf is entitled to stand, if she so wishes," said Eleanor. "But I wasn't thinking of her."

Hastings' brow creased. "I can't imagine there are many with the experience to be plausible candidates, no matter how great their desire. Please, Your Majesty, don't keep an old man in suspense."

"You know, John..." She raised an eyebrow. "I rather think I shall."

"You?" Lester tripped on a cobblestone and nearly shoved Isabel into a wall.

She straightened from her protective brace position. "Yeah, why not?"

"Wouldn't it kinda restrict your, uh, activities?"

"You're asking the woman in a wheelchair?"

"Good point." He resumed pushing the chair towards the Royal Compound. "But I never tagged you as interested in politics."

"Oh, I've always kept an eye on things. Just that..." She grinned. "There was always something more interesting to do."

He shook his head. "Anything I can do to help?"

"Well, since you're asking..."

Damn. She'd probably request something ridiculous. He'd already sought out fresh-picked blueberries and sketches of Hastings as a boy. When would he learn to think first? "Yeah?"

"I wouldn't mind an assistant, someone who can do the legwork."

"But I don't have political savvy."

She waved a languid hand. "That can be learned."

"What's in it for me?"

"Others might believe it a disadvantage, but associating with me will scare your admirers off."

Hmm. That didn't sound like too bad a deal at all.

"Ouch!" At a thump from upstairs, Susanna jabbed her thumb with the needle. She set her embroidery hoop down and reached for a handkerchief. "It's your turn to check."

On the other side of the fireplace, Jonathan swung himself out of the armchair and dropped the *Informer* on the table. "If I'm not back by dinnertime, send a search party." He planted a kiss on her forehead and left the sitting room.

As his footsteps ascended the stairs, she smiled. He'd returned from the south with a new zest for life. It manifested in unusually affectionate behaviour, as if he were making up for lost time. He was still endearingly awkward around Tabitha, who was thriving in the infirmary. When she asked him for permission to write to her parents, he'd turned three shades of pink before pointing out it was her decision.

Jonathan and Susanna's responsibilities had changed during the months since Samuel had started living here. Knowing how accident-prone the boy was, Susanna had hired a live-in couple to help tidy up after any disasters. The couple had also promised discretion over any strange drawings he might make. So far, they'd all been of Jonathan. But maybe that would change as Samuel grew old enough to train.

Jonathan's footsteps descended. There was always that slight unevenness. His steps were slower than usual this time.

He re-entered the sitting room with a piece of paper and a frown.

"Any damage?" asked Susanna.

"No, Samuel's fine, and so's the furniture." Jonathan smoothed out the sketch on the table. "Seems he dozed off and dropped a book on the floor after drawing this."

She joined him by the table. The sketch depicted a vague figure with long black hair. Its enlarged belly contained the detailed outline of a baby. The back of Susanna's neck prickled. It was eerie how the blue eyes seemed to be watching her.

Her heart thrummed. *Breathe in*... "That's obviously not you."

"No." His shoulders slumped, and his expression grew pained. "I think we know who it is. Susanna..."

She took his hand. "Whatever the future holds, we'll face it together. We'll be fine. I mean it."

Epilogue

Prime Minister Isabel Hanlon's first act was to require that summaries of governmental discussions be made publicly available and to open up the scientific archives for anyone to visit. She continued her cousin's initiatives with investments in rural infrastructure. Knowledge of powers increased exponentially.

Hanlon's abrupt departure from office the following year shocked the realm. While speaking at a public assembly, she declared herself unfit to continue because she'd previously committed regicide. She demanded a public trial. (Note: the other deaths she'd brought about had already been accepted as lawful killings.) Text analysts and mind readers confirmed the sordid events leading up to King Frederick's death. She was found guilty, of course, but because of extenuating circumstances, the jury unanimously appealed for clemency. Judge Hastings gave her a suspended sentence.

Several candidates stood at the next election, many from rural settlements. Remarkably, the rural candidates had coordinated their manifesti, making use of the improved communication system. All stood behind a push to reinstate Eleanor Samson as queen. After some protest she eventually agreed, but only on condition that she have a casting vote in the new government, rather than the absolute power she had held previously. King Artur was infrequently in the public eye, but outlying settlements grew

accustomed to him arriving at odd times with useful new
ideas and techne.
With the more widespread use of powers, the realm enjoyed
a rapid improvement in the quality of life and an extended
period of harmony.

From Queen Eleanor: The Early Years *by D. Brigham*

Acknowledgements

Enormous thanks to everyone who contributed along the way while I wrote the Numoeath trilogy, of which this is the final book. In particular, I must thank Philip Folk for his encouragement and support through all the books from start to finish.

Mistakes and inaccuracies are my own.

If you enjoyed reading this, maybe you'd like to take a few minutes to leave a review on your favourite book website. I'd also really appreciate word-of-mouth recommendations to any friends who might enjoy the world of Numoeath.

About the author

M. H. Thaung works in a pathology laboratory in London, England. When not supporting patient care or biomedical research, she enjoys putting fictional characters in challenging situations and seeing how they react.

If you're interested in exploring the world of *A Quiet Rebellion* further, please drop by:

Website: **mhthaung.com**

Twitter: **@mhthaung**

Other books

A Quiet Rebellion: Guilt (Book 1) is available in ebook and print formats.

A Quiet Rebellion: Restitution (Book 2) is available in ebook and print formats.

A Quiet Rebellion: Short Tales is an ebook-only collection of flash fiction set in the same world.

The Diamond Device is a light-hearted steampunk adventure where an unemployed labourer and a thieving noble race to foil a bomb plot and avert a war.

Printed in Great Britain
by Amazon

80739182R00185